His Duchess at Eventide

A Legend to Love

Mythic Dukes
Book 2

Wendy LaCapra

Publisher:

Wendy LaCapra

http://www.wendylacapra.com/

Facebook * Twitter * Goodreads * Pinterest * Newsletter

Cover design by The Midnight Muse

Developmental Editing by Lindsey Faber & Copy Editing by Louisa Cornell

Ebook ISBN: 978-0-9994253-2-9

Print ISBN: 978-0-9994253-3-6

Manufactured in the United States of America

First Edition December 2018

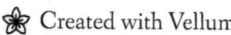 Created with Vellum

For my parents, Galen and Priscilla Gavel

Chapter One

November 1805

WIND WHIPPED CAPTAIN Lord Cheverley's improvised sail against his raft's mast. Salted sea-spray stung his lips and gusts roared in his ears. Using his shoulder, he wiped rain from his eyes and then re-wedged the paddle between his left arm and leg. Thighs straining, he gripped the groaning rudder.

He hadn't survived the unspeakable—seven years of war, a shipwreck, the loss of his right arm below the elbow, and six excruciating years of captivity—only to fail now.

Had he?

Wine-dark depths did not defer to long-serving officers of the Royal Navy. Frothy white waves were indifferent to sons of dukes. And life-hungry storms didn't give a damn if they stripped wives of their husbands, or sons of their fathers.

Penelope. Thaddeus. Vast emptiness yawned. Instinctively, he beseeched the heavens. *Please. I must survive.*

No god answered, only darkness without direction, no land, no guiding stars. The blank, shifting water beneath promised death—the same, slow demise that had claimed the lives of Chev's fellow seamen stationed with him on the *HMS Defiance*.

That gale, too, had materialized as if summoned by Poseidon's trident, without warning and yet powerful enough to devour his sixty-four-gun ship. Rocks like rusted knives protruded from a deadly shoal. Waves thundered without reprieve, breaking the *Defiance* into pieces unfit for kindling. And his ship's end had been only the beginning of his nightmare.

Tu n'es rien. You are nothing. *Je te possède maintenant en entier.* I own every part of you, now.

His raft listed. He spit over the side.

How much adversity could a man face before he surrendered to annihilation's mercy? How god-damned much?

The wind bellowed. Siren whispers sounded, sensing weakness—*supplicate, surrender, submit.*

What did he have to offer the world he'd left behind? He'd thought he'd return a hero. Instead, he was broken in body and soul. If he yielded to the storm, would it not be kinder to his family and a just restitution for his sins?

Memories feathered through his thoughts. His face buried in the softness of Penelope's hair. Her fingers, drifting in soothing circles against the small of his back.

He inhaled deep, straining against invisible bonds and roaring back into the wind. He cursed fate. He cursed God. He cursed the pirate witch who'd kept him captive. Then, he cursed himself.

His anger crystalized in breath, clouding the chilled air. He'd escaped captivity, darkness, restraints. Zephyr's winds and Poseidon's waves demanded the final say, but he would not give up without a fight.

Not tonight.

The bundle strapped across his back held what little

remained of hung beef and brandy. His cask of fresh water ran low, but he had enough to last another day.

He smothered his weakness, gritted his teeth, and held fast to the rudder.

He'd survive.

He'd survive on the pure need for vengeance.

* * *

For years, while Penelope labored to transform her husband's estate, Pensteague House, into a haven, she'd done her best to ignore the specter of neighboring Ithwick Manor, her husband's birthplace. At her worst, she'd wished the house and grounds would simply wither away. Then, however, the duke had been hale, his heir, Piers, alive, and she and her son superfluous to the duchy.

Now, everything had changed. Light filtering through the ducal library's windows chastised her for those fancies—the carpets were worn, the centuries-old relics, dust-laden, and a must-heavy scent burned inside the bridge of her nose. Hour by listless hour, time *had* been devouring what was left of her husband's boyhood world. And Ithwick's slow demise provided none of her hoped-for triumph.

Still, she had done her duty, called on the duke, and reported on Thaddeus's education and care—not that His Grace had appeared to understand a word—and she itched to leave this place full of ghosts and greed, mother to the heir or not.

Mrs. Renton—the duke's devoted housekeeper, and one of the few Ithwick residents Penelope trusted—wrung her liver-spotted hands.

"You must stay here at Ithwick," Mrs. Renton said, her pale eyes wide. "The duchy is without a duchess. The duke has lost his sense. Master Thaddeus remains too young to assume an heir's duties, and I am certain those...those..." Mrs. Renton gestured to the window, "...*men* mean to destroy everything that's left!"

Moving to the window, Penelope's gaze found the duke's closest male relatives apart from her son. The elder was Mr. Robert Anthony, who, as a descendant of the last duke's brother, was next in line to inherit after Penelope's son. The younger was a more recent arrival. Son to the duke's sister and her husband, the Duke of Warfield—Lord Thomas.

Absurd for those gentlemen and their friends to be littered about the lawn in winter, despite the unusually warm weather. Ridiculous, too, to be having a weighted disc throwing competition while attired in the latest, highly impractical fashion.

Penelope touched one of the pins in her tightly knotted hair and then rested her hand against the neckline of her outdated muslin. Unexpected discomfort blossomed in her chest. Hot, outsized discomfort.

Had Mr. Anthony, Lord Thomas, and their friends no shame? Even now, beyond the restless channel, young men were sacrificing their lives defending these craggy shores in a war that had already cost Penelope her husband.

"It appears to me"—Penelope's voice tinged with bitterness—"Mr. Anthony and Lord Thomas's only aspiration is a perpetual, decadent house party."

"It is worse than decadence! It is unnatural ambition."

Unnatural ambition? Pen knew them to be irresponsible, certainly, but to accuse them of intentionally usurping the duchy's power?

"Don't you see?" Mrs. Renton asked. "Mr. Anthony

brought suit to have your husband declared dead—you need look no further for evidence."

Penelope turned. "Mr. Anthony claimed the suit was necessary in order to free funds for Thaddeus." That was, however, before they'd discovered the surprise codicil to Cheverley's will granting Penelope full possession of Pensteague.

"Mr. Anthony," Mrs. Renton replied, "also claims His Grace is in complete accord with every decision he makes. But, you've seen for yourself—His Grace's words are unintelligible. As for Lord Thomas, he often returns late"—Mrs. Renton lowered her voice—"smelling of tipple and perfume."

Penelope frowned. The amorous exploits of her husband's cousin weren't any of her concern.

On the other hand, she could not deny His Grace's troubling condition. The duke's blank stare had sent shivers through her spine. For the first time, she'd felt a measure of compassion toward the tyrant.

But compassion for the duke and a willingness to intercede on his behalf were two very different positions.

"If *those* actions weren't awful enough," Mrs. Renton continued, "several women have left our employ so distressed they did not request references. The remaining women serve as mistresses and little else."

Penelope's flush spread to her cheeks. A man *had* to be vile-hearted to take advantage of anyone in their employ in such a way. "If you would, Mrs. Renton, supply the names and direction of those who left. I will provide references for them from Pensteague."

"Thank you, Lady Cheverley." Mrs. Renton bobbed a short curtsey. "But what of Mr. Anthony and Lord Thomas?"

Penelope gazed back out to the lawn. Were they merely reckless libertines as she'd long assumed, or were they greedy, dangerous men emboldened by the duke's illness, Thaddeus's youth, and his mother's perceived lack of connections?

Anthony had come to Ithwick following the duke's sudden illness at Piers's request and had taken over the duties of steward. After Piers's death, Lord Thomas had arrived. They'd been indifferent to Penelope and only cursorily interested in Thaddeus, and she was happy enough to allow things to remain as they were.

But what if they were intentionally robbing Ithwick? What remedy could she bring? She'd need solicitors, barristers, and witnesses to bring suit.

Though Pensteague thrived, she returned every sixpence earned to the estate...the only way she could care for the wounded seamen who regularly appeared on Pensteague's doorstep.

She'd taken the land her husband, Cheverley, had been granted as part of his mother's marriage settlement—a small cottage with surrounding forests and wastes—and transformed it into a thriving estate with choice livestock, crops, fallows, and coppiced wood. She'd raised Thaddeus without assistance from his ducal grandparents. She'd remained dutiful and loyal to Cheverley—and, by extension the duchy—all while striving to provide the wounded seamen Pensteague sheltered the dignity of a generous livelihood. And now, Pensteague was hers and hers alone.

Why should she place all she protected and all she'd built at risk?

"Mrs. Renton," she began, "you've always shown me kindness—"

"You were devoted to young Lord Cheverley," Mrs. Renton interrupted, sniffling. "I had hoped—"

"Allow me to speak plain." Penelope's own dashed hopes were difficult enough to bear, thank you. "To Lord Cheverley's family—everyone but the late duchess—I have always been an interloper. It is not my place to interfere."

"But there is no one else," Mrs. Renton replied. "Mr. Anthony acts as if he is master of Ithwick. You are the only one who can stop him."

"Mr. Anthony has been inclined to be pompous for as long as I have known him." But pompous and criminal did not negate one another, did they?

Pen attempted to rationalize again. "Isn't it natural Mr. Anthony take an interest in running the estate? He is, after Thaddeus, the next in line to inherit."

"Mr. Anthony and his coterie are draining the coffers. They are depleting the livestock. Their mismanagement is so severe, long-time tenants are choosing not to renew their leases. Please help us, Lady Cheverley. If *you* do not protect Ithwick, I fear there will be nothing left for young Master Thaddeus to inherit." Mrs. Renton paced the length of the rug, paused, then glanced up at a painting. "If Lord Cheverley were here now, it's what he would wish you to do."

Pen's lips flattened at the invocation of her husband's name. Reluctantly, she turned her gaze to the painting she'd avoided since entering the room—a portrait of Cheverley and his older brother as boys.

Though in the portrait, Cheverley's pale blonde hair had yet to darken, his stance already hinted at future swagger. His sheepish half-smile acknowledged worlds he had yet to understand, let alone conquer, but his pale blue eyes alit with a sickle-sharp cunning and an insatiable thirst for adventure.

A thirst that would rob her of a husband and Thaddeus of a father.

Tears pricked the corners of her eyes. Foolish, *foolish* man.

She did not, however, regret their brief affair and whirlwind marriage. The experience had been transformative and grand—to the extent her sixteen-year-old mind could comprehend grand—a rush that had taken her from the threshold of womanhood to the full blossom of her feminine power. And what followed, though unpleasant, had been the gauntlet that formed her character.

She sighed.

Thirteen years had passed since she'd seen her husband, six since he disappeared off the coast of France, though she hadn't known the gut-wrenching details of his final hours until the recent trial to prove his death.

Cheverley's ship had left the Channel Fleet on orders to capture a French privateer. Soon after the privateer was won, Chev ordered his first mate to sail home the prize. Then, a sudden storm parted the ships, pushing the *HMS Defiance* off her reckoning by three degrees. But three mere degrees had altered the ship's course enough for the naval gunner to meet a gruesome, rocky end.

In the horrible hours it took the hull to break to pieces, Chev sent part of his crew in a cutter, hopeful they'd find harbor. He remained with his ship...exactly what Penelope would expect of her husband—always certain he could find or forge a way, always driven to display mythic heroism, even at the expense of those he held dear.

In this case, Chev failed. The cutter capsized. The few survivors drifted for days before being rescued. As for Cheverley, after reviewing the evidence, a judge declared him dead. No man, he said, could have survived the wreck.

Then again, her husband had not been just any man.

A burst of low, male laughter rose up from the lawn.

"They laugh while they drain the duchy dry," Mrs. Renton murmured. "They wouldn't have dared to set foot in the house in the first place if...if..."

"...If Lord Cheverley were here," Pen finished quietly.

Yes, she was weary. Yes, she could not spare the expense.

But could she truly turn her back on this part of her husband's past, forever denying skeletons that were not so much in a cupboard as atop a neighboring hill?

"Perhaps," Mrs. Renton whispered, "Lord Cheverley will yet return."

Penelope's neck prickled.

If she were honest, on nights when the moon's glow brightened the sheets of her marriage bed, loneliness pierced her heart like one of her husband's hand-crafted arrows, and she sometimes allowed herself to imagine Cheverley would return.

"Mrs. Renton"—she squelched irrational hope—"we must be careful what we wish. If Cheverley survived, a terrible fate must have befallen him. If he is alive, he is suffering."

She turned away from the portrait.

What would Chev have wanted her to do? If he were here, he would have wanted her to remain tucked up in the proper little jewel casing he'd prepared while *he* forged forth to set everything to rights in a spectacular show.

But he wasn't here. He hadn't been here for thirteen years.

The better question was—what did she wish to do? How much of what she'd built in Cheverley's name could she risk?

She turned about, taking in the ducal library and considering the stern faces of her husband's ancestors glaring down from centuries past.

If Mr. Anthony and Lord Thomas were corrupt, what would she be teaching Thaddeus if she remained ensconced in comfort while corruption flourished?

Corruption bred fear. Fear bred distrust, anger, divisions and even—if left unchecked—bloodshed.

She *did* have a responsibility, loath as she was to admit it. Whatever the cost now, it would pale in comparison to the future cost if these men succeeded in fully usurping the duchy's power. She must find a way to root out and remove the corruption. Not only for Thaddeus's sake, but for the sake of those, like Mrs. Renton, whose livelihoods depended on Ithwick.

"Mrs. Renton, I concede." Lord help her. "Thaddeus and I will take up residence at Ithwick, care for the duke and keep a close eye on Mr. Anthony and Lord Thomas. Having the heir and his mother present should gentle the worst of their conduct."

"And if they ask why?"

"I will tell them I intend to weave a shroud for Cheverley on the medieval loom upstairs."

"Bless you, my lady." Mrs. Renton's brows knit. "But is it wise to bring Master Thaddeus? As Master Thaddeus's guardian, Lord Thomas could make trouble."

Let him try.

"Thaddeus goes where I go." In fact, Thaddeus was so protective, she couldn't have confined him to Pensteague if she wished. "Besides, *both* the duke and Lord Thomas serve as guardians. Thomas cannot assert himself without exposing the duke's state. And, in a few months, Thaddeus will be fourteen—old enough to choose his own guardians."

She recast her gaze toward the group of gentlemen below. Another drunken cheer rose from the lawn.

"You needn't worry any longer, Mrs. Renton." She spoke with bravado she did not feel. "I will become Ithwick's unlikely champion."

But were her adversaries indolent man-children, or were they a crawling nest of vipers?

And, if they *were* a nest of vipers—she chilled—which would be the first to sting?

Chapter Two

Lungs—Cheverley inhaled—*on fire*.

He came fully awake, coughing like a man possessed. Air pricked in his chest, stubbly as a beggar's cheek. Every attempted inhale thrust another shard of glass between his ribs. If only he could sit, he could...

He expelled a guttural *oomph* as his chin landed in straw. *Yes.* Pain rippled through his bones. *Right.*

No arm.

Yet, somehow, the sensation of a *hand* remained, right down to the jarring ache in his non-existent—though strangely fisted—fingers. He rolled onto his back and blinked into the dim light breathing in air thick with tallow's heavy scent. Above him, a roof of thatch. Beneath him, stillness.

He'd made his way to land, at least.

"He's back."

A man's voice. Not one Cheverley recognized. English, though. Which was an immense relief...for unclear reasons.

"Lord have mercy." A woman. "T'ain't right. He was dead, he was, when you pulled him out the water."

Out *of* the water.

He frowned.

Where had that come from? He didn't give a sixpence about grammar. What passed for English on his ship would have curled a schoolmaster's toes—not counting the sizable portion of the crew who had other native languages.

Wait... *His* ship? Was he a captain, then?

"He looked dead at first," the man agreed. "But he's coughin' now, ain't he?"

He was. He snatched another illusive, rasping breath.

"Should have left him. You ain't got no reason t'be dragging in strays like you do."

A cat's hiss suffused the shadows. He shivered.

"Go on," the man cooed. "She's all talk."

The feline mewed.

"Mark me, lass," the man continued, "they'll be a prize for this one."

The woman snorted. "I ain't no lass. And that one ain't worth a half-penny. Can't you see he's missing his arm?"

The man grasped his ankle and twisted. Chev cried out, punctuating with a kick.

"Areeah! Stop that." The man lowered his voice. "Look here. That is the Hurtheven crest. No telling the other two —his scars cut right through. I wager he's quality, though."

Chev stilled. Hurtheven...?

"Quality?" The woman harrumphed, dismissive. "What's he doin' with his clothes all tattered, then? He ain't nothin' more than a fisherman. Or worse." She paused. "He could be from the *other side*."

What did she mean, *the other side*? He concentrated. Ah, yes. War. Between the kingdom and France.

Chev lifted his head. "Not"—he coughed—"French."

"You see?" The man said.

The woman folded her arms. "Just what a...*Frenchman* would say, ain't it?"

Good Lord.

"What's this here on your ankle?" The man tapped Chev's bone.

Cheverley yanked back his leg. As he stared down at a trio of crests, two faces from his boyhood pieced together.

"Hurth...Hurtheven," he repeated the title the man had supplied.

Yes, one of the faces was Hurtheven. Hurtheven—whom he'd met...at Eton? That sounded correct. Hurtheven...who was a good sort, even if he had been mad enough to insist the three of them scar their ankles with pins and ink. It had *stung,* damn it all.

He frowned again.

How had he remembered that detail? And what of the other boy? He touched the second crest. The boy's family title remained elusive, but as he touched the third, the name of his own family seat came rushing back.

Ithwick.

Suddenly, he knew he was Captain Lord Cheverley, the second son of the Duke of Ithwick—not that he was going to proclaim the fact to these two. He didn't know where he was. He barely knew *who* he was.

Hurtheven would have to be enough.

"I work...for"—*Almighty!* Every dammed word was a struggle—"the Duke...of Hurth...even."

"Knew it!" the man crowed.

"*Pfft.* You said he *was* quality. Not that he *worked* for quality."

"It doesn't matter," the man replied. "Hurtheven's sure to give a prize. A shilling at least."

"A tuppence at best. What good's this one to anyone, let alone a duke?"

"Hurtheven will...reward. Get word... *Please.*" Forcing out the final word, Chev collapsed.

He closed his eyes against a wave of nausea. The louse had better provide a reward, even if it had been a long time since they'd seen one another.

But why?

He couldn't remember, and the reason was important. Very, very important. There were other things he should remember too. Things even more vital.

The image of a woman shimmered beneath his lids. A woman with blonde hair, smooth as corn silk. Graceful and willowy yet brimming with a determination that was the essence of life.

Penelope. His wife.

A prize he had whisked away to store and to protect.

In his memory, his lips touched her collarbone before sliding over to the adjacent valley in the v at the bottom of her throat.

Heaven.

His longing stretched out into the ether, grasping for balm that could soothe his soul. What returned, however, was a sense of foreboding.

He closed his eyes. Another woman's image replaced Penelope. A woman with dark hair and a voice that cut like a metal scourge.

Tu n'es rien. You are nothing.

Her whisper sliced through his ears. His blood went cold. His breath lodged in his throat. Then, oblivion claimed him once again.

* * *

The ship had resumed rocking.

That, however, hadn't felt like the list of a ship. And even a gale couldn't cause a rumble like—*bam.*

The back of Cheverley's head smacked against a hard surface.

St. George's dragon.

He winced.

Only, *had* St. George killed a dragon? Or, had it been St. Michael?

No. Not *St.* Michael. His heart surged as another memory slipped into place. The other Michael, the archangel...*he* killed the dragon. But maybe St. George had also—*bam.*

His nonsensical thoughts arrested.

"Christ!" he cursed.

He ached all over. And someone had left an anchor on his chest. Though, the weighted spot was rather small to be an anchor. Instinctively, he swatted. Air, of course.

Wrong arm.

"Keep still, would you?" The voice came from far away, not in proximity but in time.

With concentrated effort, Cheverley lifted leaden lids. He was in some sort of a carriage. A long one. Curtained. Black. No benches.

Bam—hell and damnation. Was he in a hearse? A *moving* hearse?

He struggled to rise. The anchor *still* did not move. He squinted, parsing the shadows. The anchor was a hand, and the hand was unquestionably attached to a man crouching at his side.

The man was large. Herculean, almost, though his glinting buttons suggested he was far from common.

"What the devil?"

The man's teeth flashed as he smiled. "Not the devil, though some suggest I am related to him." He lifted one brow. "And, when you rise from the dead, you're bound to increase their certainty."

Pardon? "Not dead."

"Yes." He sighed. "I am afraid you are. As far as the law and your family are concerned, anyway."

The man's words sent warning through Cheverley's blood, though his voice—not just the tone, but his way of speaking—felt very familiar.

"You needn't worry." The anchor tapped against his chest. "We'll do something about the 'your being dead' part...after we take care of your problems with the Admiralty."

The man clucked his tongue.

"You are in a good deal of trouble, you know—not that I should be surprised." He held up a finger. "At sixteen, you stole a carriage and eloped with the daughter of a pig farmer," a second finger joined the first, "at twenty-three, just before disappearing without a trace, you demanded I meet you in enemy waters so you could amend your will, and, now," he held up a third, "on the cusp of your third decade, you wash up in rags with little more to say to your rescuers than my name. Which means," The man's face loomed, "you've placed me in a good deal of trouble, too." A crease marked his patrician chin. "I detest trouble."

No, you don't. Chev's answer formed without thought. *You revel in trouble.*

Chev blinked.

"Too much, too fast?" The man's dark brows drew together. "Let's start with the main, then. Do you know who you are?"

"Captain Lord Cheverley." Chev hated the implied question in his voice.

The man, however, was pleased. "That's right. Though, to be fair, I might not have recognized you but for the helpful bit of artistry on your ankle. Do you know me?"

"Do I?" Chev asked. "Know you?"

"I should hope so. Though, if you've forgotten, proper introductions are in order." The man cleared his throat. "The Duke of Hurtheven"—he inclined his head—"at your service."

Chev blinked again. "Hurtheven?"

"Last time I checked. And you should know, you laughed like a madman after seeing me in my first set of parliamentary robes." His grin returned. "Bad form, that."

"You looked preposterous," Chev said, again, without thought.

Then, recollections rolled past like alabaster marbles, zig-zagging through time and flashing with head-splitting brilliance. Hurtheven in his robes. Hurtheven and another man, witnessing his wedding. Penelope, heavy with child and begging him not to go. The thunder of cannons. A vast darkness. A vicious sea. As best he could, he sorted them in time.

"I was in a raft." Why had he been in a raft? "Then, there was a man...and a woman...and..." a cat?

He hated cats. He was clear about that much, at least.

"Yes. Right again," Hurtheven said. "A man. And a woman." He lifted a brow. "I don't suppose you had a choice who fished you from the sea, but next time I would be obliged if you wash up closer to someone less grasping. You cost me *two* gold guineas, you know."

"Gold guineas?" What kind of fisherman demanded gold from a duke?

"Well…" Hurtheven paused, "…if you prefer to be exacting—one guinea was for your person, the other to secure their silence."

"Silence?" Cheverley asked. "Why?"

"I told you." Hurtheven made an exasperated sound. "You're dead."

"*Explain,*" Cheverley said through gritted teeth.

"Well, I couldn't have those greedy bob tails realize they'd fished *you* out of the channel. You bet your Hessians they'd have demanded more than two guineas for the heir apparent to the Duke of Ithwick, and two was all I had." He glanced askance. "Bad night at the tables."

Heir? Cheverley coughed. "Not…heir."

"You aren't *now,* of course. You are dead. The distinction of heir presumptive, therefore, belongs to your son."

His son? His heartbeat surged. Yes. He *did* have a son, didn't he?

Thaddeus.

He strained to recall a face. But, no. He'd never met his son.

The old wound broke open and other memories spilled forth.

He'd eloped to Scotland without his father's consent and then further enraged the duke by beginning to work a separate estate made irrevocably his because of a clause in the duchess's marriage contract.

Naively, Chev believed the estate would place his family beyond the duke's power.

Then came the duke's ultimatum—either Chev take a naval commission, or face a lawsuit challenging his marriage and potentially making a bastard of his child, already well on the way.

At first, he'd gambled the duke would come to his senses and place family above pride and relent.

His Grace had not.

When Chev reluctantly accepted the commission, his father demanded he not return until he had proven himself. Chev left, determined to rise above his father's power by becoming the greatest naval hero England had seen since Raleigh. And then—

Then what? Nothing came.

But he was in rags. So, not Raleigh.

And—he grimaced—Hurtheven had said *heir*.

He was certain he hadn't been heir, which meant... "My brother?"

"Devil take it. I'd forgotten you wouldn't know." Hurtheven gripped Chev's shoulder and bowed his head. "Piers is gone."

"How?"

"Nasty bit of bad luck." Hurtheven winced. "He was wandering through the woods at Ithwick and stepped into a nest of adders, poor chap. Two days passed before they found him. Coroner wasn't sure if it was the snake bites or the cold damp that got him—likely a bit of both. I am sorry, Chev."

Loss settled over Cheverley. *Ah, Piers.* His brother had loved his woodland rambles.

How could it be Chev had survived war and disaster while Piers had been killed by something so common in Cornwall as a few snakes and a bit of rain?

"Her Grace, the Duchess of Ithwick," Hurtheven continued, "passed away last year. Grief, the physician said, as if such a thing were possible."

Chev swallowed, roughly.

"The duke lives, though he is, I understand, not well. In

the absence of an adult heir, your cousins have become"—Hurtheven cleared his throat—"quite solicitous."

Both his brother and his mother were dead? He finally grasped Hurtheven's meaning. *He* must have been declared dead, too.

He wasn't *dead*. He'd been lost at sea.

That's what had happened. He'd been lost at sea for... Months? Years? More? Anyway, he'd been desperate to get home from...?

He shook his head, coming back to the idea that his wife and son believed him to be dead.

Lost was an unfinished sentence; Dead, a conclusive period. The end to one sentence so that another one could begin. If he were dead, his belongings would have been disbursed and his wife...

Good God. Was Pen still his wife? "Penelope?"

"Alive." Hurtheven's gaze slid away. "Hale, the last time we met."

"But is she...is she...?"

Hurtheven grimaced. "I judged it impertinent to ask if she'd been faithful. But she is unwed." He flashed a look. "At present."

At present? Chev coughed. "And what of my son?"

"Thaddeus"—Hurtheven's expression softened—"is a healthy lad. If you can call a young man of thirteen a lad."

Thirteen? Chev grasped his head between his thumb and forefinger. He'd been apart from his family for thirteen years?

Impossible, but true.

He was not a lost man found, but a dead man resurrected. His mother and brother, gone. His father dying. A son he did not know on the cusp of manhood. And a wife...

Not wed. *Yet.*

His whole being hung from *yet,* swaying like fresh kill on a gamekeeper's hook. He massaged his temples.

Had he really believed, even for a moment, she could have been pining for him all this time?

"Better I hadn't returned."

Hurtheven inhaled sharply. "How dare you suggest Pen would be better off if you were, in fact, dead?"

Bitterness twisted Chev's features. "Not worth a half-penny, the woman said."

"What woman?"

"The grasping, greedy bob tail."

Hurtheven snorted. "If I'd known how she felt, it would have saved me a good deal of blunt."

Nothing about this circumstance was amusing in the least. Even if Pen were to have held out hope—"How is my wife to feel when *this*"—Chev lifted his severed arm—"is returned to her?"

Hurtheven examined Chev's raised arm with interest. Then, he met Chev's gaze. "You speak," he said, "as if you were a stray package. You are her husband. Her *beloved* husband."

"I am not the man she married."

"I should hope not! She married a randy sixteen-year-old buck with a good deal more brawn than brain."

Chev's startled cough ached in his ribs. "Whoreson," he said with affection.

"Chev." Hurtheven lifted a lip. "I knew you were in there."

Cheverley's sense had started to return, anyway. Wearily, Chev set aside questions too unanswerable for his throbbing mind.

"Where *are* we going, anyway?" he asked.

Hurtheven raised an imperious brow. "Demanding, aren't you?"

"You don't have a destination in mind."

"I most certainly do! My plan—brilliant for being hastily put together, I might add—begins at the Admiralty."

The Admiralty. Chev nodded. Of course. He'd remembered he was an officer. A captain. He squeezed his eyes closed. And his ship—the *HMS Defiance*—a slight, fast beauty with a mast as tall as—

"The Admiralty will court-martial you for the loss of your ship," Hurtheven said.

Chev winced, turning his head to the side. Behind his lids, the mast swayed, and then split apart from the ship, splashing into the sea.

Suddenly he knew there was more. So much more. And he wasn't ready for any of it.

"And," Hurtheven continued, oblivious, "they will also want to know where you have been—as would, well, *everyone,* by the way."

Where *had* he been? The damp stench of a cave stung Chev's nostrils.

On an island. Or not.

He could not say for certain. However—he glanced down at his arm—his first attempted escape ended with a lead ball in his wrist...which had then led to an amputation.

Saw jaws rattled his bones and then a gravelly, female voice filled his ears.

Le pauvre bébé. The poor baby. *Je pense que je te préfères comme ça.* I think I like you better now. *Plus facile à maîtriser.* Easier to subdue.

He saw her face. The pirate.

He slammed the stub of his arm against the hard surface beneath him.

She disappeared.

"No answers." What he had was a devil of a headache and a chill that had seeped into his bones. "Hurts, Hurtheven. Bad."

"I know." Hurtheven's voice softened.

"I cannot go home." Not like this—weak and left cowering by a few phantom whispers.

Hurtheven was right. Everyone would want to know where he'd been. And Chev had locked the answer in an unfolded memory.

"You can't go home," Hurtheven amended, "before you've been to the Admiralty."

"You don't understand."

Hurtheven flashed him a startled glance. His lips flattened as he thought. "We'll store you at Ash's, then. Until you regain your strength."

"Ash?" He frowned.

"Weren't here for that either, were you? Our old friend has been fully fitted with the dubious mantle of his mad father—the Duke of Ashbey." Hurtheven stopped abruptly. He tilted his head. "For now, let's just say Ash's habits are such you could stay with him as long as you need, with no one the wiser."

Ashbey. Chev fitted the family name to the other face he'd remembered when he'd first awoken.

Hurtheven rubbed his chin. "Perhaps this isn't the worst of ideas. You, Ash, myself." He chuckled. "Who'd have thought our brotherhood would reunite?"

Eta Rho Zeta. The ink on his ankle. A name for the secret triumvirate inspired by some American society Hurtheven's uncle had founded. Three school boys, taking for themselves the mantle of gods—Zeus, Hades and Poseidon.

Poseidon. He snorted. What hubris. If the sea god existed, no wonder the waves had been intent on his death.

"You were always a bit touched," Cheverley said.

"Entitled, yes. Arrogant, often. But my mind's as sound as the king's."

Cheverley expelled a rough, involuntary chuckle. Hurtheven glanced askance with a half-smile. He squeezed Cheverley's shoulder.

"My God... Chev." His smile faded. He shook his head, and then he turned away. "It is really you."

The hearse jostled, parting the curtains and illuminating Hurtheven's face. Lines—deep cut—chiseled his forehead and wetness glinted in the corners of his eyes.

Thirteen years.

Vastness hit Chev all at once—an expanse that set him adrift in uncertainty.

In bone-deep fear.

Hurtheven wiped his eyes with the back of his hand and stiffened. "The sea spit you up. For now, be grateful."

Grateful?

There was much he didn't know. So much he had yet to understand. He turned his head to the side. Heat from Hurtheven's hand seeped into his skin. Warm. Comforting.

Grateful. Yes. *For now.*

He had made it out of the storm. He had made it back to land. As for the menace lurking just beyond the grasp of his consciousness?

That was too large to be faced—or exorcised—with weakened limbs and a mind engulfed with fog.

First, he must regain his strength. Because when those memories came, they would bring a fury stronger than the sea.

Chapter Three

Spring 1806

UNDYED WARP STRINGS stretched far above Penelope's head, giving the ancient loom rescued from the ruins of Ithwick Castle the appearance of a massive harp. Instead of producing music, however, Penelope's skilled fingers—carefully guided by the image in the mirror beyond—slowly transformed bobbins of colored thread into representations of the things Cheverley held dear—Pensteague, his longbow, arrows and quiver, Ithwick Manor, Ithwick Castle's ruins, and the sea.

Conspicuously left out of her design for Cheverley's shroud? Herself and Thaddeus.

The young bride he'd left. The son he'd never met.

Yes, Chev's father—the duke—had given him an impossible choice. But, had Cheverley chosen to stay, they might have prevailed by working together, either in the courts or through the duchess's influence.

Even the amendment to Cheverley's will had hurt almost as much as it had helped. Certainly, the will had placed Pensteague in her possession, thus ensuring her and

Thaddeus a home whether or not their marriage was challenged.

But the amended will had been witnessed by Ashbey and Hurtheven and dated just a few months before Cheverley went missing—which meant he arranged to see his friends when he hadn't taken the time to meet his son.

She pursed her lips and tucked her anger back inside as neatly as she tucked away her tightly knotted hair.

She'd had far too much time to think these past few weeks—too much time to splash fruitlessly in puddles of regret.

She missed Pensteague. She missed bearing witness to the camaraderie between the former navy men who'd taken refuge in her home. Without them she felt Chev's loss more keenly—something she had not anticipated.

Just like she hadn't anticipated how ardently Mr. Anthony, Lord Thomas, and their guests would compete for her attention. They had never shown the least bit of interest in her before, but now they showered her with praise. Their unwelcome advances left her little choice but to retreat to the loom whenever the duke rested.

Carefully, she moved her shuttle between strings and began another row of black thread—not for the first time, either.

During the day, Penelope cared for the duke or wove, but, by night, she searched for the estate records Mr. Anthony had hidden while Mrs. Renton removed half of Penelope's knots. She hoped the delay would give her more time to find something that could oust Anthony and Thomas from the estate, some proof of ill intent.

Unfortunately, Penelope had yet to uncover any evidence that would convince a solicitor—let alone a judge

—that Mr. Anthony and Lord Thomas were willfully attempting to usurp the duchy. However, she'd noticed enough oddities to convince *her* they were not merely self-indulgent libertines, consuming what they could until Thaddeus came of age.

First, there was the matter of the missing books. And, suspiciously, the duke improved under Penelope's care. She couldn't yet make sense of His Grace's words, but just yesterday, with Thaddeus's assistance, the duke had been strong enough to take a full turn about the library.

The only change she'd made had been to prepare the duke's medicines and food and provide daily encouragement and exercise. She suspected His Grace's illness had not been the sole result of accidental misfortune but had been magnified by neglect and malevolence. And, if her suspicions were correct, Mr. Anthony and Lord Thomas were far more dangerous than even Mrs. Renton believed.

She checked her progress in the mirror, startled to see Mr. Anthony's reflection.

Though cousins, Anthony bore little resemblance to Cheverley. Where Chev's features had been angular, Anthony's were round. Where Chev's eyes had been light and his gaze penetrating, Anthony's were dark, and they peered, mouse-like, from beneath a carefully greased fringe of hair.

She shifted her leg, reassured by the presence of her knife.

A woman alone could never be too careful.

"Ah, Penelope." Anthony strode into the room without permission. "I knew you would eventually sense my presence."

"Mr. Anthony"—she might be obliged to endure his

familiarity. She was not obliged to reciprocate—"is something amiss?"

She turned but did not stand.

"Amiss? No." He smiled. "I came to check on your progress. You've been working on this morbid project for how long—eight weeks?" Anthony glanced over her shoulder. "Shouldn't you be farther along?"

"Good work takes time," she said. "A tapestry of this quality would take a weaver far more talented than I months to create. And certainly, you would not wish me to memorialize my husband with anything less than my best work."

Anthony's gaze traveled over her features, lingered on her lips, and then returned to her eyes.

"Pray do continue." He seated himself on a bench against the wall. "I will observe."

She blinked. How was she to concentrate with his cloying presence? "I prefer solitude."

"That is unfortunate. *I* prefer to stay."

His intentional provocation snaked through her like a living creature. She held his gaze for a long moment, allowing the disturbance to settle.

Petulant and selfish, Anthony used provocations like arrows, weakening his opponents with repeated dings meant to induce outrage. She polished the nick to her dignity and turned to resume her work. Outrage was an effective weapon.

A weapon she intended to hold in reserve.

"What would you say," Anthony began, "if I told you Mrs. Renton unties your knots every night?"

She met Anthony's gaze in the mirror, eyes steady. "Mrs. Renton has been gracious enough to assist. I grieve for my husband, and this tapestry contains everything he held dear. Is it so surprising I find mistakes when I review the day's work?"

"Not surprising at all." Anthony paused. "As a matter of fact, Lord Thomas and I have, of late, had several discussions on the topic of your...perpetual grief."

Her heartbeat quickened. "You needn't trouble yourselves with my concerns."

"What kind of family would we be if we did not?" Another skin-crawling smile. "We all—every man present—long for your presence. How could we not? So, we've decided that one of us should sit with you, every day...as a means of comfort and support."

Her shuttle slipped from her fingers, knocking against the bobbins as it fell.

"Perhaps then," he continued, "you will make fewer mistakes."

"How surprisingly...kind."

"Come, Penelope." He leaned forward. "You must realize I'd offer more than kindness, if only you would allow."

She rose from the chair and he, from the bench.

"Must I again remind you again that I prefer to be addressed as Lady Cheverley, Mr. Anthony?"

He ignored her protestation. "Is it not time to accept your fate? Surely you have not resigned yourself to a life without love."

She flashed him a warning glance. "I am a married woman."

"Which is it?" A faint smile graced his lips. "Grieving widow, or married woman? You cannot be both." He waited. "Very well then, don't answer. But hope—unwarranted hope—is nothing more than cruelty. If Lord Cheverley were alive, would he have gone for so long without word?"

No. Cheverley had written regularly before he'd disappeared. Long letters detailing his feats of bravery and closing with words of devotion.

And, as much as she'd treasured his letters, the reminder of his absence made her ache.

Anthony lowered his voice. "I would never leave you alone, if you were mine."

She stiffened. "I belong to no one."

He veiled his lids and whetted his lips. "Penelope..."

She turned away. Had he actually intended they *kiss?*

She lifted a handkerchief to her face and pretended she hadn't noticed.

"Pardon," she sniffed. "The subject is not, naturally, an easy one."

He clamped hot hands on her shoulders. "It's well past time you made future arrangements. For the good of the duchy."

"The duchy." She kept her voice light, though the heat in his hands made her ill. "Why should my marital status matter to the duchy? And, if the good of the duchy is your aim..."

Anthony cocked a brow.

"...Aren't you concerned how rapidly your guests have been draining our resources?"

"Our?" he queried.

"Yes, *our.* We are family, as you pointed out."

"What makes you think Ithwick's resources are being drained?"

"Come now, Mr. Anthony." She repeated his phrasing while removing his hands from her shoulders. "The lavish meals you supply your guests have decimated our supply of beef, deer, chicken, and pheasant."

"I hadn't realized you'd been paying such close attention." He paused. "Did you just refer to the gentlemen staying here as *my* guests?"

"Of course, they are *your* guests. And, at this rate, to keep them fed, you will soon need beg pork from *my* home farm."

"*Your* home farm. Ah, yes. The codicil. I have my doubts about that, you know."

Inner bells clanged alarm. Sternly, she reminded herself she had the loyalty of Cheverley's friends.

"Are your doubts strong enough to challenge the Duke of Ashbey and the Duke of Hurtheven in court?" she asked.

Anthony's grin vanished. "Lord Thomas believes you are harmless. But I warned him you had a cunning little mind. Did you think you had me fooled?"

"I haven't any idea what you mean. In no way have I been trying to fool—"

"If anyone will beg," Anthony interrupted, "it will be you." He plucked a carefully folded gazette out from beneath his waistcoat. "I am afraid, *my lady,* your reputation, or what little you had, anyway, is in tatters."

The newspaper crackled as it unraveled. Bold, black letters shouted, "Captain's Widow Ready to Set Sail."

"Try running to your late husband's friends, now," Anthony taunted with a curled-lip sneer. "Let us see how your would-be lover Hurtheven responds."

She met his gaze, furious. "Why on earth would you do this?"

"*I've* done nothing." Anthony raised his brows. "You, my dear, left your little cottage and your noble naval charity scheme and willfully joined a household full of eligible gentlemen mere weeks after your husband was declared dead. Clearly, even the papers comprehend the nature of your stay."

"I spend my time caring for the duke and *weaving!* I wouldn't know your gentlemen friends one from another."

"*Please,*" Anthony scoffed. His inhale whistled in his nose. "Did you really think we believed you were here to weave a shroud? That you are driven by duty and devotion to care for a duke who tried to ruin you?"

With a huff, she wrestled the newspaper from his grip and then threw the it on the floor. "That is what I think of your attempt to besmirch my name."

"Ah." His smile returned. "*There* is the impudent little miss with the audacity to marry a duke's son."

"I beg your—" She shut her mouth. She'd never beg anything from Anthony, figure of speech or no.

"Such an odd wedding, too," Anthony mused. "An anvil marriage in the dead of night. The duke, as I recall, was more than a little displeased. Isn't that how Lord Cheverley ended up a midshipman despite being the rather advanced age of sixteen?"

The salted wound stung. But she owned Pensteague, now. There was nothing Anthony could do. "*If* my marriage could have been disproved," she replied, "the duke would have done so long ago."

"Who said anything about disproving your marriage? Such a wild imagination you have." His scent enveloped her as he leaned in. "It makes me wonder how wild you are in—"

She smacked him without thought—jerking back as an angry, red blotch appeared on his cheek.

Anthony plucked her hand from the air and ran his

thumb over the still-burning flesh. Then, he kissed her palm.

"Settle, sweet."

Nauseating. Indecent. "Let me go."

"Poor dear—first the loss of your husband, then the spectacle of a trial, and then the duke's devastating illness. Perhaps Lord Thomas is right. Perhaps all of this has made you too overwrought to properly care for the duke and the ducal heir. Perhaps we should, as Thomas wishes, send Thaddeus to school and you...to a place where you could properly convalesce."

Breathe in. Evenly. "Are you threatening me?"

"Me? I do not make threats." His gaze swept her person. "I devise solutions. However," he dangled his sentence like a lure, "I believe I could persuade Lord Thomas to forgo making arrangements..."

"If I abandon Ithwick and return to Pensteague House."

Had she thought his gaze mouse-like? Rat-like would have been more apt.

"If you agree to marry me."

"You cannot be serious."

"Why? Because you know how much I abhor your tainted blood? True, but not so much that I'm blinded to your...assets." He moved his thumb against her palm. "Think clearly, sweet. You can save your reputation in one, easy sweep. The matter is simple, really. You are a widow in need of protection. I am a man"—his gaze dropped to her chest—"more than willing to protect."

"Never," she whispered.

"We'll see, won't we?" His smile reappeared. "For now, I trust you will comply with a much simpler request."

Instinctively, she yanked back her hand.

"Oh"—he snorted—"what a delightfully vulgar mind

you have. You've no need to look so revolted. I merely ask that you preside over a soiree for our neighbors."

"Why should I preside over a gathering that proports all is well at Ithwick?"

"Because all *is* well." He lifted his brows. "I don't believe I've made myself clear. In this, you do not have a choice. You *will* preside over a soiree next week and you *will* finish this ridiculous project by month's end. Then, we will wed." His eyes flashed. "Or, you will find yourself *convalescing* somewhere even Ashbey and Hurtheven will not be able to assist...that is, until you come to your senses."

"We'll see." She did not return his smile. "Won't we?"

"You tread on ground far more treacherous than you can imagine." His nostrils flared. "Do you think you can run to Hurtheven as you have in the past? I imagine he'll be more than a little disappointed, especially as your change of heart came so soon after you rejected him. And, as for Cheverley's other devoted friend...the Duke of Ashbey has recently wed. How much time to you think he'd devote to a childhood friend's widow?" He folded his hands behind his back and then swiveled on his heel. "You are alone, my dear. Once you consider the alternative to my offer, I've no doubt you'll change your mind."

He left the room.

She shut the door behind him, turned the key in the lock, and then backed away, rubbing the palm he'd kissed against her skirts until she could no longer feel his lips.

How had Anthony known about Hurtheven's marriage proposal?

She'd given Hurtheven serious consideration—who wouldn't? Hurtheven had been kind and solicitous to her, and a life-long friend to Chev. He was handsome, powerful and, as his wife, she'd never have to worry about Thaddeus's upbringing or Pensteague's finances again.

In the end, however, she'd declined. Chev would always cast a long shadow, and Hurtheven deserved someone who could place him first in her heart.

He'd accepted her decision with grace. How would he respond now?

If Anthony's attempt to drive a wedge between her and Cheverley's friends succeeded, what was she to do?

Take Thaddeus and run.

But that was exactly what he wanted, wasn't it? To render her powerless, either by seizing control of her purse and person through marriage, by frightening her enough for her to leave, or by sending her to—she swallowed—an asylum.

He must be afraid. Otherwise, he would not be working so hard to separate her from Cheverley's friends.

Her calm returned, wrapping around her like a cloak.

She wasn't going to run. Not yet.

She was not powerless. The duke was improving. Thaddeus was strong, and smart, and brave. And, no matter what rumors Anthony had spread, her bond with Cheverley's friends could not be swayed.

Mrs. Renton's suspicions had been correct. Anthony not only craved control of Ithwick, he wanted control—through her—of Thaddeus and Pensteague as well.

But Pensteague's riches were nothing compared to Ithwick—so why?

She'd gather what information she could at the soiree. She'd enlist Emmaus—the strongest and most trustworthy of the sailors at Pensteague—as her eyes and ears in the village. And, she'd continue to scour the records.

Whatever Anthony and Thomas had set in motion, she would stop.

She was no longer the frightened young woman she'd been. She was a widow, a mother alone. She had survived more challenges than Anthony and Thomas had ever known. If they thought she would be easily intimidated, they would soon find they were very much mistaken.

Her future—and Thaddeus's—depended on her success.

Chapter Four

CHEVERLEY RECREATED A mental image of the pirate—black hair, malice-cursed eyes, and full, feminine lips in a misleading, practiced pout. Ignoring the cold sweat beading at his temples and soaking his nape, he overlaid her image on his target and focused his enmity at the center of her putrid heart.

He balanced the lower curve of his longbow against his boot and located the leather mouthpiece he'd tied around either side of the copal beads fused around the nock point. Using his right arm as a counter-weight, he nocked his arrow with his left, then shifted that hand to the bow. Then, with his back teeth, he bit down on the mouthpiece.

Feeling Hurtheven's gaze but refusing to acknowledge his fascinated stare, he pushed away on the bow at the same time he pulled back the string. The muscles in his neck corded as the already taught flax strained to breaking.

He unlocked his jaw. The arrow whizzed through the air, hitting the target with a thud and a subsequent low-toned, thoroughly satisfying pulse.

"Huzzah." Hurtheven whispered—not so much a cheer as an exclamation of awe.

Chev spit. The lingering taste was disgusting, really. Then again, after spending years believing he'd never shoot again, disgust was a small price to pay.

In the past few months, he learned to use every part of his body as he rebuilt his strength. But even his newly honed skills were not enough to silence the voice that besieged in nightly shadow, gnawing like a rodent, whittling away the hopes of family and home that kept him alive in the pirate's sunless cave.

Tu pourrais t'échapper, mais tu m'appartiens, maintenant et toujours. You might escape, but you belong to me, now and always.

He spit again.

No matter how hard he worked, the pirate's words—as much as her surgeon's saw—left him branded. Enraged. Broken.

Thaddeus believed his father a hero. Thaddeus did not need the truth.

And, Penelope, well, she'd proven she did not need him at all.

Not only did Penelope own a now-thriving Pensteague, the papers recently claimed she'd set an intention to wed.

With eyes fixed to the red-centered target, he agonized again.

The night he'd arrived at the Admiralty, he'd found those in charge deeply embroiled in scandal. Their greatest hero—Chev's former commander, Admiral Stone—had died, and the Admiralty's plans to use Stone's funeral to rouse nationalist pride were threatened by Stone's wife, his mistress, and their dual claims to Stone's estate.

Chev had knowledge of all three—the admiral, his wife,

and his mistress. Consequently, the Admiralty "requested" he resolve the matter using a false name. The last thing they needed was a concurrent scandal—one that would explode when a gently bred captain they had "lost" and proclaimed dead returned very much alive.

Chev fulfilled the Admiralty's demands—a task which had been neither as simple nor as easy as anyone expected, especially when Chev's friend, Ash, had compromised— then married—the admiral's widow.

Now, however, the thorny problem had been resolved, and Cheverley was left with a choice: He could reclaim his title at the expense of the lives Penelope and Thaddeus had created, or he could use the alias the Admiralty provided— *Captain Smith*—and risk *his* life hunting down the pirate witch.

One option would destroy the lives of those he loved, the other would destroy his soul. Both left his tight-fisted, non-existent hand in pain.

"How long did that take you?" Hurtheven broke Chev's reverie.

"Which part?" Cheverley snorted. "Finding a proper bow, or figuring out how to fashion a mouthpiece?"

"The strength," Hurtheven replied. "Your neck swelled as if you had fish gills."

Chev looked away. "I've practiced daily since I returned."

"*Just* since you returned?"

Chev ignored the question. He'd used his teeth to wrestle with his restraints the entire time he'd been captive.

"Your turn," he said.

Hurtheven made two attempts to pull back the bow string. Both failed. Cheverley corrected Hurtheven's stance, and then Hurtheven tried again. This time, he made the shot, but missed the target, though not by much.

Cheverley clapped his hand against his thigh. "I'm impressed."

"Impressed I failed at what you accomplished with your *teeth?*"

Chev shrugged. "Necessary adjustments."

"I see…" Hurtheven paused, eyes fixed on the place Chev's hand should have been.

Acid bitterness burned within—hatred for his assigned part as *The Wounded Man,* frustration he could be stranded on an island of solitude even when standing next to his oldest friend.

And then there were Hurtheven's unasked questions. *All* unasked questions charged the air much like an impending storm—force in want of a target. Everyone— even Hurtheven—expected him to absorb the strike.

"*Ask* for heaven's sake," he demanded. "I *feel* the question, regardless."

Hurtheven looked off into the distance and rubbed the back of his neck.

"You want to know how it happened," Chev said. "Well, there was a lead ball, you see, which a flint spark sent hurtling through a small barrel directly into my wrist. And I suppose you want to know how it feels to have pieces of sinew-dressed bone too small to pick one's teeth strewn across one's breeches, too. The answer? Plenty pleasant."

The pain had been excruciating. The humiliation, worse.

Pourquoi as-tu couru? Why did you run? *Tu es à moi.* You are mine.

The pirate always used *tu* not *vous*—you, familiar. You, intimate. You, shattering.

"A surgeon took it off," he finished.

"And what of prison?" Hurtheven asked, unperturbed.

"Prison?" If Cheverley had merely been in prison, he'd have been released during the *Treaty of Amiens,* something Hurtheven would have already guessed.

Chev kicked the earth. He hadn't been in prison. Not as men defined the word.

He'd been captive, yes. Held by a band of privateer pirates led by a woman who called herself Calypso. A woman whose husband Chev accidentally shot and killed. He regretted firing that ball more than he regretted the ball that had cost him his arm.

The latter was proof he'd tried to escape. Proof he'd never given into despair.

Until now?

He clenched his teeth.

Is that what he'd be doing if he did not return to Pensteague? Giving in to despair? A low buzz sounded in his ears.

"One would think," Hurtheven said, "learning to shoot with your teeth is a task more difficult than trusting your oldest friend."

Chev pursed his lips. Then, he shook his head no. "Can't."

"Can't," Hurtheven repeated. "You survived a wreck that destroyed a sixty-four-gun ship, crossed the bloody English Channel in a makeshift raft, taught yourself to fire arrows *with your teeth* but you cannot tell me where the devil you've been the past six years?"

Chev considered. Then, he shook his head again.

"I'm finished with patience, Chev. The Admiralty insisted you remain hidden for a time. But that business with the Admiral Stone, his widowed wife, and his mistress is over." He paused to catch his breath. "Don't you think it's time you return to *your* wife?"

"Can't," he repeated, voice cracking. This time, he didn't need to consider. How could he return to Penelope's pity? Her scorn?

"Can't," Hurtheven scoffed.

He grasped for something to staunch the onslaught. "Penelope has chosen to move on. You read the story in the gazette."

Hurtheven sighed. "I have *good reason* to doubt that bit of gossip."

She is unwed. Yet.

Hawk-like creatures batted their wings inside Chev's mind, clogging his throat and ears and setting his stomach to churn.

"What are you saying?"

"Do you need me to spell it out? I wager you've already guessed." Hurtheven scowled. "You know how I feel about Pen. You've always known."

"You love her." Hurtheven's image broke into two. Chev swayed. "You offered for Penelope, didn't you?"

"Yes." Hurtheven held his gaze. "You were dead. Your cousins were practically drooling for her estate. You know if I had an inkling you were alive, I never would have offered."

"Why aren't you with her, then? Did you decide she was not good enough for you?"

"Lord, you are an ass. She's too good for us both. She always has been. But, to answer your question, I would have moved heaven and earth to make her mine." His cheeks darkened. "However, there are some things even I cannot do."

"Like?"

43

"Like make a woman love me. When she's still desperately in love with someone else."

The buzz grew louder.

Pen did not still love him.

She couldn't.

Thirteen years.

How could he want to hear something so badly, only to have the words singe and crackle in his ears?

"Even if Penelope wasn't still in love with you," Hurtheven continued, "her lack of affection wouldn't be cause to deprive your son of a father, and your father, *on his deathbed,* of his proper heir."

"I don't give a damn about Ithwick."

"Liar." Hurtheven trudged off to collect the arrows and target.

Anger exploded in a constellation of red dots behind Cheverley's eyes.

Hurtheven couldn't understand.

Chev had done unspeakable things to survive. For Hurtheven. For Ash. For Penelope. For his son. In excruciating irony, the very capitulations that kept him breathing rendered him useless to anyone he loved, useless for anything but vengeance.

The thought of telling Penelope what he'd done—what he'd allowed the pirate to do—left his blood cold, his arms tingling, and his tongue stuck to the roof of his parched mouth.

"You've left me no choice." Hurtheven cast the quiver at Chev's feet, raised his hands and shoved.

Hard.

"What the devil?" Chev demanded, stumbling.

"That was for Pen." Hurtheven shoved again. "I *told* you. She *needs* you."

She did not.

"At first," Hurtheven continued through heavy breath, "I thought you complied with the Admiralty's preposterous demands because you needed time to regain your strength. But it wasn't that, was it? You became *consumed* with the Admiral's estranged wife."

"Aren't you confusing me with Ash?"

"*He* fell in love with her. You—you put her concerns above your own."

Hurtheven wasn't wrong. But he wasn't right, either.

"I did take the matter to heart"—Chev's vision blurred—"but it wasn't for the sake of Lady Stone."

Admiral Stone abandoned his wife—the woman he'd sworn to protect. Just like Chev had abandoned Penelope. He'd thought—God it seemed stupid now—righting that wrong would silence his nightly terrors.

He'd been wrong.

Nothing would silence the pirate but her death...or his.

Hurtheven shook his head. "If you feel guilty, you *should*."

"I'm *dead!*"

"*Stone* is dead. *You* are very much alive. Go"— Hurtheven shoved again—"home."

"Hit me again and I *will* hit back."

"Good," Hurtheven replied. "Violence is the only thing you understand."

Hurtheven had *no* idea.

"Coward," Hurtheven scoffed.

The buzz's pitch heightened—feverish, unbearable. The red spots behind his eyes merged into blinding rage.

With a guttural roar, Cheverley charged. He collided with Hurtheven, and for an awful, timeless moment, both were suspended in air. Then, they hit a patch of muddy earth in a tumbling, pummeling mass of muscle and sweat.

Hurtheven pinned him. But he didn't see Hurtheven. He saw *her*. The pirate witch. *Calypso*.

C'est bien que tu ne puisses pas bouger. It's good you cannot move. *Je n'ai besoin que d'une partie pour prendre mon plaisir*. I need only one part to take my pleasure.

Chev's neck muscles bulged, then came the hideous retching.

"Jesus." Hurtheven leapt aside.

Gagging, Chev dragged his torso from the mud. His empty stomach heaved, and then heaved again. He wedged his head between his knees.

Even if Pen wished for his return—and that was still very much in doubt—how could he go home?

He'd thought survival would be enough...that if he regained his strength, what happened on that island could remain buried in the dark of the past. But shame ran like an underground river, bursting though the most thickly packed earth when least expected.

Without vengeance, violence would forever rise up, destroying everything—innocent or no—in its path.

In remaining dead, he would be protecting everyone he loved.

He knew only one way to make Hurtheven understand.

"You want to know what happened?" Shaking and weak and with the taste of bile on his lips, Chev had nothing left for the truth to steal. "I'll tell you what happened, though God help us both if you tell anyone else —I was plucked from the wreckage by the wife of a man I'd just killed. She kept me alive...barely." He shook as he inhaled. "The part of me she was interested in rousing did not involve my strapped down limbs."

"Jesus," Hurtheven repeated, this time in a whisper.

Chev fixed his gaze to the mud. "My one attempt at escape cost me my arm." He swallowed. "It took three more years before I weakened enough for her to lose interest. She set me adrift to die." He clenched his teeth. "Call me a coward again, whoreson. And then tell me how the hell I am to protect my wife when *I* embody the danger."

Chev lifted his head.

He had expected revulsion. Instead, Hurtheven held his gaze with neither pity nor censure, but with fierceness, the embodiment of a demand for justice.

"What can I do?" Hurtheven whispered.

Fuck.

Chev nearly wept.

He turned away, gazing into the perpetual mists that cloaked Ashbey's land and shrugged. He had no answers, only mocking shadows of the man he had once hoped to become, the things he had once held dear, and the hollow mottos he'd once perpetuated as truth.

"Nothing," Chev replied. "I am dead, though I live."

"No!" Hurtheven inhaled, ragged. "The moment I saw you in that—that *hovel*"—Hurtheven's voice cracked—"was the god-damned happiest moment of my life. And one thing I know for certain—what I felt is a fraction of what Pen will feel when she sees you."

"You don't," Chev forced, "*know* that."

"I do, actually. I know it better than anyone." Hurtheven ran his hand through his hair. "You survived. Everything else can be sorted."

Sorted.

What did that even mean? But, by God, he'd give anything to be whole—Cheverley closed his eyes—resting in the circle of Penelope's arms.

"Trust me," Hurtheven said. "She and Thaddeus need you. I had hoped...but nothing can take your place. They need *you*." He laid a hand on Chev's shoulder. "But not as much, I think, as you need them."

Was *need* the name of this feeling? This flayed but stubbornly persistent demand?

"I can't." He closed his eyes. "I cannot let them see me."

"Well then," Hurtheven replied, "see them. Go home. Go home in disguise if you must. But go home. Go home and judge for yourself."

Chapter Five

CHEVERLEY DECIDED TO follow Hurtheven's advice though his internal war remained unresolved. He relied on his horse to journey to Pensteague. Riding a post-horse unfamiliar with the special saddle and laces crafted to accommodate his needs was too great a risk.

By day, Chev and his horse picked their way from standing stone to standing stone—crosses worn from centuries as sentinels guiding the wandering and the weary and gathering them to prayer. By night, they'd seek out a copse just far enough from the road to conceal themselves from travelers, difficult given the stretches of wide-open moor.

On the third night—the night after he'd passed through Penzance with hat pushed low—Chev swayed in the hammock he'd stretched between two trees and a faint salt-sea scent whispered in the wind, awakening his captain's soul.

He had not wanted to go to into the navy, but, once

there, he'd found a world he was a better man for having known.

Ships were manned by men whom land-life had over-looked and under-appreciated, at sea because they had no other choice—a disparate collection of souls from the kingdom—England, Ireland, Scotland and Wales—but also from Europe, Africa, India, and the Americas.

He closed his eyes, listening to remembered voices raised in bawdy song—the low, open vowels of men from the West Indies, the clipped accent of those from the East, the joined consonants marking those born in London's most neglected neighborhoods. Together, they'd blended in an unlikely harmony that soothed the stark loneliness of the sea.

He fell into slumber, wondering if any of his men from the *HMS Defiance* survived.

In the morning, he urged his horse into a two-beat gait, a clip that quieted both his fears and his regrets. By noon, the road joined the river, and by evening, the road had tapered into a less-worn bridle path.

He was close.

The silence within Chev shifted, becoming at once alive and alert.

The land itself seemed to inhale and hold its breath in recognition. Would his disguise hold?

He'd clothed himself in laborer's breeches and a rough shirt. Nature accomplished the rest. He was thinner than he'd been, not fully recovered from the years he'd lost. His sun-bleached hair peppered with pre-mature grey. Stubble concealed his cheeks. Scars—some physical, some etched into his face, some driven into his soul—toughened his once-youthful skin.

He who has suffered much, much will know.

He snorted. For all his suffering, he knew nothing. He'd only ever embraced one thing of value...a lady he did not deserve to embrace again.

From the start he'd failed Penelope. He failed to realize his father's power over them, he'd failed to keep the promises he'd made.

What was worse—he'd believed he could win—that he could return with enough riches and renown to place them beyond his father's reach.

And he'd thought glory would be easy.

Instead, he was picking his way back home, scarred and shattered.

His horse neighed and the turrets of Ithwick Castle's ruins appeared—shaded grey stone against a light grey sky. He gazed ruefully at the ruin. If even his mighty ancestors had not always won the day, was there hope he, too, could rebuild?

He urged his horse onward.

His boyhood rambles mapped the fields, streams, and woods in his soul, but when he passed the bend in the path that signaled the boundary between Ithwick and Pensteague, for a moment, he was lost.

Land that had been nothing more than unculturable waste had been transformed into lines of wooden pens around a neatly-thatched cottage. The sun broke through low-hanging clouds, glinting off the cottage's white-washed walls and twinkling in the glassed windows.

A charming, if startling, sight...but what—he wrinkled his nose—*was* that scent?

Chev spotted a man hefting a log, setting it into a broken space in a fence. The man wiped his brow beneath his hat and set his gloved hands on his hips.

"Hello," Chev called out.

At the sound of Chev's voice, dogs raced from behind the cottage, barking and snarling. His horse neighed and bucked. He landed on the ground with a thud, still tethered to the rein by the brace he'd fastened to his upper arm.

Two dogs—with dripping fangs bared—charged closer.

The man whistled. The dogs skidded to a stop.

He tested his shoulder. Bruised, but not broken.

Lucky enough, though not the most auspicious homecoming.

"Are you hurt?"

Chev squinted down the road. With a rolling shock equal to his fall, Chev recognized the man's sailor-step, his high cheekbones, his churned-mud gaze that missed nothing. Trusted nothing.

Emmaus. In shock, he nearly spoke the man's chosen name.

One of his men, at least, had survived.

Emmaus had spent his youth as a maritime pilot, guiding merchant ships through the shifting shoals off the coast of the Carolinas...and, occasionally, connecting men and women searching for freedom with captains willing to take their coin.

When caught with runaways, he'd been sent to the Caribbean. Three grueling years later, he joined the British Naval Fleet.

What the devil was he doing at Pensteague?

Emmaus kneeled. "Can you speak?"

"Yes," Chev replied, adding intentional roughness to his voice.

Emmaus' gaze held his. "I apologize for my dogs."

"No matter."

Emmaus gripped Cheverly by the elbows, helping him rise. "Hungry?"

"Do you always greet travelers this way?"

"'For I was hungry, and you gave me food,'" Emmaus answered. "'I was thirsty, and you gave me drink. I was a stranger...'"

"'...and you welcomed me,'" Cheverley finished the scripture.

"Will you join me?" Emmaus asked.

"If you will have me."

"Wanderers are welcome at Pensteague." Emmaus assessed Chev's clothes, his face. "I will extend that welcome to you, not to put you at ease, but to assure you that you need not lie. Anyone hungry enough lies." Emmaus nodded toward the horse. "There's a shelter for him behind the cottage. For you, Mr.—" He paused.

"Captain...Captain Smith."

"For you, Captain Smith, there's stew on the coals in the hearth."

Without further word, Emmaus turned on his heel and made his way to the cottage. Cheverley unhooked himself from his horse's reins and moved quickly to catch up.

"You don't look like a man at ease here," he said.

Emmaus glanced askance.

"On land, I mean," Chev added hastily. "That is to say, you have a sailor's gait."

"I was a sailor." Emmaus gestured toward the shelter. "I *am* a sailor." He disappeared inside the cottage without further elaboration.

Chev settled his horse inside the shelter and then ducked inside the low door.

Though the cottage was small, excellent workmanship was evident in the hewn timber and glass windows. The furnishings were simple but sturdy. Two chairs. A service-able table. A few racks. A multitude of hooks. For sleeping, a single hammock spanned a corner by the hearth, suspended between two beams.

Chev slid into one of the chairs as Emmaus set down two bowls. A curl of welcoming steam rose from the broth. With a spoon of silver-over-copper, he stirred chunks of meat.

Pigs. He identified the scent he'd smelled before. *Pigs.*

Of course, Pen would begin with animals she knew.

"You'll have to make do with runt meat," Emmaus said. "The sows cannot be spared, and only a few boars remain."

Chev frowned. "Why is that?"

Emmaus did not answer. Instead, his eyes moved from Cheverley's worn cuffs, to his pinned sleeve, to his dusty, worn breeches.

"A shame, isn't it, the way the Admiralty forces officers to survive on half-pay? They *can* pay, of course—a point made obvious by Admiral Stone's funeral." Emmaus's speculative gaze came to rest on Chev's. "Wasn't too long past. Were you there?"

"Yes," Chev replied carefully. "I was there."

"Did you know him—the admiral?"

Chev looked out the window to the pens beyond. "In passing." He understood Emmaus's probing. But to simply comply? He started his own line of questioning. "What manner of estate is this?"

Emmaus faintly smiled and leaned forward, resting his elbows on the table. He flexed the biceps visible through his homespun linen shirt.

Always white linen and animal skin for Emmaus. Never cotton.

Never dyed.

"I find it hard to believe," Emmaus said, "you haven't heard about Pensteague."

Cheverley shook his head no. "What should I have heard?"

"You'd have me believe you just happened to be traveling through western Cornwall and stumbled upon an estate well-known for employing injured sailors?"

"Injured sailors?"

Penelope.

Had she turned their home into a haven for men like him? Hurtheven hadn't told him. A rigging knot locked into place, roughing his throat

"If I were to guess," Emmaus said, "I'd say you are about to tell me I don't look injured."

"I wouldn't presume."

Emmaus snorted. "You'd be the first. Lady Cheverley takes in any wounded sailor, especially one who claims some connection that might lead to her lost husband." He threw his arm over the back of his chair, a posture that belied the intensity in his gaze. "I happen to have known her husband. When I heard, I appointed myself a sort of gate-keeper, if you will."

"Her *lost* husband?" He swallowed.

"Make no mistake. He is dead"—Emmaus's lids veiled his gaze—"but hope dies harder than blood and bone. Did you know Captain Lord Cheverley?"

"No," Chev said. And because lack of curiosity would be suspicious, he added, "What was he like?"

"Brave. Honorable. A leader so trusted he rarely resorted to the lash commonly used on ships."

He'd been that, hadn't he? Once. Before the pirate. Cheverley swallowed again. The knot hadn't loosened.

"I would have called him brother." Emmaus leveled his gaze. "I will not tolerate anyone who claims an unproven connection."

55

"I would not bring false hope to Lady Cheverley." Truer words he could not speak. "But if shelter is available, I would be obliged."

"Obliged..." Emmaus tapped his fingers on the wooden table. "Can you shoot?"

"Arrows, yes. Aim's not what it was," Chev lied, "but it's better than most."

"If you promise not to lie to Lady Cheverley, I'll provide shelter and work for as long as you require."

"I swear on my life I do not mean harm to the lady."

Emmaus nodded once. "I will accept that."

"How long," Chev asked, "do you expect to remain here?" Land had never been part of Emmaus's intentions.

"For now," Emmaus answered. "As for what I do, I serve as gamekeeper for both Pensteague *and* Ithwick."

"Both?" Chev had so many questions.

"Ithwick's famed deer herds have"—Emmaus paused— "thinned." He stirred his stew. "I warn you, the work is hard. And the current stewards of Ithwick are wasteful, immoral, and unforgiving." He flashed a brief smile. "On a good day."

"They intentionally depleted the deer herd and culled the boars?"

Emmaus nodded.

"Don't the boars belong to Pensteague?"

"Mr. Anthony claimed rights, as the lady and young Lord Thaddeus are staying at Ithwick. And, he insists the lands are soon to be rejoined."

"Joined?" Cheverley frowned. "How?"

Emmaus looked up. "When Lady Cheverley weds Mr. Anthony, of course."

If Pen refused Hurtheven, she would never accept Anthony. "Is such a thing anticipated?"

"Not by me," Emmaus replied. "Nor, I'd guess, by the lady."

"Are you suggesting he is forcing her hand?"

"I am advising you to be on your guard while you are here." Emmaus kicked back his chair, went to the mantle, and retrieved a knife. "I sleep with one." He handed the knife to Chev. "And if I suggest anything, it's that you do, too."

Chev frowned down at the knife's jagged edge. "Is that necessary?"

"Ithwick's last heir died after stepping into a nest of adders, after having warned his nephew—Lady Cheverley's son—away from the very area he was found. Rents and harvests have dwindled, yet still they have money to spend." He leaned forward. "I know nothing, but I find a great deal odd."

Chev nodded.

"Now," Emmaus stood, "I have work to attend before I sleep."

"I do not wish to keep you," Chev replied. "I arrived late."

"Late." Emmaus paused on the threshold. "One might say, Captain, you arrived just in time." He disappeared into the twilight.

Cheverley came instantly awake at the sounds of footsteps in the gravel. His hammock swayed as he jerked upright.

Emmaus's hammock? Empty. By the light, it was already mid-day.

He reached beneath the balled-up pig's hide he'd used to fend off the chill and carefully retrieved the knife

Emmaus had given him. Silently, he swung his legs over the side of the hammock and stood, parsing the quiet.

The dogs hadn't barked.

Whomever had arrived, they knew. The tension in his shoulders eased.

"Emmaus?" A young man called. "Emmaus!"

Through hazed glass, a boy's profile came into view. Rushing awareness seized Chev's limbs.

He'd never met his son, but he'd seen the angle of the boy's chin in a lifetime of mirrors and the boy's hair swept up from a cowlick in the same spot as his, too. The boy's nose, however—pert, pointed, and slightly upturned—*that* was all his mother.

Elation blended with loss, holding Chev beneath unnavigable currents.

Then, the young man opened the door, and Chev locked eyes with his own. Bittersweet ache seeped to the back of his knees.

Thaddeus hesitated for a moment. His gaze flicked to Emmaus's empty place.

"Not Emmaus."

"No," Chev answered.

The boy's gaze settled on Chev's knife, then returned to Chev's without the slightest hint of fear.

"No need for that," he said.

Chev set down the knife. Pride flitted through his chest. "Emmaus left before I awoke."

"He does that," the boy replied. "Though a preference for night isn't unusual in these parts." He held out his left hand. "I am Thaddeus, and I am pleased to make your acquaintance."

But for the use of his left hand, Chev might have assumed Thaddeus hadn't noticed his injury.

"Just Thaddeus?" Thaddeus had not used the heir's title, nor the honorifics of *Master* or *Lord*.

"Well, the servants at Ithwick use 'Master,' and Emmaus says 'Lord'—if only because my cousins refuse. Either will do if you wish to be formal. I choose not to use the heir's title just in case..." He paused and then changed course. "Anyway, I prefer Thaddeus, Mr.—?"

"Ch—" Chev cleared his throat. "Captain Smith." He shook his son's proffered hand. The boy had a fine grip. A man's grip.

"Captain?!" Thaddeus lifted his brows. "Well, isn't that a fine thing? We don't get many officers. Are you a friend of Emmaus?"

For nearly a decade. "We've only just met."

"I'm sure he asked his questions, then." Thaddeus's raised his brows. "I don't suppose you have news of my father, else he would have brought you to my mother at once."

Chev didn't trust himself to speak, so he shook his head no.

"Well," Thaddeus said with a touch too much brightness, "there's always a chance, now, isn't there?" He paused briefly. "My mother and I are staying at Ithwick Manor—and we never did so before and, if you'll pardon, it's dashed exciting to sleep in my father's room. I never knew him myself. But I've heard plenty about his skill. That's why I'm here."

"Oh?" Chev said, hoping Thaddeus didn't notice the crack in his voice.

"Yes! I found this." Thaddeus stepped back out the doorway and returned with a longbow. "And I thought Emmaus might be able to show me how to string the thing. You'd be surprised at all the things Emmaus knows."

Actually, he was well-aware of Emmaus's competence.

And still unsettled that Emmaus had elected to remain on land. Emmaus could catch danger's scent quicker than an owl could spot a mouse. And if he had chosen to remain, that could only be because he sensed innocents in danger.

Innocents like Thaddeus.

Chev's gaze settled on the bow, recognizing the craftsmanship right away—one of the first bows he'd ever made. Deceptively simple looking, the bow had taken two years to make. Yew sapwood formed the back two thirds of the wood and heartwood, the belly.

"I've tried everything I can think of," Thaddeus said. "I haven't been able to get it to bend in the least."

"Have you asked the other guests at Ithwick to help you?" he asked, drawing out Thaddeus's position on his mother's suitors.

"Pah!" Thaddeus made a sound of disgust. "I would not let any one of them even touch my father's bow." He set back his shoulders. "Food wasted. Servants seduced. Beggars turned away. If I were older, I'd kick the idle trespassers out on their bums." He stopped abruptly. "Oh, I apologize. I didn't mean to shock you."

Impressed, more like. "May I try stringing the bow?" he asked.

After a moment's hesitation—and a brief glance to Chev's arm—Thaddeus handed him the bow.

How sweet the weight and feel! "I can help you."

"Can you?" Thaddeus's expression turned hopeful. He stuck his hand into his pocket and pulled out a string.

Cheverley sat on the chair, rested the bow against his shoulder and instructed Thaddeus how to fasten one end of the string. The boy's rapt attention was rain on parched earth.

"Now," Chev stood, "there are many ways to bring the string to the other side, but with a longbow of this size, this is the method I'd recommend."

He placed the bow at the corner of his left foot. He stepped over the bow and hooked the top of the bow in his right arm.

"Would you mind handing me the string?" he asked.

He took the string, and, using his body weight, bent the bow while simultaneously stretching the string and then securing the string to the top of the bow. He tested the tautness of the string. *Perfect.*

"Ha!" Thaddeus laughed aloud. "You made it look easy."

"The trick"—he winked—"is steady movement."

Thaddeus grin faded. "It must be awful to be an archer and not be able to shoot."

"Who says I cannot shoot?" He nodded toward the door. "Come outside."

Chev retrieved his bow from his pack. He allowed Thaddeus to handle the bead and the mouthpiece before he strung the yew. Then, Thaddeus handed him an arrow from his quiver.

He aimed the arrow at a distant tree. He drew the string to maximum tension.

Muscles strained through his jaw and neck, banding tension that reached all the way to his spine. He shot. The arrow struck a leaf from a branch, bending back the branch and pinning the leaf to the trunk.

"Brilliant!" Thaddeus's jaw dropped. "Your neck popped out when you did that."

"So I've been told."

"Can you teach me?"

Something softened in Chev's chest. He indicated Thaddeus's bow. "Why don't you try again?"

Thaddeus ran his finger down the string. "Stiff as a switch."

"Stiffer, actually," Chev replied.

Thaddeus copied Chev's stance, properly positioned the bow and pulled. "Still nothing."

"Don't rely solely on the muscles in your arm, use your whole body."

Thaddeus tried again and pulled back just enough to send his arrow flying, but without much control.

"Well, son of a—" Thaddeus arrested his speech. "Do you have time to practice some more?"

Strange warmth passed through Chev as he agreed. By the time Thaddeus hit his first mark, they'd ventured more deeply into the wood, and the sun had hung low in the sky.

The day had grown later still when Thaddeus reluctantly decided he must return.

"Practice," Cheverley said. "And in time, you'll be quite skilled."

"How long did it take you to learn to shoot?" Thaddeus asked.

"Years," Cheverley replied. "And I've spent the last two months adjusting for my arm." Cheverley sighed into the disquieting silence that followed. "I took a musket ball to my wrist," he explained, "and, yes, sometimes it still hurts."

"I wouldn't have thought to ask." Thaddeus squinted one eye. "Actually, I was going to ask if you would practice with me again."

Extraordinary boy.

Well done, Penelope.

Thaddeus was confident without arrogance, honest without yielding authority. He'd be dammed if he didn't

wish to spend as much time as possible getting to know
his son.

And, Cheverley had no intention of leaving Cornwall
before inquiring into Emmaus's suspicions.

"If I practice with you," Chev offered, "will you tell me
truthfully about what goes on at Ithwick?"

Thaddeus frowned. "The men there are no one you'd
wish to know. Greedy. Violent. Crude."

Emmaus had intimated as much. Which was exactly
why he intended to find out as much as he could. One could
not fight what one did not understand.

"If they are so ill mannered," he asked, "why does your
mother permit them to stay?"

Thaddeus's eyes hardened. "Pardon?"

Chev's chest warmed. He softened his voice. "No insult
to her ladyship was intended."

Slowly, Thaddeus nodded. "Mother believes it is her
duty to care for the duke. His Grace has improved, but he is
not yet well enough to order them off his land."

His Grace. Spoken as if the duke were a stranger, not a
grandfather.

"If there's no rain tomorrow," Thaddeus said finally,
"the men will likely be throwing weighted disks on the lawn
—that is, if they do not drink themselves into oblivion this
evening." He flashed a grim expression. "Tonight, there's to
be a soiree. Everyone important for miles has been invited."

A soiree? With the duke too ill to attend? Just what was
going on at Ithwick?

"If you will allow," Chev said, "I would like to escort
you home."

Chapter Six

From Pen's perch at the duchess's window, she studied the edge of the forest, searching for any sign of her son. Evening shadows muted the colors of day, gathering quietly in the space between day and night.

In other circumstances, she might have luxuriated in the twilight—day's harsh judgments had hushed, night's secrets were about to be revealed.

Not today.

She stopped herself from biting a fingernail. Instead, she rubbed her bottom lip.

Why had she agreed to allow Thaddeus to return to Pensteague on his own?

Not that she could outright forbid him, even if she wanted. Thaddeus's smile sheathed razor-sharp resolve, much like his father.

In Chev, she hadn't grasped the essential nature of his need to take charge and to protect. In fact, she hadn't truly understood Chev until she mothered his son.

Through Thaddeus, she'd come to understand Cheverley in many ways. She pressed her forehead against the glass. Now, however, it was too late to make use of what she'd learned. And what she understood did not make Cheverley's loss—or the hubris he'd displayed—any easier to bear.

Thaddeus had been thrilled when he discovered one of Cheverley's first bows. He'd asked if Chev could shoot through twelve axes—a legend Chev himself loved to perpetuate.

"Not through the axes. Through holes in the axe handles." She told Thaddeus the truth, hoping the truth would sift through the heart of Thaddeus's romantic ideals. "Skill isn't magic. Your father spent years testing his strength against different combinations of arrow weight and bow stiffness until he could shoot through all twelve handles."

Men were impressed with Chev's "magical" strength.

She'd been awed by his inventive planning.

She meant to encourage the latter in her son.

So much like his father, that boy. Soon, Thaddeus would transform excited dreams into ingenious remedies. And, if she weren't careful, then, like Chev, he'd be gone.

But could anyone separate the engineer from the wanderer, the adventurer? Were they simply different sides to curiosity's coin?

Behind her, Mrs. Renton *tsked*. "Come away from the window, my lady. You aren't yet properly dressed."

As if anyone looking up from the courtyard below could tell her shift and stays were all she wore beneath her dressing gown.

"Of course," she said, moving into the room and preparing to be dressed. "I was just watching for Thaddeus."

"I wouldn't worry, my lady. He's likely occupied with the new sailor who's arrived at Pensteague."

"A new sailor?" She frowned. She preferred to question any new arrivals before they saw Thaddeus.

"When Emmaus stopped by the kitchens today, he told me a captain arrived yesterday evening. Master Thaddeus is likely peppering the man with questions about life at sea."

"No doubt." If Cheverley were a subject at Cambridge, Thaddeus would take a first.

Thaddeus requested stories from the men Cheverley had led, the men Cheverley had called friend...anyone, really. In the absence of direct information, he collected other details. In his mind, he pieced them all together like precious puzzle parts, creating a phantom father.

"Not to worry." Carefully, Mrs. Renton laid Penelope's dress out on the bed. "The captain did not claim to have known his lordship."

Penelope set aside the pang of disappointment.

"And," Mrs. Renton continued, "I doubt he'd be a harm to anyone, what with him missing his arm.'"

"Poor man," Penelope replied. The last sailor in a similar circumstance stayed only a few weeks before deciding London's gaming hells were a more interesting use of his time. She prayed for true healing this time.

Mrs. Renton picked up the dress. "Ready?"

She nodded, lifting her hands.

The heavy velvet buffeted as the fabric slid down over her torso and tumbled to the floor. Mrs. Renton fastened hooks, and the bodice cinched over her breasts. Penelope held still as Mrs. Renton then began stitching the navy-inspired braid Penelope had woven over the hooks.

"Such a wonderful idea." Mrs. Renton mumbled over pins, which disappeared into the seam one by one. "I never would have thought the duchess's court clothing would have enough fabric in the skirt alone to make you such a beautiful dress."

"Thank heaven for the panniers popular in the duchess's time," Penelope said.

"And for the new, slimmer style."

After Mrs. Renton finished stitching, she stepped back and gasped.

Penelope winced. "Was that a good gasp or a bad one?"

"See for yourself." Mrs. Renton gestured to the gold-gilt mirror.

Stepping in front of her reflection was like peeping into a different world—an imaginary world. Penelope didn't recognize the woman in the glass. The crimson velvet emphasized her lips' deep red, her cheeks' subtle flush, her hair's highlights, and her dark eyes' contrast. The effect was striking. And the white, tasseled braid served its purpose—a tribute to Chev.

"Lord Cheverley would be speechless if he could see."

Penelope's heart panged, and she turned away from her likeness.

Mrs. Renton held out white gloves of the finest kid leather. "Your gloves."

They weren't *her* gloves at all. All of this—the room, the fabric, the gloves, even the pins in her hair—belonged to the late duchess. She was, for the night, in borrowed clothes, on borrowed time.

She looked like a duchess. She felt like a fraud.

At Pensteague, she was the proprietress of a haven. In this world, she was nothing without Cheverley. But that wasn't the reason she ached.

She'd no doubt Chev would have been speechless if he could see her now—and desperately attempting to get her out of the clothes Mrs. Renton had taken such pains to get her into.

Then again, Chev had been complimentary of everything she'd worn—from her simple laborer's clothes to the breeches she'd borrowed when she'd helped him plane their bed.

Especially the breeches.

Mrs. Renton *tsked* as she withdrew jewels from the bag on the dresser. "If only you'd let me do something equally dramatic with your hair. A loose twist would be so much more attractive. Are you sure you won't change your usual style?"

"Yes." A tight, serviceable knot would do. She had to draw a line.

Mrs. Renton clasped the duchess's pearls around Penelope's neck. The beads rested against her skin, heavy and yet soft.

"Oh, my lady, they look as if they were made for you. Mr. Anthony's sure to burst in fury."

That had been the idea. "He's been intent on my discomfort. Acting in kind is only fair." And perhaps, in his anger, he would reveal something he did not mean to reveal.

"I know you don't wish to be at Ithwick at all." Mrs. Renton's eyes misted. "But having you preside over an Ithwick gathering...well, it is the *rightest* thing that's happened in a long time. If only—"

"Let us not indulge fancy." She interrupted with a pat to Mrs. Renton's arm. "Tonight, I must be on my guard."

"Yes," Mrs. Renton sniffed. "Yes, of course."

Penelope returned to the window.

Dusk made black paper cut-outs of the trees, completely hiding the path to Pensteague, but the un-doused carriage lamps glowed, creating peek-a-boo pockets of day.

She spotted Thaddeus by the stables and exhaled. Then, her gaze fell on his companion—the new sailor. The captain.

He was tall and thin with untied hair that cascaded down his back. Despite his slender frame, he moved with dangerous grace, untamed—predatory, even—as if he were aware of all things seen and unseen.

His shadowed face tilted up toward the window.

Penelope stepped back, touching the pearls at her throat. Was it fear that had soaked her with watered ice?

She shook her head. Clearly, the pending confrontation with her adversaries disturbed her usual calm.

"Thaddeus is on his way to the kitchen gardens. Will you go down and greet him? And will you thank the captain for ensuring his safe return?" Her own examination of the man would have to wait.

Mrs. Renton nodded.

She kissed Mrs. Renton's cheek, catching a whiff of lavender-scented talc. "I don't know what I would do without you, Mrs. Renton."

"Likewise, my lady."

Penelope set aside thoughts of the captain, set back her shoulders and prepared for the battleground disguised as a polite soiree. All that stood between Ithwick and ruin was one woman and an aging housekeeper.

Anything else could wait.

Thaddeus disappeared into the house and the door to the servants' entrance clicked closed. Chev moved back until entirely concealed within the shadows of the hedge.

Night had nearly settled. But the terrors of sightlessness were nothing compared to his son's safe return to Ithwick.

Thaddeus would be back in the schoolroom in no time, and with a little suavity, he might even be able to convince Mrs. Renton that he'd been there for quite some time.

Just as Chev had done more times than he could count.

Silently, he followed the garden path inlaid with stone, moving like a spirit—like a man long-dead.

But when the pathway split, he hesitated.

The stone path turned back toward the courtyard and the tall, lighted windows of the conservatory. The other way —the way he'd intended to go—wasn't marked but led to the edge of the wood.

He glanced to the heavens.

Evening stars had appeared, and the waxing moon would soon rise from the sea. But for a few hours, darkness would reign. If he chose to linger—the light of the risen moon would ease his way back to the gamekeeper's cottage. He moved toward the courtyard, not because of the moon but because of the chance he might see her again.

Penelope.

Her feminine silhouette in the duchess's window had drawn his gaze like a beacon. There'd been a brief, indescribably transcendent moment of recognition, which panic, then pain, had flushed away.

Still, he longed for another look. A closer look.

He scowled. Why entertain such madness? Hadn't being introduced to his son caused enough bitter-sweetness for one evening?

When Thaddeus sunk his first arrow into the target Chev had fashioned, the boy had whooped and smiled, and Cheverley's armor had been pierced with an altogether different kind of arrow—a deadlier arrow, an arrow that locked him into place when the only way to survive was to keep moving.

The fist-that-did-not-exist ached, hanging tight and heavy at his side.

Move. He had to move.

One footstep. Then another. Then another. And suddenly, he found himself in the courtyard, hidden just beyond the glow spilling onto the slabs of slate.

The glass separating him from the soiree guests was more than mere sand and ash, melted and then reformed. It was a barrier as uncrossable as the River Styx—the mythical boundary between the living and the dead.

The people inside were alive, glittering. He was nothing more than a wraith—a moving swarm of vengeful anger.

First, he recognized the long-time local magistrate, Sir Jerold—much unchanged but for the color of his hair. The man Jerold spoke with stood with his back facing the window, but his stance claimed authority.

Chev's gaze moved through the room until he found Lord Thomas, his cousin, in a circle of people too far away to identify. One among them, a woman, was heavily veiled.

Penelope?

No. Though familiar, the veiled woman's form was all wrong.

Then, the conversation that had filled the night air like the rumble of a distant sea, ceased. Tingling danced up his spine. He turned toward the entrance.

Breath and time ceased.

Pen. *His* Pen.

The wind in the hedges sighed, *at last*.

* * *

71

Penelope believed she possessed the power of *"right,"* and she believed that power made her capable of vanquishing men of greed and ill-intent.

But facing a sea of faces—some lustful, some hostile, and all of them marred with the volatile mix of haughty condescension and bitter envy—and armed with only a pretty dress, she suddenly understood the truth.

The men she hoped to vanquish were the same men who had written the laws and owned the courts. They were the same men who commanded *all* arbiters of power from the armies to the customs houses, to the lowly inquests in pubs.

Against them, the power of *"right"* was a meager weapon at best.

Pen swallowed as she was announced, feeling the weight of the duchess's pearls resting against her dried throat.

Give me strength.

Mr. Anthony—standing next to Sir Jerold, the magistrate—made a motion for the music to resume, and the rise of conversation followed. Then, Anthony stretched out his hand in a silent gesture screaming with authority.

Borrowed authority—less his right than the duchess's pearls were hers.

She made her way across the room, iron in her gaze, steel in her fixed smile.

"My dear Lady Cheverley"—Mr. Anthony clasped her fingers—"how good of you to join us."

"But of course," she replied, grateful for gloves.

"You have deceived me." He did not return her smile. "I thought you above such petty concerns as fashion."

"Petty?" She blinked. "I thought you would be pleased. Fashion appears to be among you and your guests' chief concerns. Did you not insist I make a good impression?"

"I'm pleased, of course."

His grip tightened. She nearly stumbled as he yanked her close and kissed her cheeks. His lips lingered next to her ear a moment longer than proper—a warning that did not have to be spoken.

"Lady Cheverley," Sir Jerold greeted, "you look like a duchess."

"Thank you," she replied, though reprimand threaded through Sir Jerold's voice. "Have your patrols been successful?"

"Not a Frenchman to be found"—Sir Jerold rocked back on his heels—"I'm proud to say."

"I sleep soundly, sir"—she opened her fan—"knowing your militia is patrolling the shoreline."

"Yes, well," Sir Jerold replied. "We do our best."

Anthony sent Sir Jerold a not-so-subtle glance and tilted his head.

Sir Jerold cleared his throat. "If you would excuse me."

"Of course." She curtseyed to his bow before he disappeared into the crush.

"I always marvel"—Mr. Anthony spoke low—"how closely you can approximate a person of noble birth."

"I have many talents which would surprise you."

He faced her with lifted brow. "I wonder what your sartorial talents"—his eyes fell to the pearls—"are attempting to convey."

"I should think that is obvious." She fluttered her fan, forcing an inviting glance. "I wish to retain my place in this household."

He studied her intentionally inscrutable expression. "Does that mean you are accepting my proposal?"

"Not yet." She looked away. "However, I am, as you so helpfully pointed out, a widow in need of protection. I must consider which man can make the best offer."

He grasped her arm.

She could not do this. As much as she needed to deceive, she could *not* feign affection. Not with a naval braid circling her waist and the duchess's pearls around her throat. She hadn't felt as much like Cheverley's wife in years.

"I do believe, Mr. Anthony," She smiled, apologetic, "that the musicians seek an audience with you. You have my sympathies. There are so many things to consider when one is in charge."

His gaze, heated, lingered on hers. He glanced to the musicians and sighed. "If you will excuse me."

"Do go on," she replied. "We all must do our part."

He moved across the room.

Placing a hand to her stomach, she suppressed a wave of nausea. What had made her believe she could prevail?

Her determined stride for the door was stopped by the vicar and his wife.

She forced a smile and exchanged greetings. Then, Mr. Rowe returned to his favorite topic—the improvements Pen had made at Pensteague. No one else ever took as much interest.

"...I must say, Lady Cheverley, you put the men of the county to shame," the vicar finished.

"Mr. Rowe," the vicar's wife said playfully, "am I to deduce that you admit a woman's management can be superior to a man's?"

"I must give credit where credit is due, Mrs. Rowe." His eyes twinkled with good cheer. "In an age when many seek quick profit that sacrifices land quality, our Lady Cheverley has proven that it is possible to invest in good cultivation practices, take measures to ensure health of those in one's employ, and still earn generous return."

"From your blush, Lady Cheverley," Mrs. Rowe laughed, "I gather such praise is rare."

"Rare, indeed," Pen replied. "I cannot, however, claim all credit. When first married, Lord Cheverley and I spent a great deal of time talking about our vision for Pensteague."

Though dreaming was, perhaps, more apt. In truth, neither of them had known much about estate management. "I've employed Lord Cheverley's approach—never saying 'it cannot be done' before exhausting all possible methods."

"Lord Cheverley's memory is important to you," Mr. Rowe spoke with a vicar's practiced cadence—and too-observant eye for the truth.

"I have heard, of course, of your husband's daring," Mrs. Rowe added. "I'm delighted to know his substance was equally impressive."

Pen looked away.

Mr. And Mrs. Rowe's twin expressions of concern were nearly her undoing. After thirteen years, how could grief remain so raw?

Then again, her grief wasn't only for the young man she'd known, she grieved, too, for the life they'd planned together. A life finally yielding pearls of achievement she could not share.

"Let us speak of other things," Mrs. Rowe suggested gently. "You'll be happy to hear we have taken your example to heart."

"My example?" Pen asked.

"I was a stranger..." Mr. Rowe quoted, "...and you welcomed me."

Mrs. Rowe's gaze moved to a veiled woman beside Lord

Thomas. "We've welcomed into the vicarage a young woman seeking refuge from the war."

"The lady is French?" Pen asked.

"American," Mr. Rowe answered, "but of French descent. She lost her husband at Trafalgar, *and* he was fighting on our side."

"Extraordinary." Pen had no idea there were Frenchmen in the Royal Navy, though with all the other nationalities, she shouldn't be surprised.

"She has no love lost for her ancestral homeland," Mr. Rowe continued. "Her grandparents were among those lost to the terror."

"Nor does she have the means to return home," Mrs. Rowe added.

"We thought, perhaps, when Emmaus is ready to return, he could escort—"

"Emmaus," Pen interrupted, "has no plans to return to the Americas." Not ones he would share with a stranger, anyway.

"Ah." Lord Thomas's approach saved her from further inquiry. "If it isn't my charming cousin. Lady Cheverley, may I introduce, Madame LaVoie?"

"Delighted, Madame," Pen replied.

"And Madame," Lord Thomas continued, "may I present my cousin's widow, Lady Cheverley?"

"Your husband was of great renown." Madame LaVoie spoke in clear English and roughly resonant tones. "I am delighted to meet you, Lady Cheverley."

"If you'll pardon us," Thomas spoke to the vicar, "I'd like to escort my cousin to the refreshment table."

"How thoughtful of you," Mrs. Rowe commented.

"Scripture commands attendance on widows," Lord Thomas answered smoothly. "Is that not correct, Vicar?"

"'Honor the widows who are widows indeed,' wrote Timothy." The vicar smiled. "However, I'm not certain he had ratafia in mind."

Lord Thomas shrugged. "Well, one must work with what one has." He held out his arm. "Shall we, cousin?"

Reluctantly, Pen placed her hand on his arm.

"Careful," Thomas said as they moved beyond the vicar's hearing, "I detect a root of bitterness in your stance."

"You interrupted a perfectly pleasant conversation."

"Are you chastising me for wishing to provide you with refreshment?"

"No," she replied lightly. "I am reprimanding you for practically dragging me away."

They stopped at the table. He filled a glass. Her gaze fixed on the almonds floating in the bowl.

"Remember"—he handed her the liquor—"there is little that happens on this estate that I do not know."

"I imagine," she said dryly, "having confidants within the staff is most helpful. And, I must refuse. Bitter almonds are not to my taste."

He froze. Then, he laughed. "Oh, you are delightful."

"You needn't humor me, Lord Thomas. Mr. Anthony has been honest enough to shed pretense. You may as well."

"Me?" he said, pointing to himself, but not so closely as to ruffle his cravat. "I only have your best interests at heart. Unlike others." His gaze moved to Anthony. "Allow me to compliment you on your use of the duchess's clothes, by the way. Anthony is both incensed *and* drooling. You have confused the enemy—Chev would be proud. But"—he turned—"Cheverley isn't here. Is he?"

"Don't tell me *you* are about to propose, too?"

"Your look of abhorrence wounds, cousin. And here I thought you wise and kind." He sipped from her glass. "Tell

77

me, if you were compelled to place your loyalty either with Anthony or with me, which would you choose?"

A Hobson's choice. "I would choose, as always, my son."

"I'd also remember, then, that Thaddeus is under my guardianship."

"You *and* His Grace," she pointed out.

"We both know that the duke cannot tell a cat from a dog."

"He improves."

"Yes." He downed the rest of the glass. "But will he improve in time?"

"In time for what?" she asked.

"A storm is coming, cousin. You'd be wise to batten down the hatches." He bowed slightly. "My offer stands."

* * *

Had Cheverley thought himself in pain when he'd dreamed of Penelope?

His dreams and memories were watercolor and canvas —a pale copy of her vividness in flesh and blood.

Excruciating heat seeped from his wrung-out heart.

Physically, the years had altered her little. Her face was, perhaps, more rounded. Her skin, however, remained unlined. And what he could see of her blonde tresses—sadly twisted into a tight knot—showed no hint of grey.

Yet, a hardness he did not recognize effused her presence. A hardness transferred into the molten mess of his own sentiments, floating like crusted flakes of metal—little, doomed ships on an inward, storm-battered sea.

He could reach her in little more than ten steps, though he was no longer as close as he'd been when he'd heard her speak to Anthony with calculated invitation, a spider, confident in her web's allure.

I am, as you so helpfully pointed out, a widow in need of protection. I must consider which man can make the best offer.

He should leave. Go back to sea. Forever silence the pirate—a mission, unlike his time here, with a distinct beginning and end, a clear measure of achievement.

But Thaddeus—

He inhaled in silence.

But Thaddeus wanted to learn to shoot.

Lord Thomas bowed, turned and walked away, his triumphant smile growing wider as he strode.

Penelope touched her forehead. All traces of her earlier confidence vanished. She moved toward Cheverley—or, at least, toward the doorway to the courtyard. She reached for the door—

Anthony called the room to attention.

With a grimace, she turned, and then rested against a pillar in the shadow of a potted palm.

Anthony spoke, but Cheverley could not understand his words over the rushing in his ears, the over-loud thudding drum inside his chest.

Then, the music began again. The words ran together, but their tone resonated. A mournful song. Anger. Longing. Grief. He couldn't stop the flood any more than he could tear away his gaze.

Penelope.

Her body tensed—she shoved away from the pillar.

He caught the words—*The HMS Defiance*—and turned his attention to the stage. In shock, he listened as his terrors were folded into softly spoken rhymes.

A sob that could have been his own wrenched from his wife's lips.

"Stop," she whispered. Then louder, "Stop!"

The music came to a jagged end in domino succession, a cacophony that intensified his chill. All eyes turned to Penelope. She gripped her pearls, and for a moment, Chev expected her to rip the strand from her throat.

"I—I can hardly bear my grief." She appeared lost. Hunted. "I miss him. I *miss* him." She sobbed again. "All the time."

Anthony moved back to the front of the room.

"The music will continue," he said to the crowd. Then, to Penelope, "do you think you are the only one who has lost anyone?"

Penelope placed the back of her gloved hand to her lips.

Go to her. The command was instant, undeniable.

Then, Chev saw his son.

"Her ladyship said to stop the music," Thaddeus spoke in a low, controlled rage.

"What I've said is true," Anthony replied. "You and your mother are not the only ones here who have suffered a loss." Anthony raised a brow. "Do you seek to challenge me?"

"I seek," Thaddeus said with quiet authority, "to rule my house."

Thaddeus placed his arm around his mother's shoulders and then led her from the room.

Chev gazed after them, an unexpected stinging in his long-dry eyes.

"Please disregard my cousins." Anthony broke the silence. "The trial has placed Lady Cheverley at wit's end, and young Thaddeus is quite at a loss. However, let us not allow her frailty to dampen this excellent tribute to the

bravery of his lordship and the many others who have sacri-
ficed so that we may someday live in peace."

For a heartbeat, the room remained silent. Then, Sir
Jerold pounded his cane upon the ground.

"Hear, Hear," he said.

"Hear, Hear." A smattering of guests replied.

There hadn't been an ounce of surprise in Anthony's
reaction. No doubt, Anthony had anticipated Penelope's
tears.

There was more here than he understood. And he must
stay until his questions were answered.

Melting back into the garden wall, Cheverley spit the
foulness from his mouth.

Chapter Seven

CHEVERLEY THRUST THE stick he carried ahead of him and limped forward with shoulders hunched. The path to the village widened at the end of Pensteague land. Fields of low grass stretched out on either side, sloping down toward the hollow that sheltered fishermen's cottages from the worst ravages of the sea.

With rough-spun dirty clothes that covered his muscle tone, he'd appear little different from the other men left in the village.

"I must hand it to you," Emmaus's well-worn boots dug into the gravel with a rhythm matching his sailor's gait.

"Hand what to me?"

Emmaus flashed a sideways glance. "You look every inch a beggar, Captain."

"Captain Smith," Chev corrected. "I'm not *your* captain."

Emmaus stopped walking. "Not anymore you're not."

Chev stopped as well, not truly surprised. "How long have you known?"

"Since you turned a shade of violet when first I mentioned Anthony's intention to wed your wife."

Chev looked out to the horizon, leaning heavily on his stick. "Emmaus."

The name was neither a request nor a reproach, but an invocation, as if Chev could somehow reach certainty on his friend's integrity alone.

"I cannot tolerate your deception indefinitely. I expect you, at least, to pay me the courtesy of revealing your intent."

"I should not have deceived you." Chev squinted. "Trust I have my reasons, will you?"

"Do you think I would have gone along this far if I did not trust you?"

Chev shook his head no. Not Emmaus. Emmaus always did as conscience, not man, directed.

"Do you think they'll recognize me in the village?" Chev asked.

"I don't know," Emmaus replied. "You were already weathered when we met. I assume you looked quite different before your years at sea."

Chev nodded. "Right."

So, possibly he'd be recognized. But possibly not.

And every additional day he spent the risk he'd be revealed increased.

"You went to Ithwick last evening," Emmaus said.

Chev swallowed. "I delivered Thaddeus home."

"She saw you, you know."

Chev stopped breathing.

"That is to say she saw a man with Lord Thaddeus crossing into the gardens."

He exhaled.

"Did she ask pointed questions?"

"Just the usual," Emmaus replied. "But she will. She misses little."

Chev bristled. "How well do you know my wife?"

"Well enough." Emmaus raised his brows. "Better than you, if you believe either of us would betray you—or if you truly believed Anthony's assertion she wishes to wed."

"I apologize to you," Chev replied. "As for Anthony—I heard her court my cousin with my own ears."

Emmaus snorted. "He that hath ears let him hear."

"I wish you wouldn't do that."

"Quote scripture?"

Chev had meant see through him, actually. He nodded anyway.

"It's how I learned to read." Emmaus shrugged. "Now that you're here—"

"*I* am not here."

"Which brings us back to your intent, does it not? Why exactly are you *here* and *not here?*"

"I don't yet know if I *can* stay, even if I wished to." Chev sighed roughly. Not only was he a different man, he wasn't certain he'd ever be able silence the pirate's whispers. Not without hunting her down. "I—I have unsettled debts. But"—he fixed Emmaus with an even gaze—"something is wrong, here. And I don't intend to leave until I am sure Penelope and Thaddeus will be safe."

"I've felt something was wrong since I first met Lady Cheverley at the trial." Emmaus nodded slowly. "Later, she told me Anthony had gone white when he found out about your amended will."

"It's Pensteague he wants? Why? It's worth a fraction of Ithwick, barely self-sustaining."

"Perhaps," Emmaus replied, "he just wants Lady Cheverley."

Chev considered, and then shook his head. "He values his bloodlines too much. He wants something more—something worth the sacrifice of marrying a farmer's daughter."

"A farmer's daughter whose son will one day be a duke."

"My father insisted on family guardianship—I'd rest easier if Thaddeus's fate were not in Lord Thomas's hands —what do you know of his intentions?"

"Not much." Emmaus shrugged. "He's shown special interest in the widow staying with the vicar. Beyond that, he appears to be content to be included with the bacchanal celebrations. Do you think you can pry answers in the village?"

"No. Any direct question asked in these parts isn't likely to be answered. And the person probing would be lucky to leave with teeth intact." He chewed on his lip as he thought. "When I was a boy, smugglers ruled this village. My father gave his blessing...and his permission to use the tunnels that led from the sea to Ithwick Castle's ruins. Even His Grace— scion to the leadership of the House of Lords—was opposed to paying one hundred and twelve percent tax on his tea. But the smuggling ended when the tea tax was repealed."

"What makes you think the smuggling stopped?"

"Dwindled, is perhaps more accurate. The duke closed the tunnels by setting off explosions within the entries. You've got to be pretty determined to climb up those cliffs, especially when there are easier ports of entry in Kent. And the profits can't be nearly be as high."

"Might I remind you we are at war? Demand for French brandy hasn't exactly disappeared."

Chev lifted his brows. *Of course.*

"Dwindled, is definitely more apt," Emmaus continued. "And, don't you think I cannot see what you are speculating, Captain. I'm not a part of any smuggling operation. Those insular villagers wouldn't allow me within their ranks if I wished to join them. Just to be clear—I do not."

"Because you respect tax laws?"

Emmaus grinned. "Because I don't respect their navigation skills."

Chev snorted.

"In all seriousness," Emmaus continued, "you can't possibly learn very much by simply sauntering through the village."

"I'm not going to ask questions—I'm going to observe the militia, and whatever stragglers happen to be left."

Emmaus nodded. "You won't like what you see. I imagine they're paid well to be at the wrong place at the right time."

"I haven't liked anything I've seen so far—Pensteague excepted. I'm not expecting that to change. If there's time, I'd like to see if I can find what's left of those tunnels."

"I can't help you there," Emmaus replied. "This is the first I'm hearing about them."

They resumed walking in silence, and then the fishermen's cottages came into view, squat and tidy and tucked up into the crags as if they, too, had been formed by the sea. The houses were empty, of course. The men were out on the water. As for the women, today was washing day—they were all by the stream.

Apart from the militia, only the loafers, the old, and the lame remained.

As they stopped at the fountain in the village's center, a herd of goats appeared around the bend.

The goatherd's eyes narrowed on Emmaus. "I say! Didn't I tell you you weren't welcome here?"

"You did." Emmaus did not move.

"Then what are you doing here?" the goatherd asked.

"The fountain," Emmaus replied, "exists for the benefit of all, travelers and residents both old and new."

"This man," Chev added, "has as much right as any to be here. More, in truth. He fought to defend our shores."

"Pah!" the boy scoffed. "And who are you—beggar-man? We don't welcome the likes of you here, no matter what welcome that crazed harpy at Pensteague hands out. Mr. Anthony's going to empty her madhouse of cripples one day. He says we must leave the weak behind."

Chev's rage—always at a slow burn—flared. In his mind, he grabbed the boy by the throat and squeezed until he spoke no more.

No. He inhaled deep. No matter what the lessons of war, death could not *"win"* over death.

"Silenced you, didn't I?" The boy jeered.

Perhaps just push him down...

Chev glanced to Emmaus. Emmaus's returned glance did little to hide his accusation—*this is what happens when you shirk the duties of leadership.*

Chev gathered remnants of remembered calm. He met Emmaus's gaze, gauntlet accepted. If he didn't want his family in danger, he must work to find the danger's source.

"Anthony will fail." Chev surprised himself with his even tone. "You cannot leave others 'behind.'" What did 'behind' even mean? "If Anthony doesn't want beggars, he must ensure work with adequate pay."

The goatherd stepped back. "What's this? Are you a beggar or a bloody MP?"

"Where are you taking those goats?" Cheverley demanded.

"I don't have to answer you."

Chev lifted his stick and pressed it to the center of the goatherd's chest. "Your elders are due your respect."

Goatherd's hostile gaze moved between Emmaus and Chev. "To Ithwick, of course," he replied. "Anthony pays good money. Gold, if I bring enough."

Gold. The only accepted currency among smugglers.

"I suggest you get on, then," Cheverley said.

"I'm going." The goatherd lifted his chin. "But only because I cannot bear your stink." He nodded to Emmaus. "His either."

The animals brayed as the goatherd moved them away.

"He'll take the ocean route," Chev said. "Let's return to Pensteague through the woods. I think it's time I paid my cousin a visit."

Emmaus smiled. "I couldn't agree more."

* * *

Mrs. Renton groaned and folded her arms, her eyes fixed on the lawn below. Penelope looked up from her reading.

"What game are Anthony, Thomas, and their guests playing now?"

"They've set goats loose in the courtyard. Anthony and Thomas appear to be judging a race."

"Goat against man?"

She glanced back. "Hard to tell the difference between the animals and the men."

Penelope smiled. "Well, it's a change, anyway. Those weighted disks leave crevices in the earth. I've nearly tripped a dozen times."

"And just what do you think those goats are leaving behind?"

Pen snorted. "We've a competent gamekeeper, remember? Emmaus will round up the goats when he comes."

Mrs. Renton frowned. "Do you trust that man?"

"With my life." Penelope set aside her book. "He was one of Cheverley's crew. He went with the privateer they captured, and if it was not for him, I'd know little about Lord Cheverley's last hours." She'd only wished she'd met Emmaus sooner than at the recent trial.

"But how do you *know* he sailed with Lord Cheverley?"

"Really, Mrs. Renton. Emmaus accurately described the buttons on a shirt I had given Cheverley before he went to war."

"I apologize." Mrs. Renton sighed. "These days I just do not know who I can—" She stopped abruptly, leaning toward the window. "What is Anthony about, now?"

Penelope went to the window.

Thaddeus, arms crossed, had arrived at the edge of the courtyard. Anthony and Thomas were motioning to have him join the revelers. Still scowling, Thaddeus joined the fray to raucous applause.

"Thaddeus took charge last night," Penelope said. "They've changed tactics and are trying to placate him."

"I don't like it," Mrs. Renton breathed.

"Neither do I." Penelope pursed her lips.

Thaddeus took a seat at a table apart from the others. He glanced back toward the forest and then broke into a wide smile.

Pen leaned forward, following Thaddeus's gaze. "Can you see who he is looking at?"

"Emmaus, most like," Mrs. Renton replied.

"I'm not sure." Thaddeus respected Emmaus, but that smile... She'd never seen that smile.

"There he is!" Mrs. Renton exclaimed.

Emmaus was, indeed, heading toward Thaddeus. But Thaddeus's smile had been for the man by Emmaus's side—the captain. As he came into view of the other guests, he began to limp.

"Anthony," Penelope said, "isn't the only one up to something."

Thaddeus motioned Emmaus and the captain to his table. After a brief discussion, they all sat. Then, the group caught Anthony and Thomas's attention.

"I can't hear what they are saying," Penelope said.

"Open the window," Mrs. Renton suggested.

"They'll know right away why we opened the window," Pen replied. "That won't do. I'm going down to the conservatory."

However, by the time she reached the conservatory, Thaddeus's table had been overturned. Emmaus was restraining the captain and Thomas was restraining Anthony. As for Thaddeus...his expression was pure glee.

Silently, Penelope opened the door.

"Homeless vagabond," Anthony sneered.

"I used to be rich," the captain replied.

Deep, rough and somehow familiar, the captain's voice sent shivers to Penelope's toes.

"Your fortune, too," he continued, "may change. Why do you complain? The others are unconcerned that this young man invited us to share his food."

"Easy for them," Anthony replied. "They give of the wealth I gave to them."

"And what of you? Whose wealth do you give?"

"Get out!" Anthony roared.

He tossed his chair in the captain's way.

Behind Penelope, Mrs. Renton gasped.

"Go!" Anthony commanded again.

"Only His Grace or His Grace's heir can order me to go. What do you say, Lord Thaddeus?"

Thaddeus bowed heads with the captain, speaking in low tones. The captain listened and then nodded.

"Until we meet again." Mockingly, he bowed to Anthony without looking down.

Fire-filled challenge emanated from his gaze.

"Mrs. Renton," Penelope reached behind her for the housekeeper, "go out the back and stop them before they leave. I *must* meet this captain. I must meet with him *at once.*"

* * *

Pen swiveled as the door to the kitchen gardens opened.

"Oh," she said, disappointed. "It's you."

Emmaus chuckled. "You wound me, Lady Chev."

"I am sorry, Emmaus, it's just that for a moment..." For a moment what? She'd thought something miraculous had happened. "I am a fool."

Emmaus took her hand. "You are far from foolish."

"I—I had hoped to meet the captain, he's..." She frowned, "...singular."

"That he is." Emmaus cocked his head. "Would you like me to deliver the message he gave me?"

The hope that had deflated catapulted her heart back into her throat, fluttering like a fledgling. "Yes, please."

"He did not acquiesce to your summons because he did not wish to cause more trouble with Anthony and Thomas at this time."

At this time?

"However," Emmaus continued, "The captain would like to meet you."

91

"Where? When?" *Now, thank you.*

"I suggested fairy rocks—a place quiet and private that would not threaten your reputation. I will escort you there, and stay close enough to hear your call, that is, if you wish me to stay."

The thrashing continued. "Do you trust the captain?"

Emmaus pursed his lips. "I do." He turned. "I will await you by the stables. Make sure you bring your knife. Not for the captain, but for any other threat that might linger in the night."

With that he left.

She gazed after him in stunned amazement.

Emmaus trusted no one.

Just who was this mysterious captain?

How had he so quickly captured the imaginations of Emmaus and her son?

And how was she to ensure that the same did not happen to her?

Chapter Eight

As Penelope approached the stone circle, she sensed the captain waiting for her in the shadow of the tallest rock.

She didn't know how she recognized the captain's presence, but she knew him. Just like she knew the captain was different from the other broken sailors she'd sheltered. He stood apart the same way the carefully placed stones stood apart from the pebbles littering the field.

Like the stones, he made her pause, part in wonder, part in fear.

"You came."

The deep tenor of his voice disoriented, intrigued.

"I came," she responded.

"And is Emmaus waiting down by the dip in the moor?"

"No," she replied. "He said I could trust you."

The captain stepped out from the shadows. Not enough to see him in full, but enough for the moon to illuminate the silver-and-sand hair falling past his shoulders. He was arresting, even in silhouette—so much more than Anthony, the excuse-for-a-man he had allowed to insult him.

"You could easily have put an end to Mr. Anthony's persecution, if you had wished." She imagined even Emmaus could not have restrained this man if he'd been intent on a fight. "Why did you let him taunt you?"

After a long silence he answered, "Why do you allow him to court you?"

She bristled. "I have not."

"I heard you tell him you were a widow in need of protection."

She sucked in chilled air through her teeth. "A gentleman doesn't eavesdrop."

"I was merely passing through the courtyard." He dipped his head. "And what gave you the impression I am a gentleman?"

Sending him a wary glance. "Am I in danger?"

"No." His voice softened. "And it was not my place to ask such an impertinent question. What is between you and that man is none of my concern. Consider me chastised."

He did not sound chastised in the least.

"I did not *allow* Anthony to court me. I repeated his words to me."

"He told you that you were in need of protection?" Anger vibrated through his voice. Anger he barely contained. "In an overt threat?"

She nodded.

"I hadn't considered—"

Her huff interrupted him. "Of course you hadn't. No man can understand what it is to be a woman alone. To need escort or approval for the simplest—"

"I've been imprisoned," he interrupted back. "You cannot *imagine* what I understand, Lady Cheverley."

The edge in his voice rendered her mute.

"Would you explain?" he asked more softly.

"The duke is not yet well, and I haven't the authority to oust Mr. Anthony or Lord Thomas. Mr. Anthony is serving as the steward. Lord Thomas is Thaddeus's guardian per my husband's will. The rest are their invited guests."

"Can't you depart? Turn to someone for help?"

"I cannot leave...not without abandoning—" *Blast!* She hadn't expected the swell in her throat. The sting in her eyes.

"Without abandoning what?" he whispered.

"Without abandoning my son's inheritance. Without abandoning my husband's"—her voice cracked—"home."

That *was* why she could not leave, wasn't it? Because leaving meant abandoning all hope. And some small part of her expected Cheverley to return.

Some small part of her had even hoped—she eyed the captain and then shook her head.

"I..." He stopped. "I see."

Did he? She doubted. "And you? I asked a question, and you have yet to answer." She did not even care how petulant that sounded. "Why did you suffer Anthony's taunts?"

"You could say I lost a battle to win the war." He tilted his head. "The humblest are often underestimated."

"But why? Why bother engaging him in the first place?"

"He made me angry on your behalf—sitting there, acting as if he had every right to claim what—" He twisted his shoulders—not so much a shrug as a sign of discomfort. "You—through Emmaus—gave me shelter."

"*I* gave you nothing," she replied, uncomfortable with the idea of giving anything to this man. "Pensteague was built for shelter."

A trivial distinction perhaps, but necessary.

Necessary because—for reasons she could not fathom—she wished to give the captain more than shelter. She wanted to draw him out of the shadows, to brush his hair from his face, and to look into his eyes...

"Pensteague." He looked out over the field. "Beautiful Headland."

"That's right," she said slowly. "Most people think it was named for me."

"Yes, well." He rolled his shoulder again. "I picked up bits of many languages on the seas—Cornish included."

"Who are you really"—she took a step closer—"Captain?"

"Do you doubt my name?"

"No, but your name tells me little." If only she could see his eyes. But their color—and their secrets—were veiled by the mist and by twilight's subduing grey. "Where were you born? Who are your parents?"

"Please do not ask me of my past." His coiled-spring stillness belied the supplication in his voice. "There is too much grief."

"Grief," she repeated. "I do not wish to intrude on your grief, Captain Smith, but I'm afraid I must insist on knowing *something* of your past. If, that is, you intend to spend time with my son."

He moved fully into the moonlight. Her gaze settled on his shoulder.

He'd changed clothes since he'd sparred with Anthony in the courtyard. Though nowhere close to a gentleman's finery, his shirt, coat, and breeches were clean and fitted. On his right—the side of his injury—his sleeve had been cut short and sewn shut.

She frowned.

Shrugging into that coat must have been awkward. The seams, as sewn, would restrain his ability to balance. Couldn't his tailor have come up with a design more suited to his comfort? A more liberal cut, perhaps. And a seam that would allow him to—

Abruptly, she cut off her thoughts.

First, she'd wanted to give him whatever he asked. Now, she was mentally designing him clothes. What would the captain think if he knew?

The night—thank God—hid her blush.

"Far be it from me to dishonor a mother's instinct," he said finally. "I suggest an agreement. A trade, if you will."

Her heartbeat quickened. "What kind?"

"Truth for truth."

"Very well," she agreed. "If you answer first."

Though too dark to see, she fancied he smiled. "What do you wish to know?"

Everything. His deepest secrets. "Let us start with the name of the ship you captained?"

"My ship is no longer. My crew perished. I did not."

She inhaled sharply. A ship's crew perished—but the ship's captain survived? The wound to his honor would be keen. The wound to his reputation? Shattering.

That much, at least, Cheverley had been spared.

"You were court-martialed, then?" she asked.

"Yes," he replied.

Odd. She had not read about any recent court-martials.

"I'm told to expect honorable discharge," he finished.

"Then the Admiralty believes you did everything humanly possible to save the ship."

"It doesn't bring back my men."

"No."

Intrigue hung about the captain like a scent—tempting, cajoling.

If he fascinated her as much as she fascinated him, she could not say, but he chose his words as carefully as

Emmaus laid rabbit traps. Even his silences were calculated.

"I believe it is your turn, Captain."

"Tell me something about your husband."

"Speaking of Lord Cheverley is hard"—especially to the captain. Not speaking of Chev to the captain? A betrayal. An admission the captain had stirred something inside that made her very, *very* aware of him. As a man. She stepped back. "I grieve my husband. I grieve the past we might have had, and the future we will never see."

"You and your husband were parted for far longer than you were wed."

As if that made a difference. "I take it you have never been married."

"What makes you think so?" he asked.

"A day. A year." *Thirteen* years. "In love, time stands still. Anything—everything—can bring Cheverley close to my heart. Last night, for instance, a mere line from a song sliced open the wound." *Enough.* She inhaled with a tremor. She intended to lure the captain into his own revelations, not drive herself to tears. "My turn."

"You asked of my family." He paused. "My mother and sibling are dead."

The disbelief lacing his voice kept her from chiding him for choosing her question. The shock had been recent. "I am very sorry."

The captain cleared his throat in acknowledgement. "Let us speak of happier things. Tell me how you met your husband."

"How I met my husband?" she repeated, surprised.

"Why not?"

She couldn't think of an answer *why not.* "I usually

question sailors about Cheverley, not the other way around."

"Would you rather I ask something else?"

"No," she sighed. "Which version of how we met do you prefer? I could tell you the story he would have told you. Or, I could tell you the ducal version."

"I prefer your version."

Her version? She didn't have one. No one ever bothered to ask.

He folded his arm behind his back and leaned against the rock, disappearing entirely into shadow. "Why did you choose Lord Cheverley?"

"I didn't choose Cheverley. Cheverley chose me."

"Still, you could have refused."

That made her smile. "I'm not sure anyone *ever* refused Cheverley."

"He was arrogant, then?" He did not share her amusement.

"No," she answered. "Not exactly."

"I am not sure I understand."

Strange, conversing with a man she could not see... The experience contained echoes of another night, long ago.

"You still have not told me how you came to meet?"

"If you are seeking a light, buoyant tale," she replied, "you will be disappointed."

"Perhaps I merely seek to listen."

To listen. How long had it been since anyone listened?

She'd hadn't allowed herself to think of that year. Of her father's death and her introduction to the bewildering, crowded city. Of the wretched loneliness. Of the grueling work. Of the nights she'd escaped to the public assembly rooms and danced with abandon. Her only hope? A few, elating moments of forgetting.

"First," she replied, "you must know something about my past. My mother died when I was a child. My father was a farmer—though not of any consequence. And, when I was fifteen, Parliament passed an act of enclosure on behalf of our absent landlord. The loss of the right to pannage rendered father incapable of paying rent. He lost the farm."

"So, your father was a pig farmer. And yet you married the son of a duke."

"Well"—she raised a brow—"I'm back raising pigs, aren't I?"

With help, this time. No matter what her troubles, she refused to take for granted the means to pay for help.

"I am certain that is a disappointment."

"A disappointment?"

"Had your husband lived, you could have been a duchess."

She scoffed. "Why does everyone assume I married Cheverley in some bid to be rescued by wealth? Cheverley wasn't heir when we married. I did not marry him because I was poor. I did not marry him because I was alone." She backed up against the rock by the captain's side. This hurt too much to stand.

"Why did you marry him?" he asked quietly.

"I married Cheverley because I was in love. Because Cheverley chose me, and I simply couldn't refuse." The rock was cold against her back, and its rough edges bit into her arms. But it was the captain's proximity that discomfited. "Truth for truth," she said. "And, after all that, you owe me a *big* truth. A monumental—"

"I have been in love, too."

Her heart stopped.

"But," he continued, "I'm afraid it is too late."

Her heart broke for the young woman he had loved.

Her heart broke for him. "What was she like?"

"She was beautiful. Mysterious. An enigma. I thought" —he snorted—"I thought she believed I was her hero."

"What did she believe?"

"I don't know. I'm not sure I ever thought to ask." He paused. "What did you believe about your husband?"

How could she answer that?

The night they met, every woman—eligible or not—had taken note of Chev, Hurtheven, and Ashbey the moment they entered the public assembly rooms. She'd only seen Chev—his blonde hair ruffled, his curls falling askew just-so over one eye, poet-style.

Chev's swagger had amused, but Chev's focused admiration? That had been sweetness that left her craving more.

Always more.

When they finished their second dance—all pink and panting—he'd met her gaze with an intensity that still caught her breath. She'd led him into the alley behind the assembly rooms, where the air was cool and the concealment complete.

"Would you like me to kiss you?" he asked.

"Would I have led you here if I did not?"

"You are surprisingly bold," he murmured, "for a blushing young maiden."

Impatient, she'd gathered him into her arms. "And you're surprisingly solid...for a toff."

He brushed her lips with his in a tender, careful kiss.

Not what she had expected. "You surprise me—"

"Chev."

"Chev?" she queried.

"My name. Cheverley."

"I've never heard that one before."

"My Christian name, actually."

"Even good friends do not call one another by their Christian names, Chev."

"They do if the Christian name is preceded by 'Lord.'"

"As in Lord Cheverley?"

He nodded. "Though I am merely a second son."

Merely? She'd never even met a proper baron. The most rarified gentleman of her acquaintance was a barrister whose wife sometimes purchased meat from her father.

The titled were shadows from another world. A world with awesome, terrible power...

"Have I silenced you with my consequence?"

"Second sons can be called 'Lord'?" she managed to ask.

"They can if their fathers are dukes." He'd leaned close to her ear. "Are you impressed?"

"Do I look impressed?"

"I can't see you. But you don't sound impressed at all." He ran his fingers down her cheek. "It's dashed attractive."

"I'm not trying to be attractive."

"That is exactly why it works. Is there anything I can do to impress you?"

"No," she'd replied truthfully. She did not like the aristocracy. She especially did not like dukes. She was about to tell him. Then, he laughed, and everything changed.

His laugh. Good God, his laugh. It rumbled in her belly. It made her come alive.

"Kiss me again, Chev." What could a short dalliance hurt? "And do try and give this one a bit of effort."

"What's your name, vixen?"

"Penelope."

"Miss Penelope..."

She'd liked that. Miss Penelope. In fact, she'd gone a little gooey inside.

"I choose you, Miss Penelope." He kissed her again. Hotter. Lingering. "Do you choose me?"

"I can't."

"Why not?"

"You've stolen all my words."

"Mmmm." He tightened his hold. "You, Penelope, are the embodiment of words I've never understood."

"What words?"

"Enchantment." He'd kissed her forehead. "Quite possibly, love." He kissed her temple. "Would you marry me—?"

"My goodness, you must be mad. Of course not!"

"Let me finish. Would you marry me if I court you properly?"

"Still no, you goose. I don't belong in your world. You do not belong in mine."

"Why does everyone dwell on impediments? If I don't belong in your world, and you don't belong in my world, we'll simply invent a new one."

Foolishly, she allowed him to court her, falling further and further under his spell, *knowing* no one had the power to invent a new world, knowing all anyone had was the broken mess their parents gave them.

And then, she'd discovered she was with child, and she'd wanted to give that child his shiny new world.

When she told him about the baby, Cheverley had whooped as if he was thrilled. In that moment, he'd sparkled. She changed her answer to yes.

Yes to love, to transformation, to the new world he promised.

She teared.

"Lady Cheverley?"

"It was unwise to come here." She sniffed. "Unwise to speak of the past."

"Are we finished trading truths, then?"

"What more could you possibly want to know?" If the song played last night had opened a wound, the captain's questions sliced open a vein. "Cheverley was brilliant. Infuriating. He made everything seem possible. And, if it weren't for Thaddeus"—she pushed away from the stone—"I would dearly wish we never met."

That night, in the darkness, every instinct then had told her to run.

She hadn't listened.

She would not make the same mistake again.

* * *

Red dots gathered once again, blindingly bright.

Loss.

It hung in the air. Moved with the shifting winds. Whistled within the unheard, ancient tones resonating from the stones.

His monster had a face, a name—Calypso.

Penelope had her monster, too—his absence. A wraith-like silhouette that had sucked the air from her life like a hungry storm. And, if there had ever been a chance he might atone, that chance had passed.

She was angry at the captain and she was angry at him.

So angry, she practically frothed.

"It's late," she said, brushing her check roughly with her palm. "I will be missed."

He held out his arm.

She brushed past him—as if he'd needed more proof of her disdain.

Earlier, when he stepped forward, she'd stepped away. And, when he came into the light, she'd stared at his shoulder in discomfiting silence, as if she couldn't bear to look at his injury.

She held Cheverley in contempt. She wanted nothing at all to do with Captain Smith. He could not argue with either choice.

She strode toward the circle's edge. "You needn't escort me," she called over her shoulder.

He ran to catch up. "Nonetheless," he said, breathless, "I intend to see you safely home. Would you slow down, please? I know you cannot bear to look at me, but—"

She stopped abruptly. He did not. They collided and she, quite literally, fell into his arms. The jolt weakened his knees as he lifted her body to his. Years broke away like spinning discuses, landing with jarring thuds.

Where was he? Who was he? *When* was he? Past and present collided, but all that remained was her heat.

"Oh," she said in distress. Then, "oh," and "oh" again, both in entirely different tones.

She inhaled. Then shuddered.

"I have the worst impulses," she said. "I refuse, do you understand?"

He did not.

"I refuse to—oh, it's no use." She worked her hands beneath his coat and balled his shirt in her fists. "The seams are all wrong. But it's not like I can just tell you, can I? That would be entirely improper and completely inappropriate."

She set her brow against his breastbone.

"You even *smell* like him, not that I can remember what he smelled like because that would make me sound mad, but your scent makes me confused, and hot, and longing, and I'm fairly certain his did as well, but that could have been the fact we were sixteen and sixteen is entirely too young to know better and, oh, blast, I can't, I tell you! I just cannot do this—"

"Shh," he soothed. Tentatively, he rested his hand against the small of her back.

"No! Not *shh!* It's terrible. A complete muddle." She splayed her hands against his chest. "I'm still bold and you're still impossibly hard but you aren't a toff—and I'm me and you're *not* you and I'm—well—I *am* going mad, aren't I? That's the only explanation."

"Shh," he repeated, crumbling inside.

"Stop shushing and just—" she grabbed his wounded arm and wrapped it around her waist. Then, she placed her hand on his nape, curled her cheek into his neck and sighed. "There. Now. I will shush. *This* is right."

This was anything but right.

He hadn't intending on asking her questions. They'd been a betrayal of trust, considering. And a gross impertinence.

But he'd wanted to know, needed to know, had she loved him? Did she love him?

Could she love him once again?

"I'm sorry," he whispered.

"That helps," she replied.

"Helps make you feel better?"

"No. It helps to make you *you*, not him." She sighed. "Chev *never* apologized, you see."

Fuck. He hadn't. Had he?

He hadn't apologized. Not for bringing her into a world that despised her. Not for underestimating his father's rage. Not for leaving her to fend both for herself and their child alone.

He told her he had a duty and asked her to trust that he'd return.

And she had trusted. Hope had long since passed. Still, she waited.

"And I do not *really* wish I never met Cheverley. It's just that, well..."

"Loss hurts."

"Exactly."

"I know."

"You do, don't you? You've been in love. And—bother it —if you are you, and I'm me, then we shouldn't be—"

"I thought you said you were going to shush."

She sniffed again. "I don't want you to think badly of me."

He could barely think at all. "You are weary, my lady."

"Weary, yes." She snuggled closer "*So* weary sometimes I ache all over. But I'm not a lady. Not really."

She was definitely a lady, just not, at this moment, *his*.

And he wanted her to be his.

Her breasts crushed against his chest and she traced those circles he remembered so well against the top of his spine.

Christ. Blood pooled in his groin. Temptation.

Torture.

His cock would fill. Then came despoiling, humiliation.

Tu es impuissant. You are helpless. *Tu ne peux pas te controller.* You have no control of yourself.

Instinct—born of countless assaults—demanded he thrust Penelope aside.

"Don't." She held him tighter. "Please don't pull away."

The red dots began to coalesce.

"Penelope," he whispered through clenched teeth. *Pen.*

If he could tie himself to the mast of her name, the whispers would not kill him.

Chapter Nine

PENELOPE RESTED HER head against the captain's chest. His warmth was as solid as the stones, and her body responded by releasing, for a few blessed moments, her cares.

It was as if she'd been taken out of time, out of body. This wasn't her. This wasn't him. This was a meeting of two lost souls in an ancient, mystic place, a brief sojourn amid the chaos of life. Around them, the moon shadows danced with the mists, above them, a vast sky, glittering with celestial jewels.

Then, he withdrew. The chill rouged her cheeks.

He searched her face, his expression severe in the soft moonlight. She had no answers for questions he might ask, no truth to trade. All she knew for sure was that something inside her, something that had been buffeted and tempest-tossed, was suddenly still and quiet.

Anchored.

He bent down and kissed her temple—hot lips against a cool brow.

She whimpered.

"If we do not return," he said gently, "you will be missed."

The enchantment was slipping away. The shadows grew longer. The jewels muted, transforming back into plain stars.

She grasped his cheeks as if in holding onto him, she could hold to the magic. She raked her fingernails through his stubbly beard.

Penelope.

Had he said her name again, or had she just imagined it?

She wanted to hear him say it. She loved the way it sounded on his lips—like a spreading vine, living thing. She stared at those lips, doused in darkness.

"Penelope."

A vine, yes, with tendrils that pulled her in.

She brushed her lips against his in a feather-light kiss. A kiss of gratitude. Of reverence. Of acknowledgment for whatever it was they'd just shared.

He touched her hair. A tremor ran through his hand.

"I think it best if you walk on ahead." He spoke like a man at odds with himself. "I will be near, and I promise you will make it safely back to Ithwick."

Ithwick. He spoke it like a curse. The estate's specter rose—a menace, a thief.

"Very well." She sighed, but a question mark remained. She knew, just as sure as this circle of stones, there were truths between them yet to unfold. "May we meet again?"

"If you wish to meet, we will," he replied, barely audible. "I will not deny you."

She nodded, bowed her head, and then turned. The mist cloaked all but a few steps of the bridle path. There

109

was no way forward but to walk, to place each step with the faith that the next would unveil.

Faith was not among her strengths.

Perhaps all would be well; there was no way to know.

She resisted the urge to look behind. She would not be able to see him anyway. But he would be there. He said he'd be near. She trusted his word.

And, what was more—the peace she'd found in the stones. *That* peace she could recall. It wasn't faith, but it was something to hold.

Somehow, she reached the house. A candle burned in the window of the duchess's rooms. Silently, she thanked Mrs. Renton, and entered the house. As soon as the door closed, his presence was gone.

* * *

Penelope fluffed her pillow for the nineteenth time. *Why* couldn't she sleep?

Why?

She *knew* why. She'd been terribly bold. She'd placed her hands just above the captain's hips, on the swell of his chest muscles, on the planes of his cheeks. She'd taken his injured arm and wrapped it around her waist.

The pang that lingered in her heart was not regret.

To be held again had been a marvel. And to be held by the captain?

She sank into the pillows, curled her arm against her face and rolled to her side, grateful, for once, to be at Ithwick.

She could not imagine lying in the yew bed she and Cheverley had carved and thinking such thoughts about another man.

She set aside thoughts of the captain and turned to her memories of her marital bed, and of the great yew tree that had spawned not just the bed, but many of Cheverley's bows. Young, newlywed, and giddy with love, they'd built a cottage—the single room to eventually serve as the heart of Pensteague.

The yew's roots formed part of the cottage's foundation. They'd wanted their bed—like their home—to be immovable—a veritable symbol of an ideal world they wished to create. Then again, an immovable home must have been only what *she* had wanted. Not long after the thatch had been set, he had gone.

But she had not been alone forever, had she? First, the duchess had sent Mrs. Renton to help. Then later, the sailors began to arrive—each one in need. And Pensteague had grown, room by room, resident by resident. She'd had Pensteague, her son, and the sailors to love.

But none had replaced Chev in her heart.

That ungiven love had been spooling within for over a decade. Carrying all that hoarded love left her volatile, unstable. That lop-sided mass was what had gone still when she was standing with the captain inside the circle of stone.

That knowledge was the source of her unrest.

She fell into a restless slumber. And then, she dreamed of Chev.

In her dream, their limbs entwined under the sheets of their bed, knotted together, entangled like the yew's roots as they dove deep into the earth.

Her hair was loose and flowing. She was a flower, opening, with trust, to the man by her side. The man that caught her breath with a single wink. A man whose laugh was the sound of bliss, whose touch was transcendent fire.

No man now or ever could take his place, even if she wished.

And she did not wish.

How could she?

Chev had been her first love. Her only true love. Father to her son.

She reached up to caress his face, but his cheek was not clean-shaven.

She dropped her hands to his chest, finding lean muscle, not brawn.

And the hair that flowed past her shoulders was not only hers, but his.

"Penelope," he said, in his gruff, other-worldly voice.

This time the vine choked.

She awoke, her skin damp with sweat, blinking into the harsh, late-morning light.

Had your husband lived, you could have been a duchess.

She did not want to be duchess—she yanked the duchess's pillow from beneath her head and threw it across the room—and she did *not* want the captain.

She squeezed her eyes closed.

She wanted Chev.

The door opened. She barely had time to erase her scowl.

"Lord bless me, my lady." Mrs. Renton held her hand against her heart. "I thought you were up hours ago."

"I overslept."

Mrs. Renton's gaze moved to the pillow, resting askew against the window sill.

Pen cleared her throat. "Is Thaddeus awake?"

"Master Thaddeus was up at dawn and to his studies. He's determined to finish in time to make his appointment with the captain.

"The captain?" She wasn't the only one falling under his influence, of course.

"Yes. I believe they intend to hunt rabbits." Mrs. Renton stepped into the room and closed the door behind. "There's something else you should know. Lord Thomas has just returned from London. And"—she lowered her voice—"he is not alone. There's a woman with him in the drawing room."

"Honestly!" she huffed. "You'd think he'd at least *attempt* to observe propriety while Thaddeus is under this roof... I'll go down once I dress."

Carefully she wound her hair into the tightest knot yet. It pulled from her nape, from her forehead, from the place behind her ears.

A quarter hour later, she approached the drawing room ready to face Lord Thomas armed with a riding habit, a stiffened spine, and a furious scowl.

The couple in question were already speaking in low tones, though she would not have been able to understand them even if they were shouting.

She spoke only the most basic French.

She recognized the petite, thin-but-amply endowed form of the widow staying with the vicar, still dressed and heavily veiled in grey.

The widow stamped her foot. Lord Thomas reddened. The widow made a slashing gesture with her arm. Thomas grabbed her by the shoulder and then tossed aside her veil. The widow smacked him hard across the face.

Pen gasped. Lord Thomas and the widow turned in unison.

The widow's face was beyond beautiful. She had naturally puckered lips painted a deep, unnatural red. Her thin brows delicately arched, and she had chiseled cheekbones and eyes so vividly green their color was unmistakable.

Sin.

The widow possessed a face carefully sculpted for sin.

The widow lifted her lips into something akin to a smile, but smaller and more knowing, as if she were as fully aware of Pen's secrets as she was her own. Then, she arranged the veil back over her face.

Penelope blinked to recover her balance.

"Forgive me," the widow said in her indistinct accent. "I beg your pardon. I have a...loose temper."

Thomas huffed and looked away. "Among other things."

"Forgive my intrusion," she continued. "We arrived early and did not wish to disturb the vicar. I was on business in London. Your cousin recognized me and was thoughtful enough to bring me home."

In a carriage? "London is more than a day's drive." Travel to London was *far* easier in a boat.

"Oui."

A moment passed before Pen realized the widow had merely agreed.

"Perhaps, Lady Cheverley," the widow asked, "you would accompany me back to the vicar's?"

Madame LaVoie.

She exhaled as she remembered the widow's name.

Lord Thomas's glance to the widow spoke volumes— volumes Pen could not decipher. Clearly, however, he did not wish Pen to comply.

"Of course," Pen replied.

"Lord Thomas," the widow practically purred, "you are no longer needed."

Madame LaVoie glided across the floor, and then took

Pen's arm with a firm grip. Pen strode quickly, following through the hall, out the front door, and down the steps.

Then, Madame LaVoie climbed into Lord Thomas's carriage and settled in beside the window. She rapped on the front as if she owned the conveyance and employed the coachman.

"You, too, are, I understand, a widow."

Something about the way she said widow set Penelope's teeth on edge.

"So," the madame continued, "you understand a widow's...particular needs."

Penelope arched a brow. "I am not sure I know what you mean."

"Oh, you English. So prudish."

"You owe me no explanation," Pen said. "Your...friendship with Lord Thomas is none of my concern."

"No indeed?" Madame LaVoie chuckled softly. "And yet I was under the impression he was one of your many suitors."

"You are mistaken."

The widow shrugged. "If you do choose him..." A breeze lifted the bottom of her veil, revealing another small, but vicious smile. "You should know he appreciates a lady with a firm hand."

"Madame LaVoie"—Penelope faced the veil as if she could see through the layers of heavy gauze—"*I* would appreciate it if you do not return to Ithwick."

"I am sure you would."

"No matter what Lord Thomas has told you—"

"You would like to know what he told me, wouldn't you?" She interrupted. "Well, I did not believe a word he says and nor should you. Lord Thomas is a bad boy." She emphasized each *b*. "He tells bad lies."

"You lovers' quarrel is no concern of mine."

The widow turned her face toward the window, though Penelope continued to feel her gaze. "I will not trouble you at Ithwick again. I do not intend to stay in Cornwall much longer."

Pen frowned. "I was under the impression you were unable to return home."

"Now *you* are mistaken." She chuckled softly. "Home. Such a quaint illusion."

"Illusion?" How could something as important as home be an illusion? She longed for Pensteague. For her own, marvelous bed. "I am sorry for you."

"What you call *home* is wherever I am." Madame LaVoie leaned forward as the carriage slowed. "And make no mistake, I always rule my home. *Au revoir, ma petite.*"

The grey veil swished as she climbed out of the carriage. In the sunlight, the color reminded Penelope of a storm-churned sea.

Lord Thomas's warning echoed in her ears. *A storm is coming, cousin. You'd be wise to batten down the hatches.*

* * *

Chev had slept little and hungered much. All his unanswered longing had vibrated in the body he'd denied.

All. Night. Long.

And the triumph of mastering his desire without humiliating himself or Penelope had eventually given way to questions he could not answer—hopes he did not know he could fulfill.

Using his leg and his left arm, he hefted another piece of wood onto the chopping block. Stepping back, he aimed and swung his ax. The impact sent spurs prickling up his arm, but the wood's crack-and-tumble satisfied.

He grunted in approval.

Behind him, Emmaus whistled. "What did that log ever do to you?"

He glanced back—a warning.

"Easy now." Emmaus shook his head.

Chev set one of the halved pieces of wood back onto the block.

He struck again.

"Are you splitting wood, or are you serving as executioner?"

Chev swiveled to face Emmaus. "Are you still here?"

"I take it," Emmaus said, "the meeting did not go well."

The *meeting* had passed like a dream after she'd stumbled into his embrace. The atmosphere had been something out of a myth, and the night infused with inspiration. If he were a different kind of man, he might have believed some goddess had intervened.

Athena, perhaps.

Then again, Athena was the goddess of wisdom and holding Penelope had not been exactly wise.

Emmaus clucked. "Quite the conversationalist this morning, aren't you? Very well, I can see I am not wanted. There's stew on the coals. And"—his gaze raked Chev's dripping torso—"I'd wash up before Lord Thaddeus arrives."

Again—*fuck*. He'd forgotten his promise to hunt with his son.

That was how dangerous Pen was. One would think she has harmless, given her slender form and those soft, inviting—

He cast aside his ax.

"I apologize," he said, catching up to Emmaus.

"No need," his friend held up his hand. "I understand. *Women.*"

"I only wish *she* were the problem."

They stopped at the pump. Chev drew a bucket of water.

"She isn't the problem?" Emmaus asked.

"Of course not. The problem is me." Holding his wife had unleashed something within. He had no words to describe what was happening. "Douse me, would you, please?"

He bowed his head as Emmaus poured earth-cold water down over his back. The water ran in rivulets and then dripped down from his chest.

Now *that* was what he had needed—to work himself into a sweat and then be refreshed, washed clean.

Contrast. Life was full of it.

Like an expert naval navigator who'd taken work as a game keeper.

Like a pig farmer's daughter who'd make an excellent duchess.

Like leaving a second son and returning as heir to a duchy in desperate need of a duke.

Like the chaos that ate away at prosperity when a leader refused to lead.

"Have you cooled down?" Emmaus asked.

"Yes," Chev replied.

"Good," Emmaus replied. "Because I have something I have to tell you—I must leave for a day or two."

"Leave?"

"I received a message this morning. A naval summons." Emmaus squinted off into the distance. "I've been arguing for my portion of spoils. My solicitor believes an arrangement can be made."

"Will you travel all the way to London?"

"No, just to the Vice-Admiral of Cornwall."

Chev nodded. He'd be on his own. He didn't relish the thought. "Good luck."

Emmaus snorted. "We'll see."

"I have faith in you," Chev said.

Emmaus clapped Chev on the back. "And I in you, my friend. And I in you. Just promise me I'll find everyone alive and standing when I get back."

"I won't lose my temper."

"I didn't expect you would," Emmaus replied. "But try not to break my ax."

Emmaus sauntered back toward the house...*whistling*.

If Cheverley claimed his place as heir, he could make right several wrongs. For one, he could help Emmaus get his due. He'd no doubt Emmaus would eventually prevail, but it never *hurt* to have the heir to a dukedom on your side.

He ran his hand through his damp hair and turned his face to the sun.

If he claimed his place...

Was there still, realistically, an *if*?

Was he capable of abandoning Penelope again after he'd held her close?

But *should* he forgo hunting down the pirate like he planned, making sure she could never hurt anyone else? Vengeance was its own duty and would impart honor and great relief.

Last night, he'd gained one, small triumph over the pirate.

He'd mastered his desire before it exploded into rage.

He now knew he was capable of holding and

119

comforting his wife, but when—*and if*—the time should come, would he be capable of lying with her?

Of giving her pleasure?

The sun turned his eyelids to red—not the red of rage, but the red of warmth. Of fire.

He listened for the pirate's whisper and heard only silence.

But would the silence last?

Chapter Ten

PEN RETURNED THOMAS's carriage to Ithwick and then traversed the pathway through the woods, listening for signs of her son. Halfway between Ithwick and Pensteague, she spotted Thaddeus through the trees in the distance.

She stopped.

First came the unmistakable sound of a plucked string; next, the near-simultaneous strike of an arrow into the earth. A white tail flashed and then the lucky rabbit disappeared.

"You were closer, this time," the captain said.

"Close doesn't end my hunger, does it?" Thaddeus replied.

The captain laughed. Pin-pricks danced over Penelope's skin. That laugh...

It could not be.

She closed her eyes and shook her head.

The captain *was not* Chev. Another trick of her imagination.

Chev had been large, with smooth, pale skin. The

captain was tanned, slim as a cord. Lines of hardship had been etched into his face—he looked older than Chev would have been.

"Another instruction," the captain spoke to Thaddeus, "if you will allow."

"Yes?" Thaddeus sounded hopeful.

"Never turn your back on a man with a weapon."

"But it's just you—"

"Nonsense," the captain replied. "An affinity is no reason to grant your trust. If I were a villain, the first thing I'd do is try to make you like me. Try to make you put down your guard. I am a still a stranger. You do not know my intent."

"My own father could be a traveler in a strange land. Are men to mistrust *him* wherever he goes?"

Ah, Thaddeus. "You needn't grant your trust"—Penelope ventured into the clearing—"in order to be kind."

"Mother!" Thaddeus whirled around. "You gave me a fright."

But she hadn't surprised the captain. From the look on the captain's face, he'd known she was there since she arrived.

The captain was not a man to underestimate.

"Thaddeus, didn't we agree that you would catch up on your studies today?"

"I did," Thaddeus replied. "And now I am studying the English longbow. Captain Smith says I have the makings of a fine hunter."

Thaddeus gave her a look she hadn't seen since he graduated from pony to horse.

"Did he?" She turned her gaze to the captain.

She'd been caring for Thaddeus for years. She'd been protecting him. Raising him. Educating him. And in the space of a few days, this man had made Thaddeus flush with excitement

"Your talents appear to be quite broad," she said.

He lifted a brow. "Have I done something to cause your ire?"

"No," she said, finally. Though he might *attempt* not to be so attractive.

"Would you like to try?" He indicated his longbow.

"You must think I'm a fool," she quipped. "That longbow is strung to match your strength."

"Do I look like a man who can shoot?" He lifted his injured arm.

She snorted. "You look like a man who could do just about anything he put his mind to."

His surprised expression melted into a smile. A dazzling smile, a smile that melted her insides, so they dripped like hot wax all the way down to her toes.

"Honestly, Mother," Thaddeus said. "Your cheeks have gone all red."

"Try," the captain offered, still smiling. His eyes communicated a deeper, unspoken plea. For a moment, she found herself lost in his questions, transported.

He crossed the distance between them.

Perhaps it was the dream she'd dreamed last night. Perhaps it was his closeness. Perhaps it was the wails of feminine needs long-denied. But when she blinked, she saw Chev. She blinked again. The captain returned.

She searched deep into his gaze. Not a sign of recognition—of shared past. The only plea leeching from his gaze was challenge.

Try.

Well, one thing she'd learned from Chev—never agree to a challenge unless you can define the rules.

She leaned down and drew out her knife. Not the one long knife, thin enough to fillet a fish or an intruder, but a shorter one she kept tied to the other leg. This knife wasn't nearly as sharp, but it had its uses.

"Thaddeus, love, would you set a clump of dirt between the v of that tree over there?"

For once, thank goodness, her son did as he was told.

"If you would step aside, Captain."

He acquiesced.

Closing one eye, she aimed. She flicked her wrist and then the knife hit the tree, sending the dirt flying in every direction.

"Impressive." The Captain wiped a clump of dirt from his cheek.

Penelope shrugged. "We all have talents."

He flashed another melting smile. "Remind me not to cross yours."

"I thought I just did."

He chuckled softly. Despite her annoyance, she warmed.

Most men would have been insulted. Or frightened. Only one other man had watched her perform the same trick and clapped with a whoop.

The captain turned away.

"Cheverley," she whispered.

He did not turn back.

Then, Thaddeus yelped.

"Thaddeus!"

"Don't move!" The captain's held her back with an iron arm. "Either of you."

Thaddeus answered a quiet, "Yes, sir."

Sir?

Furious, she met the captain's gaze. There was not time to argue.

"Trust me." An order, not a request.

Taking in a shaky breath, she nodded.

Thaddeus hung from one arm, lifting as much weight as he was able but hanging above a now partially-exposed pit. Glancing down into the hole, she saw a poacher's spring trap. A piece of a branch used to cover the pit had wedged into the trap and was arcing in a dangerous bulge.

"Come around my right and crouch near the boy, but do not reach for him until I say so," the captain said.

"What are you going to do?" she asked, moving into place.

"I am going to lay myself across the opening while you pull him free."

She blinked, her eyes misting. One false move and he'd be missing another limb—or worse. She met his gaze.

Trust me.

She nodded again.

On his knees, he examined the pit and the trap within. His breath slowed.

He crouched into position, leaning his weight on the elbow of his severed arm. And, with a foxlike pounce, he landed across the opening.

"Now," he yelled.

Penelope grabbed Thaddeus's legs and swung him down.

Behind her, the captain roared. Then, the spring trap snapped closed.

* * *

Chev stared at the single spot of blue visible through feathery clouds while his heart whipped against his ribs. Somewhere close, his wife murmured sounds of comfort to their son.

He was alive. With remaining limbs intact.

Which, oddly enough, did not even rate.

There had been a moment, a lightning second, when he'd thought Thaddeus would not clear the pit before the spring trap snapped closed. Everything Chev had survived up to that moment was nothing more than a flickering candle next to that explosion of pure terror.

Spring traps were nothing more than a trigger and hinged jaws that closed like teeth when the trap went off. They were simple, but unforgiving.

He rolled to his side and glanced down into the shallow pit. The trap—pit and spring together—had not been created to catch small game. The branches used to cover the opening would have supported a rabbit or a fox.

But not a man.

Or a boy.

He hung his head. He hadn't known if he had strength enough to support Thaddeus if Thaddeus fell. All he'd known was that he must trust Penelope to do all she could. Either way, the jaws of the trap would have closed on him— not on his son.

He reached up to wipe his eyes. *Wrong arm.* He slammed his elbow against the ground. He rolled back, prone and vulnerable, quaking like an untrained child.

C'est comme ça que je t'aime. This is how I like you.

No. *No!* He refused to listen.

Her voice returned nonetheless.

Le capitaine grand et courageux, impuissant et frémis-

sant. The great and brave captain, helpless and quivering. *Et donc très irrésistible.* And so very irresistible.

No. *No...*

This time, not so much a protestation as a whimper.

The pirate would always return, especially in the times he most needed strength. As long as she lived, she'd remain a leech in the shadows of his mind.

A feminine face blocked the sun. "Captain," she said. "Captain!"

Not the pirate, but Penelope.

Penelope.

She was within inches, but an ocean lay between them. An ocean he, an expert mariner, could not fathom a way to cross.

Slowly, Penelope came into focus. Worry etched onto her face, echoed in her hollow gaze.

What would she say, if he told her the truth? What would she do if he cried out, my wife, my son?

Tu ne possèdes rien. You own nothing. *Tu n'es rien.* You are nothing.

He turned away from the glare threatening to destroy everything he valued.

"Captain, are you—?"

"I am fine," he interrupted. He fended off her touch. He couldn't bear the weight of her gaze.

Look away, Pen. Please, look away.

The scarred end of his limb brushed along her arm. He flinched. Even in places numbed by scars, she burned.

"I am fine," he repeated, this time in a voice that brokered no objection.

She sat back, pained with uncertainty.

"Mother?"

Thaddeus's voice broke the awful spell. She moved

away, leaving Cheverley aching for—and fearing—her return.

"Thaddeus?" He asked without rising. "Are you injured?"

"No, sir."

Sir. The boy was either a radical or he had started to suspect the truth. All the more reason to end this before it was too late.

"Pe—" *Damnation.* He cleared his throat. "Lady Cheverley, are you able to take him to Ithwick?"

"I had already determined to do just that," she answered coolly.

He raised himself to his elbows. She assessed him, detached, but all authority.

Ah. There she was—the knife throwing, pig-farmer's daughter who could build a cottage and, with equal ease, fool the *ton* into believing her blood blue.

A woman who deserved to be a duchess, even if he did not deserve to be a duke.

A breeze ran fingers along his forearm, taunting him with the closeness he could have felt, if he were not broken beyond mending.

He used the tree's trunk to help him stand. Facing Thaddeus, he gripped the boy's shoulder, resisting the urge to pull him close.

"Fine courage," he said.

"Thank you." The boy beamed. "And thank you for saving my life, too."

He nodded once. "Your mother played an equal part."

"I've already thanked her," Thaddeus replied.

"A word, Lady Cheverley?" Though torture, he drew her aside and lowered his voice. "Keep him inside and occupied for the next few days."

She lifted a brow. "And where will you be?"

"Scouring the woods for traps." And finding out who was responsible for setting this one.

"Very well."

She tried to turn. He tightened his grip. She glanced down at his hand.

"Forgive my presumption." He released her arm. "It was not my place to tell you what to do."

Penelope looked away. "Yet you did not hesitate to do so."

"Not for the reasons you think." He hadn't been lording. He just—he sighed heavily. Yes, he had been lording. Arrogant. Everything she had accused. "Listen," he said, "I've seen sailors younger than Thaddeus bludgeon enemies without batting an eye, only to crumple in feverish nightmares once the danger was past."

"The reaction is not immediate, you mean?"

He nodded.

She glanced to Thaddeus, and back again to him.

"The soul pays the price," she said. *What has yours paid?*

She didn't have to ask the question. It was in the air between them. In the tension he'd created when he'd shoved aside her concern. But only Cheverley could answer those questions. They weren't in the purview of Captain Smith.

"Thank you for saving him." She took a deep breath. "I don't expect you to acknowledge my thanks, but I hope you can feel it. Now"—her breath stuttered—"if you will excuse me, I must attend to my son."

He let her go.

He did feel her thanks, and her thanks crushed him with a deadly blow.

Chapter Eleven

CHEV FOLLOWED HIS wife and son until they disappeared into the entrance of the Great Hall. Only then did his shaking cease.

Blank windows stared outward from the manor house, eyes in a soulless shell. In the distance, above the dull, slate roof rose the remaining ramparts of Ithwick Castle. From this aspect, castle and manor appeared as puppet and puppeteer—both grey structures, both foreboding, both meant to instill awe and respect in men of different generations.

Without the privileges nor the responsibilities of being heir, he'd been spectator to Ithwick's true cost, watching as Piers stumbled beneath the weight of the power that had left their father avaricious, acquisitive, and mean.

The soul pays the price.

Indeed.

But—he turned back to the wood—was the prize valuable enough to make a man—or woman—kill?

Slowly, he made his way to the clearing and the pit. Careful to watch his step, he leaned over the pit and lifted out the spring trap by its closed jaws. Beneath the trap, something hissed.

Adders.

He backed quickly away.

The beautifully marked black snakes were poisonous, but not usually aggressive.

Not unless one stepped directly into a nest.

Had this been the spot where Piers had lost his life? When Emmaus returned, he'd have to inquire.

He cleared the spring trap of debris, removing grass from the iron hooks placed there for just that purpose.

Disgusting.

The trap was several times the size of a trap meant to ensnare a rodent. He'd seen its like only once before. It was a man-trap, meant to ensnare poachers.

As if there wasn't enough game to go around.

To his knowledge, man-traps had never been needed or desired at Ithwick before. And even if the duke had ordered them placed, there wasn't any need to make the trap even more deadly by placing it in a shallow pit.

So, who had brought the trap here? And why?

Had this been a trap set for Piers? Or had it been meant for Thaddeus? Or Emmaus? Or him?

Strangers were neither welcomed nor liked in Cornwall, especially not in smugglers' country. But to wish any of them maimed or killed?

That didn't make proper sense, either.

Not that any of this made sense.

He glanced back at the pit. What would have happened to Thaddeus—to Pen—if they'd been wandering through the woods alone?

To *that* question, at least, he had an answer: The same thing that had happened to Piers. He hooked the trap on his arm and turned to head back toward Emmaus's cottage. Then, something flashed within the tree.

Penelope had forgotten her knife.

Unsurprisingly, the knife did not dislodge with ease, but he managed. He held it up to the light, seeing Pen in the way it had been lovingly polished, carefully sharpened. She'd never been one to take anything for granted.

Would he have taken the same care with his possessions if he'd been born poor? Or would he have been wasteful, embittered?

No matter what her protestation, he'd always believed he'd rescued her, in a way.

He'd intended to whisk her away from the hardship to which she'd been born, to protect the jewel he'd found by creating a lovely setting just for her. When his father had given him the choice—Navy or exposure, he'd told himself she and their child would be better off where he'd placed them while he ventured off to bring home the prize.

Instead, he'd left her alone in this world. A world with far more ease by many measures, and yet, a world of treachery and deceit.

What if—he hefted the knife—he had trusted her strength? What if he had taken them both to a world even his father's power could not reach?

And, if he were to trust her strength now, what would that mean?

He slid the knife into his belt.

Before turning back, he scanned the forest one last time.

How could he prevail when he could not answer the enemy within and he could not see the enemy without?

* * *

Penelope passed three days at Thaddeus's side following the incident in the forest. Three *excruciating* days. Thaddeus had collapsed almost as soon as he reached his room and had only just begun to recover.

She hadn't even noticed the snake bite until Thaddeus had vomited so much that she and Mrs. Renton had to remove his breeches.

She dipped her cloth into the basin at Thaddeus's bedside, wrung out the excess water, and carefully wiped her son's brow. Even if the captain had not encouraged her to keep watch, she couldn't have left her son's side.

At least Anthony, Thomas, and their guests had left for a few days at Portsmouth, for the expressed purpose of viewing the infamous hulks where the French prisoners were kept, but Pen suspected they were more likely to indulge in gaming and whores.

What kind of men traveled that far to simply to gawk at those less fortunate?

She returned the cloth to the basin.

Before the fever broke, Thaddeus had been flushed, and cranky, and insisting he must get out of bed.

"Why?" she'd asked.

"To find my father," he'd replied.

"Your father is dead, love."

"He's not," he'd repeatedly insisted. "He's out there. He's in trouble."

She closed her eyes and exhaled, grateful that trial, at least, had passed.

She stood and stretched her back, eyeing the stitching she'd thrice abandoned.

She hadn't been thinking clearly when she'd started cutting and sewing. She'd just needed something—anything —to occupy her hands. But now, the coat she'd made for the captain was finished, the shirt nearly so, and she wondered if she should give the captain so intimate a gift.

Why shouldn't she thank him?

After all, he'd saved Thaddeus's life. And, the high stakes of the moment forgave his discourtesy in the aftermath, even if he hadn't apologized.

She drew the shirt into her lap and plied her needle.

After a few failed starts, she'd settled on a design that had seams that, instead of circling the shoulder, ran from under the arm directly to the collar, allowing, as she'd hoped, for a wider range of movement.

She placed the last stitch, tied off the thread, and then shook out the shirt.

Mrs. Renton came into the room. "I'll take over for a while. You rest."

"Thank you." Penelope folded the shirt and picked up the coat. "I believe I'll take some air."

Halfway down the stairs, she heard the rattling of carriage wheels and raised, raucous voices.

Her heart sank.

Her reprieve had ended. Anthony and his coterie had returned.

The butler Anthony hired rushed to open Ithwick's door.

Anthony was first inside. "What? No sign of the intrepid Mrs. Renton?"

"Mrs. Renton's seeing to the young master," the butler replied.

"What has the miscreant done now?"

"He's been ill, sir. Following a nasty encounter with an adder in the forest."

Anthony cocked his head in a way that made Penelope's blood run cold.

She read in his expression the truth she'd only just suspected—the man-trap had been intentionally set and purposely concealed, and the target had been her son.

As for the adders—they could have been an accident, or they could have been insurance.

She set down the shirt and coat on the stairs and then strode down the rest of the steps and across the hall.

"Do you think you are clever?" she demanded of Anthony.

All chatter ceased.

"You aren't clever." Tears threatened in her eyes. "You" —she shoved him with all her might—"are a brute."

Anthony restrained her with ease, twisting both of her hands behind her back. She didn't care. He could hurt her all he wished. In the end, he would get his due.

"What"—he seethed—"are you talking about?"

"How dare you threaten my son's life?"

He paled. "Penelope, sweet," his voice was soft, "you know I would *never* do anything to harm the boy. Thaddeus is like a son to me. I'd protect him with my life. Wouldn't I, fellows?"

His friends joined together in a chorus of agreement.

"Are you telling me you had nothing to do with the poacher's trap intentionally set on Ithwick land? Either you're an even poorer steward than I thought, or you're lying."

"If someone did set the trap," Lord Thomas spoke from the rear of the group, "my money is on the lame beggar."

"Not a bad thought," Anthony replied, his gaze never leaving Penelope.

"What lame beggar?" she asked.

"Why your newest stray, of course." Anthony squinted. "We just saw him in town, dressed in rags."

"You're mad. What would the captain gain by harming my son?"

"Gain?" He shrugged. "Why need he gain?"

"Only a madman would harm a child without reason," Penelope replied.

"Oh, I heartily agree." Anthony smiled. "And, now that I consider, your beggar more than fits that bill."

"Just because he taunted you—"

"That?" Anthony interrupted. "I'd forgotten all about that. After what all of us witnessed in the village, if the magistrate sets the beggar free I would be very surprised."

Her heart leapt in her throat. "What's happened?"

"I keep telling you, sweet. Those sailors cannot be trusted. Your beggar nearly killed a man today."

She yanked out of his softened grip. "I don't believe you."

"Believe what you will." Anthony shrugged. "I know what I saw. Irus challenged him to a fight."

"Irus, the drunken fisherman?" The captain wouldn't harm an old man. Would he?

"Yes." Anthony snorted. "I suppose there simply isn't enough room for two beggars in the village."

Pen narrowed her eyes. "You encouraged the fight, didn't you?"

Snickers sounded among the gentlemen.

"What if I did?" Anthony replied. "A man has got to have *some* entertainment. Settle." He held her back by the shoulders. "Settle! My God, Penelope, I almost believe you *care* for the beggar."

Blood crept into her cheeks she dropped her hands and looked away. "I find your behavior repugnant, is all."

"*My* behavior? It wasn't *me* who nearly killed a man. Irus may well be dead."

"He's right." Lord Thomas moved to the front of the group. "You should have seen the bloodlust in the captain's eyes. I shiver just to recall. He beat Irus until Irus could not stand and then dragged him half-conscious from the town."

No. It couldn't be true.

Not the captain. Not *her* captain.

I am still a stranger. You do not know my intent.

The captain had even warned Thaddeus not to give him his trust. Had she been a complete fool?

She turned away. Anxious to reach him. Anxious to discover the truth.

"Where are you going?"

"Back up to Thaddeus." She would take the servants' stair out. She picked up her the clothes from the stairs. "Do you object?"

Anthony held her gaze for a long moment.

"Carry on," he finally said.

Chapter Twelve

CHEVERLEY GRITTED HIS teeth as Emmaus laid another stich, slowly closing the shallow gash on his side. Enduring the needle never got easier, no matter how many cuts one survived.

Listening to the howls of Emmaus's first patient hadn't helped, either. And Irus, who was unconscious again by the fire, on a heap of pigskins and deep in gin-infused sleep, only suffered a split lip.

"You're lucky Sir Jerold did not arrest you," Emmaus said.

Chev scoffed. "For defending myself?"

"For nearly killing an old drunk. And don't bother attempting to deny your rage. I saw how close you came."

Chev glanced askance at Irus—whose swollen face would, no doubt, purple long before he woke.

Chev had, once again, seen red.

Although he'd also tried to avoid the fight. He'd done everything he could to discourage Irus from throwing the first punch. But Anthony and his coterie had egged on the old man's belligerence, and, once Irus had pulled a knife, Chev had little choice.

Emmaus looked up. "Can you control your rage?"

"Can you?"

Disappointment flashed in Emmaus's gaze. "If I could not, I would not be alive today."

Chev nodded, chagrined. Even what Chev endured was nothing compared to Emmaus's tale.

"Forgive me."

Emmaus snorted. "Just promise you'll stop landing your foot in your mouth."

"Best not to speak at all, then."

Chev leaned back and closed his eyes.

Why was it, when standing on the helm of a ship, he could read a hundred risks and opportunities in the weather, in the waves. With quick calculation, he could discern the balance of enthusiasm and trepidation in his men and know how the result could affect a planned attack. But on land—though risks aplenty abounded—all opportunities were shrouded.

He'd no idea how to deduce something so simple as his reckoning, nor did he have any rudder he could shift that would change his course.

Irus snored deeply, interrupting Chev's thoughts.

Throwing punches had been far easier than bringing justice to his life and his home. Irus had been but a proxy for Anthony, for the pirate. He understood that, now that the red had passed.

"Irus will recover," he said aloud.

"Once he sleeps off that gin you bought him, yes," Emmaus agreed.

"I'm lucky you showed up when you did."

"I'll say." Emmaus tied off, and then cut, the thread.

Chev took another swig of well-earned gin. "You haven't told me what happened between you and the vice-admiral."

"Is anything having to do with the Admiralty ever quickly resolved?" Emmaus returned his needle to his leather packet. "I was not given my share of past spoils; however they did provide me with an opportunity."

Emmaus wiped his hand on a rag. He didn't touch the gin. He never did. "They've been watching a ship not too far off shore—a purported merchant ship flying a Danish flag. They want help bringing the ship in without drawing too much attention or risking their own men."

"Why?"

"Because the ship is neither Danish, nor does it belong to a merchant."

"A privateer?"

"Possibly." Emmaus nodded. "If I take it, they say it will be mine."

"You get your spoils without them having to give you anything at all."

Emmaus snapped his fingers. "Two problems solved."

"It's suicide."

"Maybe, maybe not. The ship's crew have been transferring goods to smaller vessels and receiving goods in return. Customs intercepted one of the cutters and the resulting interrogation led the vice admiral to believe the captain is a person they've sought. The captain, however, is not currently aboard the ship. In fact, he's been absent for some time." Emmaus drummed his fingers against the table. "With a proper plan, and an adequate number of skilled men, I'd have a fighting chance."

"You are going to attempt to take the ship?"

Emmaus had always wanted his own vessel.

"I've spoken to a few men who are willing to assist. But my decision depends."

"On what?"

"On you." He leaned forward. "I swore to Lady Cheverley that I would not leave until I was certain she and Thaddeus were safe. Before I commit, I want your word you intend to claim your place, your life."

Chev turned his gaze toward the hearth, eyeing a man he almost killed.

What if he failed? What if he claimed his place and the duchy remained in chaos, with a possible murderer in their midst?

And was he just supposed to forget about the pirate? Allow her to roam free and harm others?

Tu n'es rien. You are nothing. *Je te possède maintenant en entier.* I own every part of you, now.

He spit into the coals; They hissed and steamed in reply.

"While you were gone," Cheverley said, "Thaddeus nearly lost a limb by stumbling into a man-trap for poachers."

"What?" Emmaus exclaimed.

Chev rubbed his forehead. "I needn't ask if you set it."

"The *last* thing I'd do is use a trap designed for an animal on a man."

"I know," Chev replied. "Which can only mean you were right about Piers's death not being an accident. But what I cannot understand is, if Anthony planned to kill his way to the top of the inheritance line, why is he courting Pen?"

"As I suggested before—what if it's as simple as lust?"

"Possible. But"—Chev's blood ran cold—"he could satiate lust without marriage." Anthony—if the murderer was Anthony—had to have another reason. "When did Anthony first show interest in my wife?"

Emmaus considered. "Not until she moved to Ithwick."

Chev was missing something, something that connected Pensteague and Ithwick, Anthony and Pen. The answer remained elusive.

"If you revealed who you are you'd have all the resources of the duchy at your disposal. Two lives will stand between Anthony and his prize. Even Anthony isn't mad enough to attempt to stage *two* more accidents."

Chev ran his hand over his face. "It's not that simple."

"Isn't it?" Emmaus asked. "It seems simple enough to me. However, I am not you. I haven't land. I haven't a wife. And I most certainly do not have a son."

Cheverley swallowed, accepting the bitter censure.

Their gazes locked. Outside, rapid footsteps sounded in the gravel.

The door flew open and Penelope stepped inside, breathless...and so breath-*taking*, Chev did not think to cover his exposed chest.

Her gaze dropped from his eyes to his scars—moving from the new one on his side, to the ones that crisscrossed his arms just above the elbow, and then to ones that slashed across his wrist.

His breeches and stockings covered the ones on his thighs and ankles. Even so, she gasped. Her expected horror was almost a relief.

"Lady Cheverley," Emmaus moved to take the door. "Perhaps it would be better if we stepped outside while the captain dresses."

"It's all right, Emmaus," Cheverley said. "Let the lady look if she is so curious to see."

"Is it?" she asked, voice quivering. "Is it all right? Because it doesn't look like it is all right." She lifted a hand to touch her lips. Her fingers shook. "Anthony says you *killed* Irus. Did you?"

Chev tilted his head toward the hearth. "Look there. You'll find Irus very much alive."

"I saw the fight," Emmaus added. "The captain attempted restraint until Irus drew his knife."

She exhaled and closed her eyes.

"If you cannot bear what you have seen," Chev said, "You may hand me my shirt."

Emmaus glanced between them and then cleared his throat. "I believe that is my cue to check on the pigs."

She and Emmaus shared silent communication Chev could not decipher. She nodded, moved aside, and allowed Emmaus to pass. She clasped her hands behind her back and then turned her gaze on him.

Her heightened color made him aware, not just of his scars, but of his near-nakedness and all the things his nakedness implied.

Though sitting while a lady stood was considered the height of inconsideration, he did not think he could stand.

"Developed a taste for the hideous, have you?" he asked, acid in his voice.

"You are anything but hideous."

She moved forward until she—unlike his shirt—was well within his reach.

The hooded cloak that tied at her throat hung unevenly. Several locks of her hair had come loose and curled down over her shoulder, resting against her nearly-untied bodice, and the right hook on her bib was one, deep inhale from breaking free.

He swallowed.

143

This was not the time to begin mentally undressing his wife.

"Did you rush here from Ithwick alone? In the dark?"

She nodded.

"I wish you would have a care for your safety."

"How *could* you admonish me for not thinking of my safety when I was only thinking of yours?" Her voice fell to a whisper. "But *my* concern doesn't mean anything to you, does it?"

Her question slayed.

He imagined pulling her onto his lap and kissing her until she understood she—not just her concern—meant everything to him.

Which was why failing her once again was not an option.

And why he was frozen in indecision.

"Hand me my shirt, would you?" he asked.

"No." She blushed a telling shade and softened her voice. "What I meant to ask was, will you try this one instead?"

He hadn't noticed the folded clothes beneath her arm until she set them onto the table. Warm air wafted over his skin as she shook out a linen shirt and a dark blue coat. She laid the coat aside and then held the shirt up against his shoulders.

The linen was smooth. Fine lawn, actually. But what fascinated him was the cut.

She frowned down, avoiding his gaze and focusing on his shoulders. "I—I think the seam will keep you more comfortable."

She belied her cleverness.

The shirt would not only be more comfortable, but

because of the way she'd designed the seam, the way the fabric fell would allow a greater range of motion.

He'd be able to shoot his bow—or handle a sword—without restriction.

And, for the times he did not wish to suffer piteous stares, he could leave his jacket resting on his shoulders without concern that it would fall.

She bit her lip—clearly uncertain of his reaction.

"I don't know what to say. I'm stunned." He wet his lips. "And honored."

Her blush deepened, pinking the tips of her ears. "I—I was confined to Thaddeus's room until his fever broke. I cannot be idle."

She had never been able to be idle, worried or not. And yet, she'd waited for him for thirteen years.

"Is Thaddeus recovered?"

"He is much better. Begging to see you, in fact," she said. "May I help you try on the shirt?"

Allowing her to dress him was a terrible idea.

He lifted his arms anyway. She slipped the shirt over his head and then smoothed the linen down his chest like a lover.

Like a wife.

"There are hooks, you see." She fumbled with the ones on his right. "You may leave it down, or pin it back, as you require."

Her care warmed him deeply. "Thank you, Lady Cheverley."

"Penelope," she corrected.

He ran a knuckle down her heated cheek. "Pen."

One minute, he was sure she knew he was her husband.

The next, he was not.

The old spark flamed between them, but, while secrets

remained, they could be nothing more than emissaries of their true selves.

She traced the puffed white lines across his wrist. Her lip trembled. Then stilled. Though his scars muted her touch, the pain ran deeper than the physical.

"You said you were imprisoned. Were you cut then?" she asked.

"Yes," he whispered, raw.

"You must have fought quite hard." She sniffed. "You were not easy to restrain."

"No." He blinked over stinging eyes. "I wasn't."

"I thought—I thought officer prisoners were treated with respect."

"Sometimes," he answered. "Sometimes not. I wasn't in a regular prison. And yes, though I struggled until I bled, I was kept restrained."

She frowned. "To a wall?"

God help him, he could not lie. "On occasion."

And on other occasions, to a long, thin plank the pirate could easily straddle.

His memories simmered—a messy stew of fear and shame and hatred.

Tu n'es rien. You are nothing. *Je te possède maintenant en entier.* I own every part of you, now.

Pen lifted her gaze to his.

Her eyes contained no guile, no pity, no disgust. Yet they stung worse than Emmaus's needle. Would it be easier to tell her behind this veil of partial anonymity?

"Please," he choked. "Don't ask any more questions."

"Truth for truth," she whispered.

"I can't." *Fuck.* The sting in his eyes eased as dampness collected between his lashes. "You don't want to know."

"Will silence protect me? Will my ignorance make everything right?"

"No." He swallowed through a dry throat. "Nothing can make everything right."

"Then what do you have to lose?" She placed her cool palms on either side of his face. "Trust me. Please."

Trust. Yes. Save me, Pen.

"My secrets—they are vile. I was—I suffered—I suffered—"

Damnation.

Truth, when able to be put into words at all, came out a halting, sticky substance. He could not gentle what he'd experienced. There was no polite way to describe what he endured.

"I can't."

"Will you let me ask questions?"

He nodded.

"Your jailor...did he defile you?" she asked.

"Yes." The word was a serrated knife forced through his mouth.

How could she know? He scowled furiously. What had she experienced that could possibly allow her to *imagine*...?

She dropped her gaze. "A friend—a fellow seamstress, spent time in Bridewell." Her brows drew together with concern. "She told me stories—terrible stories—about the ways the guards would humiliate the women...and the men."

Now, he was shocked.

Shocked and ashamed. He'd never considered such things could happen. Not here. In his own country.

Then again, how many would lift up their voice in defense of those who had broken the law? Most would shrug and look away.

Unless they, too, had been brought low.

Demeaned. Forgotten. A mistake, a lapse in judgment— even a lead ball mis-fired—did not negate a person's humanity. Life—all life—was sacred.

"My jailor," he spoke quietly, as if a whisper could lessen the blow, "was a she."

Penelope glanced up, confusion in her gaze.

"Certain physical responses can happen"—he waited until the tremor in his voice had passed—"without a man willing them to happen."

Her eyes widened. She bit her lip and looked away.

Unanchored, he trembled.

"I *said* you would not wish to know." And now it was too late.

"You misunderstand." Her eyes flashed with tears of her own. "I'm angry for you. I turned away because..." Her brows drew together. "I was thinking—fearing, really—is what happened to you—is *that* why it's too late for you and your love?"

Lord have mercy. "Yes."

She bent down to look into his eyes. "I cannot imagine what you went through—"

Thank God.

"I cannot *know* how you feel. But you—you cannot let that evil person rob you. You should go to your love. You should not leave her"—her voice broke— "waiting."

His mind struggled to form words.

"It's awful, I tell you," she said. "The waiting, I mean. The desperate hope—"

His heart beat became labored, as if he were climbing a dangerous cliff. "I betrayed my vows."

"But you aren't at fault!"

A tear snaked over his cheek, dropped from his chin onto the shirt she'd made. "Aren't I?"

"No!" She grasped his cheeks again. "Go to her. *Please* go. If there were even a chance my husband—" She stopped speaking abruptly. She released him. "You *should* go to her," she repeated, as if convincing herself. "You will, won't you?"

He swallowed through a bone-dry throat. "I haven't decided."

"You *must!* You must...even if, when you leave, Thaddeus and I..." She shook her head again. "Well, I don't *want* you to go. You realize that, don't you? But I can't keep you. Because even if I *truly* want you to be, you aren't—" Her voice dropped. "Are you?"

Tears welled in her eyes.

"Pen."

He pulled her down onto his lap. He brushed her hair from her face.

"Look at me, Pen."

She lifted her eyes. Her lashes webbed with wet.

Sentiments welled up inside him—sentiments he could not name. The cottage shrunk again, very small. Too small.

Suffocating, in fact.

He'd be strangled if he remained indoors.

"I need to go," he said.

"Now?" she exclaimed.

"Yes, now. I need to go to the sea."

Irrational. But by the sea, he'd be able to breathe. Unlike here.

With his tears, Penelope's tears, the fire, and Pen's desperate wishing that he was who he really was. His terror would shrink against the vast horizon, the churning waves.

"Ride with me?" he asked.

"Pardon?" She hiccupped again.

"Ride with me. Under the moon. Come with me to the seaside. It's a different world out there. A new world. Can't you ride?"

She held his gaze for a long, solemn moment. "I can. Mostly, I prefer to walk."

"But why? You used to—" He cleared his throat. "You seem like a woman who would enjoy a gallop in the moonlight."

"I don't have a horse."

"I do."

Her eyes dropped to his arm.

"I assure you," he continued, "I can manage."

"Yourself, certainly, but two? With your injury?"

"Yes." Damn his injury.

He lifted them both to standing. He held out his hand. Everything depended on her answer.

He wanted her to place her hand in his.

He wanted her to give him her trust—the same as he had given her his.

And—by God—he wanted so much more.

She placed her fingers into his and stared down at their joined hands with a riveted, peculiar expression.

"Let's go," he said, pulling her to the door.

He helped her up first, and then swung up onto the saddle. Tentatively, she placed her arms around his waist, careful to avoid his wound. But her hold tightened as soon as they started to move.

They made their way slowly through the wood to the field, while his horse became accustomed to two, and he became accustomed Penelope's warmth against at his back.

She held him like she had those last few miles of their mad dash to Gretna Green, when they'd had to abandon the stolen carriage and the four of them—Chev, Pen, Ash and

Hurtheven—had ridden through the darkness on three horses as his father's men searched the inn.

As soon as they reached the field, Chev urged his horse to gallop.

Pen yipped involuntarily and buried her face into his neck.

His spirit soared. And that was *before* she started to laugh.

Her startled laugh rang out like crystal bells—free, full-bodied, whole.

Her laugh rent him straight down his center and sewed him back up with a new kind of hope. He'd forgotten the sweetness of feminine joy. The rare beauty of a woman's bliss.

The moon shined down. An effervescent moon. Bubbling all around like champagne, dissolving what was past.

Chapter Thirteen

PENELOPE'S CHEEK CHAFFED against the coat she'd made for her husband.

Her husband.

She was glad of the darkness. Glad of the wind.

The first hid her tears, the last dried them. The steady rhythm of the horse's hooves drummed out her fears. She resolved to hold Cheverley close, leaving questions for another time.

For now, she would seize sensation.

They flew over the field. Each time Chev's horse jumped she made a sound of unfettered joy. Each time, Chev answered with a low-bellied laugh.

His laugh. Sweet mercy, his laugh.

His laugh had always run though her like a spring—fresh and deep and cleansing. Her fingers bit into his ribs, wanting to clutch him so close, she'd never lose him again.

But such ownership was impossible. Hearts were but borrowed things, never belonging fully to anyone but the one in whom they were born.

She wiped her cheeks against his coat.

They'd spent so many nights apart, had matured living vastly different lives. But hadn't there always been a vast difference between them?

Could they face adult fears with adult wounds and without the trusting openness of youth?

The world could wound in so many ways. Every human heart held emptiness and light, just as sure as the heavens held blank spaces and stars.

She dried her eyes as they approached an outcropping of stone that marked the beginning of the cliffs that spilled to the sea. If any tears remained, he would know she knew he was Cheverley, that she was now certain.

As it was, she wasn't sure she could keep the knowledge from her face.

But he hadn't told her. Not yet. And Chev never did anything on a whim. Every decision was calculated. Every choice carefully parsed.

If he'd come home in disguise, he must have good reason.

He slowed the horse. She leaned back, allowing him to dismount, marveling at his ease. His injury had changed him, yes, but his new body had found a rhythm all his own. She had no doubt she'd fail to notice, in time.

Time. Years. *Oh, heavens.* They would have *years* ahead of them. Years of nights, of moonlit rides, but *years.* Together.

She moved to dismount on her own.

"Now, please," he chided. "Don't you trust me?"

She did. Enough to continue with this ruse. *For now.*

"Place your right arm around my neck, and your left on my shoulder.

She did. He scooped up her legs with his left arm and held her up with the crook of his right. If she hadn't held

153

him tightly, she might have rolled from his grasp, but together, they managed a reasonably steady dismount.

She let her arms slide from his neck, but she kept her hand against the top of his shoulder.

"You can move to the other side."

His uninjured side.

"There's no need. I'm—I am—" She placed a shaking hand over her mouth, unable to say the word fine.

"Oh—oh," he soothed. "Did I frighten you? I am sorry. I should not have gone so fast."

She shook her head. "The ride was beautiful. It's just that... It's just that I feel—

He grinned. "Free?"

The opposite of free, actually. Was there a word for happily bound? She felt, if he remained by her side, she could surmount any obstacle. Conquer any foe.

It was happening again. Because of Chev, she could see doors of possibility where before there had been only walls.

But, would history repeat?

Would those doors shutter and leave her alone?

He spoke soothing things to his horse, as led them all to a sheltered area within the rocks. He secured his horse's reins.

"Come," he said to Pen. "Let us find a place where we can be out of the wind."

As they rambled around the rocks, he frequently stopped to give her his hand. He chose a place for them to sit between two large outcroppings, where they had a partial view of the horizon.

How had she not known him at once?

And now that she was certain, how could she keep from taking him into her arms and covering him in grateful kisses from head to toe?

"Tell me, Captain," she said. "Of all the places you've traveled, what do you think of Ithwick?"

His teeth flashed in the moonlight. "What proper Englishmen doesn't love a good ruin?"

"You are jesting," she said.

"Only in part. You must admit history's shadows run long in these parts. The standing stones alone have been there for thousands of years."

"Yes," she agreed. And still they retained their magic.

"What did you think of this place when you first came?" he turned around her question.

Always a specialty of his.

"I was not welcomed," she replied. "Not at first."

"But what did you feel? Of the landscape?"

"Ah," she breathed. "Stark beauty. The moors, and rocks, and woods have settled into my soul and will never depart."

"This is home, then?"

"Yes," she replied. "I never want to go anywhere else. I will wait for my husband to return."

"And what if he returns—as I have?"

"Dressed like a beggar?"

"You know that is not what I meant." He rested the elbow of his injured arm on one knee.

"Captain," she said, almost scolding. "I miss his heart. I miss the warmth of his body beside me in bed. I miss the way my heart lifted when he smiled."

She turned away. She could do this no longer.

"Penelope," he said softly.

He moved behind her, so she was sitting between his legs. She leaned back against his chest and turned her face upward toward his.

Stars sparkled around the shadow he made in the night,

just they had on that first night in the alley behind the public assembly rooms.

Then, like now, she fancied he could be hers.

But that was the danger, wasn't it?

Even now, even after the terrible complexity of the wounds he'd revealed, even knowing he had not yet told her the truth, she would turn over her heart to him and accept him without reservation.

Once again, she'd pluck out his shiny pieces, and set them into a constellation of her own making, forgetting the terrifying power of the vast places between the stars, the emptiness that frightened.

But not enough to stop her desire.

"I don't want to talk of the past, or the future. I just want..." She paused.

The power of their first night together mingled with the power of now.

"What, Penelope? What do you want?"

She unfastened her outer cloak and pushed it off her shoulders. "I want you."

* * *

He shouldn't comply. Before he walked through the door she held open, he should be sure she knew who he was.

She reached up and curled her finger around the back of his neck.

"You said you could not deny me."

"No." He concentrated on the small circles she drew. "I said I *would* not deny you." One indicated helplessness. The other, choice. "If I acquiesce to your wishes, I will do so, not because I must, but because..."

"Because?"

He dropped his voice, "I wish to hear you laugh."

"Make me happy, then," she said. "Kiss me."

Again, he could not breathe, even in the sea-scented air. Penelope, the moonlight, the desire that simmered low— they vined around his heart and squeezed.

"Would you like me to kiss you?"

"Would I have led you here if I did not?"

When he'd held Pen in the shadow of the standing stones, she'd been confused by her reaction to "the captain."

Pen did not show an ounce of confusion, now.

He'd wager his last sixpence Pen knew who he was, though his secret wafted between them thin as candle smoke.

"I'm waiting," she said. "You *cannot* know how much I *hate* waiting."

With a rueful smile, he bent his head, brushed his lips against hers. A prickling sensation shot from his lips to his groin.

"Soft," she said. "Like a whisper."

"Like a secret." He feathered his lips along her cheek to her ear, marking her sweet face as his.

"Secrets *must* be whispered, mustn't they?" she asked. "Held sacred. Treated with the utmost care."

Care, like she'd taken with his new shirt and coat.

Care, like she'd taken with his son.

Care, like the way her fingers soothed the back of his neck in a firm, gyrating dance.

"And," she finished, "secrets must only be shared with those you treasure."

His head remained giddy, but dread pooled his stomach.

"Just kisses," he said—more to himself than to Pen.

"Just kisses," she replied. "And anything else you wish."

He froze. "Pen, I—I cannot."

She adjusted her legs, turning within his embrace until they faced one another.

"What *can* you do?" she asked.

His mind went blank. Then, flashes of yellow fire— flames that followed her fingers as they threaded through his hair. He couldn't bed his wife—he did not wish to even try. Not here.

Not yet.

Not until the truth between them had been acknowledged. Not until he was fully prepared to return home.

She tilted her face toward his in trust. "I will take whatever you can give me."

The other night, when he'd held her close, her name had kept him breathing.

Tonight, could her breath become his guide?

He claimed her mouth in a deeper kiss—releasing fears as if he were bailing water, trusting her breath to keep them both afloat.

"I can give you pleasure," he said.

Her chest rose and fell as he trailed his lips down her proffered neck.

He loosened the left side of her bodice; the right, he freed with his teeth. Nibbling soft kisses against the side of her throat, he slid his hand beneath the fabric and cupped her breast.

She whimpered as he ran his thumb over her nipple.

A stab of desire sliced through to his stomach. Sweet torture—she sighed into his ear—his cock filled, draining his head of blood, his lungs of air.

He stilled, cradling her gently between his thighs, riding the rise and fall of her breath, listening for soft sounds, her desire packed within her breath's ebb and flow.

"Captain."

Her whisper turned to groan as he draped her across his thighs.

"Open for me." He moved his lips to her breast. "Please."

She inched her skirt up around her thighs, though one arm remained around his back, holding on, fingers digging into his shoulder.

He reached beneath her skirts. Even before he reached the cleft between her legs, he met with heat. Her pale legs fell apart artlessly.

More memories slipped into place—like the clicking of an opening lock.

All the times they'd come together in intimate union, she'd never cared how she looked. Pen poured her all into sensation—both her own as well as his.

When she made love, when she danced, she was unaffected joy meeting complete, immodest surrender.

That had been why she'd entranced him from the first. Why he'd wanted to rescue her, protect her, keep her. But he hadn't.

And now she was rescuing him.

She writhed against his fingers, joining with him in search for her pleasure. Then, she found it—untapped and unable to be contained.

Fever broke in her breath, in her trembling limbs, in the sound of bliss that pillowed his ears.

He clasped her close, keeping his lips pressed to her temple as he rocked her back to this time.

He'd done it. He'd given his wife pleasure.

He hadn't thought of his terrors, his injury, of anything else but Pen. He had remained anchored by her breath.

He blinked until the evening cold tingled in the dampness between his lashes.

He could have done anything in that moment, even leap from the cliffs and flown.

And the final, hidden memory slipped into place.

Limitless possibility—this was how Penelope had always made him feel.

Shameless.

She nearly chuckled.

She hadn't a hint of shame.

She'd exposed herself to the captain, let the him shatter her into tiny pieces, let him hear her unfettered cries. *Let* him? She'd practically begged him. And she hadn't told him she knew.

She hadn't needed to tell him.

Truth existed between their bodies, a recognition that went beyond words.

He'd known it. Felt it.

Hadn't he?

She shivered with a dawning chill. She flicked her skirts down over her legs and then moved to adjust her bodice.

"Allow me."

His voice returned some of her warmth.

She looked up into his face. He smiled.

Oh yes. He knew. Her Chev. He would tell her soon. He must. He would tell her, and they would oust those rotten men and start to rebuild. Together.

Just as they were working together to refasten her hooks.

"You must think—" she started.

"Hush," he said against her temple. "I'm endeavoring not to think at all."

She nodded and sighed. Silent recognition would be enough for tonight.

He'd suffered so such—had so many scars. She must trust that he would, in small measures, continue to reveal the truth.

Faith again.

And waiting.

"I'm not very good at faith," she said aloud.

"Aren't you?" he asked.

She shook her head no.

"Where do you get your strength?" he asked.

"From the hope that—" she stopped.

"Well, then." He lifted his brows. "Hope *is* a kind of faith, isn't it? And, you are very good at dwelling in hope."

Dwelling in hope. She liked that.

She *was* very good at hoping. Who else would have waited for an absent husband for *thirteen* years?

She glanced up. "I may be too good at hoping, in fact."

"My dear—" he stopped abruptly, and his smile disappeared.

"What is it?" she asked.

He placed a finger over her lips, tilting his head as if encouraging her to listen.

They were no longer alone.

Silently, she pulled her legs up to her chest, and he drew his dark coat over her petticoats, whose light color practically screamed in the moonlight. Even in this, he was thinking of her.

He was her Chev but changed.

Together, they inched back into the shadows.

A few more moments passed before she heard them distinctly.

Voices. Men's voices.

Wedged between the rock and his body, she could see nothing, but the sound of the voices grew louder.

* * *

Pen moved back into the shadows entirely without sound. What Chev could not hear, he could feel. She tucked her silver-blonde hair beneath her black wool cloak, even as he'd covered her petticoats with his, both ensuring nothing light-colored would accidentally reveal their position.

He placed the strange sense of connection—of comradery—it was like the bonds he shared with his naval brothers...the knowledge that one did not work alone, but in concert.

In trust.

As captain, he held the primary responsibility for his crew, but he worked with confidence, knowing he was not alone.

He experience the same with Pen.

He could work, knowing she would be working beside him, thinking with him, beyond him, even.

As with his fellow officers, he could trust her to fill gaps he missed, making their combined defenses impenetrable.

In the past, he'd failed to understand their mutual dependence. Failed to trust her strength. This time, he vowed, would be different.

The voices were close now—men, moving not-so-silently through the night, their whispers fizzling like ash into the darkness.

Chev's heart thudded in his throat.

Smugglers. The unseen. Smuggling had dwindled, not stopped. The goods could even have come from the ship Emmaus had spoken about.

And, from the path the men had taken up from the harbor, they would have had to walk right past Sir Jerold's militia.

Then again, why should he be surprised?

Officers and smugglers often worked in consort. Most of the time, the only way a man ended up caught smuggling was if he went against his own.

The men passed by in groups of two—one man in front, one behind, a chest between each pair. Two, four, six, eight.

One of the men stumbled and cursed.

The line came to a halt.

"That's the last time, I tell you." A man spoke.

"You whine like a woman." A second man said.

Penelope's spine stiffened.

"I almost *died* back there," the first man spoke again. "Could've been you and you know it. There's no way an inexperienced man could climb down that cliff."

"Shut it, would you?" A third man called. "I *told* you they won't be going down that way."

"Then how—"

"I said"—the third man lifted a flintlock—"*shut it*."

Silence fell among the group.

"Now," the third man said, "let's get these to the storerooms, shall we? *Quietly*."

The line of men moved slowly across the field, not bothering to hide themselves in the least.

"Looks like we'll be here for a while," Chev whispered into Penelope's hear, "you had better get comfortable."

Penelope nodded, turning her face into his chest.

He held her head beneath his chin as he considered what he had just heard.

Why would one of the smugglers complain that the cliff was too difficult for an inexperienced man to climb down?

The smugglers only transported goods.

Or were they planning to transport men?

Chapter Fourteen

PENELOPE RETURNED WITH Chev—as the captain —late the night before. On the way, they'd discussed everything they'd seen and heard.

Smuggling had returned to Ithwick, with the cellars beneath the castle ruins being used to store the goods.

Pen and Chev had come to the same conclusion—there was only one way smuggling could have resumed, and that was with Anthony's express permission.

The smugglers had also unwittingly provided the answer that had been troubling her for some time—the reason for Anthony's courtship.

If Anthony gained control of both Pensteague and Ithwick, he could reopen the tunnels the duke had destroyed. Concealed within the earth, they could smuggle even more. More goods. More *people*.

Hundreds of French naval officers were held in parole towns, under curfew but mostly by their honor. A smuggler who successfully transported an officer out of England could charge three hundred guineas or more. Suddenly

Anthony and Thomas's trip to the prison hulks made a great deal more sense.

Avoiding a tax on goods was one thing, abetting Napoleon was quite another.

The captain—Chev—had left her with a kiss to the brow and a promise he would do everything he could to protect her and Thaddeus.

That kiss had left a brand—a stamp that had comforted as she had drifted off into a restless slumber.

Last night she'd trusted Cheverley.

She'd been dazed by his presence, the very fact he existed. She'd absorbed the horrible blow of his suffering and then opened to his tentative care.

In his embrace, the heavens cracked, and she'd caught a glimpse of a vastly reordered world. Beneath the stars, in the romance and magic of night, she had trusted Chev would, eventually, reveal the truth.

What if she'd been wrong? What if he'd *never* intended to reclaim his place?

How had he answered when she'd asked him if he intended to return to his love?

I have not decided.

As Ithwick emptied of suitors for an excursion to Penzance, even dawn's rosy fingers could not pierce her heavy gloom.

And then, the duke began to thrash. His turn seemed a bitter omen.

She stood with Mrs. Renton in His Grace's bedchamber, worrying her lip with the edge of her thumbnail.

"His Grace is worse," Mrs. Renton said. "He'd been doing so well. Yesterday, he called me by name and even told me to go to the devil like he used to and now, he's confused again..."

He was more than confused. He was flushed, sweating. And he looked so very small in the middle of his massive, golden bed.

"He's vomited up everything I've tried to feed him," Mrs. Renton finished.

"You prepared the meals yourself?"

"I prepared them," Mrs. Renton chewed her lower lip. "But with Thaddeus ill—and you gone most of the evening, there were times he was alone. Do you think—?"

Penelope went to the side of the bed, placing her palm against the duke's forehead.

"You cannot be everywhere," she said to Mrs. Renton. "And I confess I've been...distracted."

"Piers!" the duke cried out suddenly. "Cheverley!"

"Please, your Grace," Penelope murmured. "Rest."

His fevered eyes met hers. "You," he said. "*You.*"

The accusation was present in his tone, his gaze. The accusation had always been present. Even when he couldn't speak at all, he'd gazed at her as if she were something he did not trust.

Like a sorceress or a witch.

He held her responsible for every curse brought down on the house of Ithwick because she'd disrupted his plan for Cheverley.

But why should she accept sole responsibility? Here at Ithwick, His Grace had been king-like in his power.

"You, too," she replied, with equal accusation.

If Ithwick had been cursed with death, dissipation, violence and greed—His Grace had played more than a small part.

In creating a world devoid of anything that resembled true affection, he had made his elder son a devotee of drink and his younger, a man chasing some illusion of male perfection.

The duke held her gaze for a long, horrified moment. Then, he stilled.

He closed his eyes and moaned. Many of his words she could not understand, but one name stood out.

Cheverley.

"Bring me my son!" The duke's sob echoed through the cavernous chamber, melding fury, frustration, and pain.

"Piers is dead," Mrs. Renton said, calm as ever. "You remember. He stepped into a nest of adders last year."

The duke shook his head no. "Cheverley. Bring Cheverley."

Mrs. Renton sent Penelope a pleading glance.

"Cheverley is not here," Penelope replied.

The duke inhaled—an awful, gasping sound.

Mrs. Renton glanced to Penelope. "Please," she said. "Please allow me to administer the doctor's tonic. He said—"

"The doctor," Pen replied, "was paid by Mr. Anthony." She picked up the bottle of Fowler's solution. "And I don't trust this—not for a second."

"But it's the same one he prescribed Her Grace."

"It contains arsenic in trace amounts," Penelope replied. "But if improperly mixed..."

She glanced down at the bottle.

The doctor insisted the tonic was safe. But the duke had sunk back into the state he'd been when she first arrived—confusion, red skin, cramps, vomiting. She strode to the window, and then tossed out the contents.

"Mine!" The duke roared.

Mrs. Renton lifted a pewter mug from the bedside table and leaned over the duke. "How about a nice bit of broth—"

The duke threw the cup across the room, spattering the dark brown liquid across the wall. The empty pewter mug made a clanging sound as it hit the dresser and then the floor. His gaze shifted to Penelope—an unspoken challenge.

"That's enough, Your Grace," Penelope said. "Leave us, Mrs. Renton."

Mrs. Renton frowned. "Will you be all right?"

Pen nodded. Mrs. Renton left the room and quietly closed the door.

Penelope sat down by the duke's side. He shrank back into his pillows.

He'd always been so large, so invincible.

He glanced at her in horror. His hands shook as he held them against his face.

She imagined suffering his confusion—a prisoner in his own aching body, in his own over-large bed. She laid a hand against his arm.

"No more medicine," she said. "You are, in fact, much improved. You could barely speak when I first came to Ithwick, do you remember?"

"No," he replied, stubborn.

"Do you know me, Your Grace?"

He put down his hands. He stared for a long time, her name shivering on the edge of his lips. "P-Penelope."

She sat straight. "Yes," she replied. "I am Penelope, Lady Cheverley."

He winced as if in terrible pain and sunk back into his bed. "Piers." His chest rose and fell with uneven breath. He lifted his hand to his forehead. "Dead."

"Yes, Your Grace," she replied.

"Cheverley?"

She hesitated. "Lord Cheverley is your second son."

The duke scowled, eyes still closed. "Daft!"

169

"Cheverley was lost at sea six years ago," she answered carefully.

His lids flew opened. For a startling moment, he appeared shrewd as ever. He gripped her arm. "Dead?"

How could she lie to a dying man? "I have reason to hope he survived."

"Hope?" His grey eyes—so much like Cheverley's and her son's—pierced. He slurred through a sentence, his tone all condemnation.

"I don't understand—"

"You've learned nothing!" He said clearly.

Oh, she'd learned. She'd learned that power corrupted. That privilege did not lead to appreciation. That love could hurt and confuse as much as love could inspire.

"Was there something you intended to teach me?" she asked.

"Foolish." His breath cracked in his lungs. "Both." He tapped his chest. "*My* rules. *Mine.*"

The duke blinked, confused again. And then he hung his head.

Yes. Yes, they'd been foolish. The duke had laid down rules, Cheverley had seen only impediments.

"We thought," she said gently, "we were in love."

His Grace made a dismissive sound. Then, he turned his mournful gaze to the door. "Duchess."

He heaved a wracking sigh, he placed his hands back over his face and then the most fearsome man she'd ever encountered in her life began to cry.

"The duchess warned—." The duke's shoulders shook. "But—but I knew *best.*" He spat the word. "Cheverley is dead."

His shaking sob alarmed. If not calmed, she feared his fevered frustration could strangle out his last breath.

"Please, Your Grace," she said. "I just told you there was reason to hope—"

The duke fixed her with an uncomprehending stare. Then he glanced about the room, surprised, lost. He closed his eyes. "I ache."

"I know, Your Grace," she said soothingly. "Food would help. Mrs. Renton can bring up more broth."

She rose to ring the bell. He reached out and grasped her arm.

She looked down at his hand. She doubted the duke had ever voluntarily touched her before.

"Stay," he said, urgently.

She removed his hand from her arm and covered it in both of hers.

"I won't go," she replied.

"You didn't go, did you?" Regret laced his voice. "I wanted," he winced, "you to give up. Leave."

She might have dropped the cold hand within hers, had it not been feather-light. She might have told the duke to go to the devil, if it were not so clear he was already there.

"I killed him." He resumed weeping. "I killed my son."

She did *not* like the sound of his breath. She may be running out of time, but the duke was nearly out.

"He is alive," she said quietly. "You don't deserve a decent end, but you will have one. Cheverley is alive."

He dropped his hands. In his expression she read the mirror image of the hope she'd carried for so long.

"Bring him to me," he pled. "*Please.*"

* * *

Cheverley followed Thaddeus up the servants' stair.

Thaddeus moved through a short corridor off a landing.

"This one goes to His Grace's chamber. That one"—he indicated door on the other side—"takes you to the duchess's room. That's where my mother sleeps."

Chev had often used the servants' stair to sneak in and out of the house, but he'd never before entered either the duke or the duchess's chambers. They'd been hallowed places. Forbidden.

Especially for a mere second son.

"Shall I take you inside?" Thaddeus asked, clearly hoping the answer would be no.

"Your mother asked me to come alone."

"Yes, well. You better get on," Thaddeus replied.

Cheverley eased open the servants' entrance to the duke's bed chamber, and then shut the door behind him. Hidden halls and stairwells snaked throughout the manor, built specifically so that the servants would be little seen.

All scions of Ithwick preferred the illusion they existed entirely on their own.

The air within the bedchamber had a heavy feel. The abundance of gold didn't surprise him. Nor did the over-large bed, though he knew for a fact the bed had never been occupied by anyone but the duke. Alone.

An outsized bed for a man with an out-sized sense of his power. Only, the person in the bed did not seem powerful at all. Gone was the commanding force of his presence. All that remained was a withered body, mouth ajar and sheets anxiously clutched at his chin.

Across the room, the doorway to the duke's sitting room stood open. Penelope lay asleep on a chaise. In contrast to the duke's ragged breath, hers was deep and even.

Quietly, Chev closed the door.

She'd given Thaddeus no explanation why Chev should

meet her here. Thaddeus's message was only that Pen
needed him.

As for why—the answer lay in the horrible rattle in the
duke's breath.

She may not have acknowledged Chev as her husband,
but she had known. And now, she was giving him this
chance—a private moment with the father who he'd feared
but not respected, who he'd loved but never admired.

He sat down on the duke's bed. How could someone so
fearsome appear frail?

"Your Grace," Chev whispered. "Father."

The duke opened his eyes, his body stilled. His breath
stopped. Then, slowly, his pale gaze settled on Chev.

"Cheverley." The syllables of his name broke into
distinct peace within the duke's labored breath.

"Yes, Your Grace," Chev acknowledged. Leave it to the
duke to be the only one who recognized him at first sight.

Why did words disappear when most needed? Why,
when Chev had so much to say, could he only stare into his
father's gaze, wrestling with the overwhelming urge to
weep?

"Hades." Fear flickered behind the duke's eyes. "Are
you here to take me?"

His Grace's voice was halting. Labored. As if it took
great pain and thought to say each word.

"No." Cheverley's gaze flicked to the door to the sitting
room and back. "I believe I've been summoned to bring you
back."

"I sent you away."

Chev inhaled sharply. "You did."

His gaze took in Chev's face, his form. "You've
suffered."

"I have." He was not going to lie.

He'd staggered so close to death, he was often surprised to wake from sleep.

He'd danced with oblivion, gazed—shamefully longing —into the emptiness.

He knew humiliation. Desperation.

When banished, he'd resolved to return a hero...

He blinked.

What, exactly, was a hero?

Did strength make a hero? Skill? Cleverness?

At the height of His Grace's power, the duke had embodied all three, and yet there'd been little in him to admire.

His father moaned. He rested his wounded arm against his father's chest and covered the old man's forehead with his other hand. "Cheverley."

"I am here," he said. "Penelope is here."

The duke opened his eyes—fearful again. "She is kind."

Chev lifted a brow. Undeserved kindness had a peculiar burn, did it not?

"She?" Chev queried. The duke had sworn he would never, ever acknowledge Penelope by her title. "Who do you mean by *she?*"

The duke grunted. "Lady Cheverley. She was not my choice—"

Cheverley snorted. "You made that quite clear."

The duke pinned him with his gaze. "But she was a good choice."

"The best choice I made." Chev swallowed with difficulty. He shook his head no. "If I could—" He stopped before his voice quivered. "If I could go back, I would not have left her, no matter what you threatened. If I could go back, I would make a different choice."

The duke closed his eyes and laid back into the pillow. "As would I."

Had his father just acknowledged his wrong?

Violence rose up within him—urgency that lashed every sinew to readiness. Pain, with the metallic taste of blood, flooded his being.

His breath, deep, even, and heavy, coasted over his father's deadly rattle.

Then, cool pressure settled against his brow—as if his wife were present as an angel, with her hand placed against his head.

Anger had stolen much more from them than his family's greed.

Cheverley lowered his forehead on the duke's right shoulder. He laid his wounded arm across the duke's chest.

Home.

But no. Not quite home, was it?

Home was Pensteague. The great yew bed. Home was Penelope.

And he had yet to reach that shore.

He remained by the duke's side until he was certain the duke slept. Then, he quietly withdrew.

The sitting room beyond had not changed in thirteen years, if he did not count the musty scent in the air. The last time he had been in this room, he'd agreed to take the naval commission.

In return, the duke had signed papers acknowledging his marriage.

He knelt beside his wife. His clever, loyal, intrepid wife. A wife he did not deserve.

He touched her face.

Her lids fluttered open.

"Oh," she said, blinking. She lifted her head, gazing into

the duke's bedchamber before sliding her gaze back to Cheverley. "What's happened?"

"You bid me come and speak with the duke."

"And you spoke with him?'

He swallowed. "Yes."

She frowned. "Will you go?"

He hesitated.

"Please don't," she whispered.

Quick calculations flitted behind her eyes.

Always planning, his Pen.

"You've calmed him. The least I can give you in return is a proper bath. You haven't had one, have you? Not since you returned home?"

He shook his head no.

The terrible readiness still clenched in his shoulders. His back. His gut. Her cool hand touched his cheek—matching the sensation he'd had before. He allowed himself to be guided.

"A bath would be welcome." He rubbed his chin. "And, perhaps, a shave."

"It's settled then." She rose. "I will send Mrs. Renton to you."

Chapter Fifteen

STEAM CURLED UPWARD from the large copper basin full of heated water, beckoning Cheverley like a lady's crooked finger. He cocked his head, observing the bath as if he were an interloper—a Peeping Tom gazing on something never meant to be his.

He closed his eyes, drifting back to the days when salted sea frothed in every direction. On the ship, the air so thick with salt spray, his skin had become rough as sand. A tub full of fresh, hot water?

Such was luxury. And extravagance. Something beyond his means and his imagination.

Purposely, he called forth the pirate's whisper.

Tu n'es rien. You are nothing.

He waited, suspended in a heartbeat of silence. Then, his blood surged in response.

He wasn't nothing. He was Penelope's husband. He was Thaddeus's father.

He was—for all his ambivalence—His Grace's son and his heir.

And, he was Cheverley, no longer captain of the *Defiance,* but still captain of his fate.

Whatever restraints remained, they existed only in his mind.

He shrugged off his coat—the coat Penelope had made for him. She'd poured care into every stich. Sewing him into his future, leaving him nowhere to hide.

He yanked his shirt over his head and cast it to the side.

He caught his reflection in the mirror—gaunt, lop-sided, mottled by the glass. The external dirt would wash away; the internal, he alone could dissolve.

Had he not earned every sinew, every scar? Did he not deserve the comfort of a god-damned tub?

Fuck the pirate.

Mrs. Renton had heated the water. Penelope had helped carry the buckets brought up from the kitchens into the chamber that connected the duke and duchess's rooms to the landing of the second floor. He refused to allow any ghosts to exist between himself and this gift.

How many times had he bathed like this as a boy? Unheeding of the effort someone had taken to heat the water, to carry it up the stairs, to fill and prepare the bath. Now, he was aware. Fully aware. Aware of the sacrifice of others, aware of the privileges he possessed.

And, he was aware of the responsibilities connected to those privileges.

He stripped out of his breeches leg by leg, fully naked for the first time since the cave.

Water swished as he stepped into the tub. He braced himself with his left arm and eased into the water. Warmth enveloped him, heat curled the hair at his temples.

Holding his breath, he submerged.

His heavy hair swished as he turned his head from side

to side. Sound muffled beneath the water. He stilled in the warmth, as if suspended between everything that had been, and everything he alone could set in motion.

He emerged with a chest-expanding inhale, blinking into the sunlit room as if seeing it for the first time.

Gold. On wall paper.

Everything heavy and dark and expensive.

How could a soul stay strong against such a claiming of wealth and power? Among tokens of authority, how could a man remember he was but a man—flawed, as much prone to injustice as justice, subject to unpredictable elements without and within?

All men were creatures on the deck of a ship, sorting a hundred choices—significant and not—that could mean destruction or survival.

Against such overwhelming mystery, the best armor was humility.

What was a hero?

He didn't know.

But one day, he would be duke. If he seized his place. One day soon, if his father's condition did not improve.

He'd possess unimaginable power, power he could employ entirely differently than his ancestors.

He could lift others up. Make a haven of Ithwick as Pen had made a haven of Pensteague.

Were those the qualities that made a hero?

Stewardship? Care?

He ran a cake of lavender-scented soap along his arms and his legs. The water clouded, and the scent eased tension from his shoulders. His skin tingled as if new.

He leaned back and closed his eyes, taking another deep inhale.

Lavender.

He placed the faint sent that had lingered in Penelope's hair, enhancing the scent his body remembered. He slid lower into the warmth of the tub.

His wife was remarkable in ways he'd never understood. Loyal. Inventive. Competent. Few men would have been able to create what she'd created out of Pensteague. And, if they had achieved such a feat, fewer still would have risked those accomplishments and taken leave to provide care to a man who had only ever caused her grief.

Where had she found her strength, her fortitude?

He wanted to learn by being by her side.

He wanted to begin, now.

Could he?

He stood up in the tub. Water ran down his sides in rivulets. Cool air, revitalized.

He grabbed the towel from the stand, lifted a leg up against the side of the tub, and began to wipe away the damp.

A knock sounded on the door.

"Yes?" he called.

"Lady Cheverley wished me to bring you clothes, Captain Smith," Mrs. Renton replied.

He whipped the towel around his lower half. "Come in."

Since he'd returned to Ithwick and Pensteague, he'd seen the woman who had served at Ithwick since before his birth, but never up close.

Strikingly, she'd changed little.

He skin may have thinned a bit, but she moved with the same brisk efficiency he remembered.

She kept her eyes lowered as she set the clothes on a chair. She turned, froze, and then gasped. Her face drained of color.

He followed her gaze to the ink on his ankle and then cursed silently under his breath.

"Lord Cheverley." Tears sprang in the old woman's eyes.

He grabbed a shirt from the pile and pulled the soft linen over his head, expelling a puff of air as the shirt slipped into place.

It wasn't fashioned like his new shirt—this—this was a shirt from a long time ago.

Thirteen years, to be exact.

"Your lordship." Mrs. Renton raised her gaze. "I *am* sorry. I should have known you from the start."

"I didn't wish you to." He hadn't wished anyone at Ithwick or Pensteague to know him. *Ever*.

Hurtheven had been right.

He was an ass. An ass who'd been running from the people who loved him.

The people he loved.

Mrs. Renton sounded as if she were struggling to hold back a sob. He sighed and placed his arm about her shoulders.

"I took pains," he explained, "to make sure no one would guess."

"Oh, Lord Cheverley, my dear boy, *why?*"

The crease between her eyes said she didn't understand —could never understand. And, in truth, he hadn't any answer that could satisfy.

"When did you return?" she asked. "How long have you been home?"

In a way, but a few, short minutes. Also something beyond his ability to explain.

But even though he couldn't find words, he couldn't lie to her—not to the woman who had practically raised him.

"After the wreck, I was imprisoned for six years," he said. "Several months ago I escaped." Or, rather, a woman—not the pirate—whose form had been sheathed in darkness had loosened his binds enough for him to finally break free.

"Months?" she said with a heartbreaking sob.

"But please, Mrs. Renton. There is more than you can possibly understand." He pushed wet hair over his shoulders. "Promise me that you will not tell anyone. Not yet."

"As you wish, of course." She sniffed. "But her ladyship deserves to know."

"Yes," Penelope spoke from the doorway. "Yes, she does."

The full weight of Pen's dark eyes, so large, so full of conflicting emotion, landed like a punch to his gut. This was what he had hoped for and feared—the storm in her gaze, windy, and rainswept, and unnavigable.

But better a storm than no feeling at all.

"Would you leave us, Mrs. Renton?" Cheverley asked.

* * *

Pen didn't hear Mrs. Renton's reply.

She leaned against the doorway for support, clutching her basket against her chest.

She'd known the captain was her husband. She'd even accepted Cheverley had his reasons for coming home in disguise. But she had *never* imagined he'd been back on England's shores for months.

Months.

And nothing prepared her for the raw reality of gazing on Cheverley's agonized features free of his filter of lies.

Blood rushed in her ears. Anger met grief, met pain, creating a storm she did not know how to survive.

Then, they were alone.

"Pen—"

"Don't speak." She pushed back the swelling internal chaos. "I promised you a bath in exchange for speaking with His Grace. And now, I intend to give you the shave you requested."

His wary eyes dropped to the towel, soap, brush, and razor in her basket and then returned to her.

"Don't speak," she repeated, preemptive warning replaced her command.

She wouldn't believe anything Cheverley said in this moment.

Months.

What the devil had he been doing?

Her current anger placed at risk all the future moments she'd embraced last night in giddy glee. How had she—even for a moment—been able to overlook the unanswered questions, the inevitable accusations and recriminations?

Then, she looked into his eyes. And his presence filled her with such immense solace she couldn't speak—the same great solace she'd experienced when he'd first taken her into his arms.

Her pair. Her partner. The mirror image of her heart.

Who'd crushed her when he'd left.

She dragged a wooden chair beside the tub and dropped the basket on the floor.

She was dizzy—so dizzy she nearly claimed the seat. If dizzy could be an adequate description the collision of past and present, of loss and love, of anger and pure, primal relief.

"Just sit." She indicated the chair. "Please."

His damp hair appeared darker. The dim light dulled

his wrinkles. Like this, it was impossible to believe she had not known him at once.

Then again, perhaps she had.

Hadn't her breath quickened when she saw him striding across the courtyard? Hadn't the power of her response drawn his gaze to the window?

"I wish—" he started.

She lifted her brows. "Not now, Chev. Not yet."

He fell silent and, after a brief hesitation, took the chair.

He leaned back his head and blinked into her eyes. She'd always loved his eyes. Storm-grey. Fathomless. How many nights had she wished she could conjure him back into existence and experience this very expression—a blend of sorrow, apology, hope and—*heaven help her*—love?

She was lost.

Drowning in his gaze.

She would capitulate, acquiesce. *Surrender.*

There'd never been anyone else for her but him. There never would be.

"May I speak now?" he asked.

She considered. "One sentence. *One.*"

"I wish I had been the one to tell you who I was."

Foolish clod.

She'd given him one sentence and that was what he'd chosen to say?

"How could you?" She looked away. "How could you believe I did not already know? Do you think I would have let you touch me like you did last night if I did not know who you were?"

"When did you know?" he asked.

She chewed on her bottom lip until it hurt. *That* pain was easier to bear. "I wasn't absolutely certain until last night, when I placed my hand in yours."

She'd felt a spark, an invigoration she'd finally managed to place.

She'd felt the same at the stone circle, but she hadn't been ready to believe. Or perhaps, certainty had remained elusive because they'd come together by accident, opposed to last night, when Chev had *chosen* to reach...

But he hadn't chosen to reveal himself.

He'd played the part of another man.

For months.

"I'm furious with you," she said.

"You don't mean that."

"I do." She frowned, even now unable to resist his pull. She captured his gaze. "I mean it in this moment. What I'll say in the next, I cannot be sure."

He smiled, rueful. "You were always fearless about telling the truth."

"And you have always embraced deception."

"No," he replied. desperate. "Not always. I told you the truth about what I suffered."

Is that why it's too late for you and your love?

Yes.

She turned away. His suffering outsized her anger, but still—"When, exactly, *did* you return?"

His sigh raked her skin.

"December," he replied.

December. *December?*

"If you had come home directly, none of this—" She struggled to contain her voice. "You could have prevented Anthony from—"

"I could not have come," he interrupted. "I *told* you— when Hurtheven delivered me to the Admiralty, I was immediately court-martialed. But it wasn't just that. The

Admiralty gave me a mission to complete before they'd set me free."

She'd heard only one word. *Hurtheven.*

"I see," she said quietly.

He sent her a doubtful glance. "What do you see?"

Her eyes flashed. "Again, you had the opportunity to choose me—to choose your son. And again, you chose *Hurtheven.*"

"No." His throat moved as he swallowed. "It was the scar on my ankle. The man said his name and then I remembered him."

"Of course you remembered him first," she said bitterly. "You made time to have him witness your will, but you could not make time to meet your son."

"I was protecting you," he replied. "That's *why* I amended my will. That's why I went to war in the first place. Would you have rather our son be a bastard?"

"Still, you cannot see."

He ran his hand through his hair. "That's not what I meant. Believe me, if I could do things differently, I would."

Would he?

Right now, he believed he would.

Surrender.

The slow melting to the iron-pointed arrows that were her only defense. Because if she succumbed and he left again, she'd have nothing to keep her from being bludgeoned to pieces by grief.

She turned away and filled a small basin with water from the tub. She wet her towel and scrubbed the towel with soap until small bubbles foamed between the woven threads. With hand aloft she returned to Chev.

"These past weeks, you've watched me struggle with

the truth I both hoped for and feared. You saw me drowning and you never threw me a line."

Her anger was a dinghy against the tidal wave of emotion in his eyes.

"It wasn't like that."

She dropped her gaze.

"Look at me," he asked.

"No."

"Look at me. Pen, love, *please* look at me."

The last of her resistance crumbled.

How could she resist him? A part of her wanted to hold him close. To clasp his face to her chest, smooth his hair down his back, and make him promise to never, ever leave again. She lifted her eyes.

He took a deep breath. "I am sorry. I am so, so deeply, and fully filled with regret, I'm sorry does not begin to express how I feel."

Of course, she warmed all the way to her toes.

Cheverley had never apologized. Not as Chev, anyway. But any apology could only be grossly inadequate.

Sorry did not lighten the burden of her loss.

Sorry did not find her within the years she'd spent lost.

And sorry did not heal her greatest wound.

"You may be sorry for going to war. Sorry for your deceit. You may even be sorry that I believed you dead." Her voice fell to a whisper. "But, have you changed? Can I trust you? Can you give me your trust?"

* * *

Was he capable of giving Penelope his trust? Last night, he'd believed so.

But her anger had punctured him, painfully extracting

187

his essence. His soul filled the space between them, pulsing weakly, like a disembodied heart.

He'd spent six years with a woman who'd fed on his terror, who'd violated him in darkness, who'd cut off his hand.

Saw jaws rattled against his bones. Straps burned against his shoulders. Cave stench stung in his nose.

But he wasn't in a cave.

He was in the duke's sitting room.

With his wife, who smelled of midsummer lavender, even as she gazed down on him with a Fury's anger.

He removed the warm, soapy towel from Penelope's hand, and draped the fabric over the tip of his injured arm.

Could he give Penelope his trust?

Slowly, he soaped his cheeks. Warm water tingled on his skin. His beard spiked through the towel, rough against his scars.

He lost awareness of everything else but Penelope. With his left hand, he lifted the razor from the basket. A tremor ran through his fingers as he transferred the razor from his shaking hand to hers.

"Do what you came to do," he said quietly.

Her eyes went wide. "Good heavens, Chev. You cannot be frightened of me! I'm angry. I'm not *Bedlam*-mad."

Hell yes, he was afraid.

His fear was a tar-like mess—thick, peaty, and hot—clinging and confining when everything in him was desperate to rise. He would be nothing, own nothing, have nothing, if he could not conquer his fear.

He sucked in his cheeks and swallowed. "I trust you."

She frowned, glancing to the razor.

"You can't think I would—" She gazed back into his

eyes. "Good God, you *do*. You think I could actually *hurt* you."

He didn't believe Penelope would plunge that razor into his neck. His body, however, responded as if he did.

"You can hurt me"—his voice lurched—"more than anyone else. I fear,"—panic and mastery teetered on the pivot point of his trust—"but I place myself in your hands."

She took a step back. "Perhaps another time—"

He seized her by her wrist.

"Now." He spoke gruffly. "I trust you." He released her. "I trust you with my life and I *swear* I will never doubt again."

She glanced down at the razor in her hands. If she refused, he would not force.

"You told me to go to my love," he said. "I listened. I'm here." He held her pained gaze as long as he was able. Then, he leaned back and closed his eyes. "Show me it's not too late."

His ears attuned to her movement, the gentle whisper of her skirts, the trickle of water off the razor.

She will not hurt me.

He could expose his scars, his neck, his heart, and still, she would not hurt him.

She touched him beneath his chin and moved his face to the side. *She will not hurt me. Breathe in. Breathe out.*

The warm razor skimmed slowly across his cheek. The scraping sound crackled in his ears. *She will not hurt me. Breathe in. Breathe out.*

If he moved, if he even flinched, he'd be cut. *She will not hurt me. Breathe in. Breathe out.*

With infinite care, she sliced away the past. *She will not hurt me.*

Another swish of water. She lifted his chin and lathered beneath his throat.

The thin line of the razor's edge traveled up his throat once—the water swished again—then twice, then a third and final time.

She wiped his now-smooth cheeks with a warm towel.

He exhaled.

"Cheverley," she whispered. "There you are, my love."

Chapter Sixteen

PENELOPE HELPED HER husband rise from the chair and then she led him into the duchess's bedchamber. She placed the candle she carried on the bedside table and then looked up into his eyes.

She'd never asked her husband to lie with her.

She didn't even know how.

She reached up and removed the pins from her hair.

The first—her bun grew heavy—the second, a lock drifted down onto her neck—the third—the knot unraveled, and her hair fell down onto her back.

She put the three pins next to the candle and withdrew the rest. Then, she sat down on the bed.

Wariness remained within her husband's gaze.

He'd allowed her to press a sharpened knife to his throat and still he held some part of himself apart. Now *she* trembled. He'd come halfway across the bridge between them.

What if halfway was as far as he could go?

"I am not the same," he said.

She placed the final pins on the bed stand. Holding his gaze, she removed the knives and sheathes from her thighs.

"I asked you before who you were. And though I know you are my husband,"—the essence of what she understood to be love—"I will ask you again, who are you, really?"

He swallowed. "I am not fully yours."

Chev. *Dear* Chev. "Nothing of you is *mine*. Just as nothing of me is *yours*." She smoothed the back of her hand down his cheek. "People are not possessions. And marriage is but an agreement to face the world together—a pact to search for the *ours*. You promised"—mortifyingly, her voice shook—"we'd invent a new world."

"Nothing could be better in this world than when two minds, husband and wife, are united in harmony and spirit, they bring grief to their enemies and happiness to their friends," he quoted.

She sniffed and then nodded.

"Not my own words, I'm afraid."

"They belong to Homer. The Odyssey."

"Yes." He knelt down, placing his forehead against her knees.

His damp hair fell around her thighs. Emotion rushed into her throat, clogging against a thickened knot that thieved her breath.

His shoulders shook with a sob.

"Stop," she whispered.

He gripped the back of her calf. And threw his injured arm next to her thigh. He turned his head to the side, struggling to staunch his tears.

She touched his face.

One moment he was Chev. The next a stranger.

His grip simultaneously kept her close and pushed her away.

She ran her finger over the scar on his wrist. He flinched.

What had happened to her husband was deeper than the physical scars he bore.

Too deep to heal?

She refused the thought.

Disloyal at best. Moot, in any case.

She'd hadn't given up on him when he was lost. She certainly would not give up now.

"Cheverley," she whispered.

He glanced up, face stilled, harsh and jagged, his gaze, still raw with the kind of hunger that had driven humans to hunt animals that could devour them whole. If any other man had looked at Penelope with an equal amount of proprietorial desire, she would have sunk a dagger into his throat.

She loosened the string at her throat, and the fabric fell away from her shoulders, catching between her body and the bed.

How much of him had the pirate robbed?

And, to reclaim her husband, how much was she willing to risk?

Everything.

She lifted her hand. He winced before she touched him.

Very well, then.

She folded her hands in her lap.

"You are beautiful." His face twisted. "Soft."

"Soft as a lioness," she replied. "And just as willing to defend her pride."

Her words earned...if not a smile, at least a gentling of his features.

"Lioness," he repeated.

"Will you remove your shirt?" she asked.

He did. His chest was a solid wall of muscle.

193

"I want to be close to you, Chev. What would you prefer?"

"What I prefer..."

He shook his head no. His face hardened again.

He made a sound of frustration. Latent power rippled through his muscles. He could crush her if he wished.

The Unknown—the unknowable slinked through her like a demon, weaving a trail of fear in the pit of her stomach.

Any thought she had, he seemed to know. She veiled her eyes with her lids.

There were pieces of him she did not know, might never know. She'd asked for his trust. And the cost had been higher than she'd expected.

The question was, did the man she knew and understood and loved still exist beneath all this rough water?

She'd made choices before and she would make choices again, none would matter as much as the choice that she made in this moment.

Could she be vulnerable?

Could she open to him now?

"Penelope." He reached up and gripped the back of her neck, his fingers, so powerful, she couldn't move her face.

She wet her lips and forced herself to be pliant.

This is a dance. I'll move as he moves. They'd mirror one another—opposite but moving as one to the same tempo.

"Trust for trust," she said.

Roughly, his mouth met hers.

His kiss ravaged—her lips would be raw. The rush that shot through her limbs was unlike any she felt before. He pushed forward in a kind of prowl until she lay back on the bed. Still they kissed—one long, unbroken kiss, strong enough to stoke a fire that could melt away the years.

She thrilled to his muscle, to his arousal, to his very scent.

A thrill so vibrant, the tingle could have been fear.

This was the man who'd ridden with her through the moonlight countless times. The man who'd danced with her in the dark. The man she'd trusted to lead her to worlds she had never known before.

To create new ones for them to explore.

No matter what transpired, he was that same man.

And she was that same girl.

He pulled away, panting. She savored the sweet ache in her lips.

"Husband," she said with a sigh.

* * *

Husband.

Not Captain. Not Chev, nor Cheverley. But husband.

Something he'd been only to her. Always.

"Penelope..." Her name was a gruffy query. A plea. "Wife."

He wanted her.

The evidence of his desire pulsed thick, hard, and aching against her stomach. He savored the pressure, the tense, heavy soreness.

He denied relief, battling the feeling he must take her or die.

He would not roughly thieve what she willingly offered.

She wove her hands into his hair, pulling the strands back into a plait so they hung down his back. He wanted this. He wanted to sink inside Penelope's body.

Yet couldn't bear her touch.

He held himself up by his elbow and tore her hands

from his back and pinned them over her head. She whimpered in protest.

His humiliating memories had no place here—but they would not be denied. They haunted like a question. Like a challenge.

He squeezed his eyes closed and drew back. The pirate and her evil whispers closed in.

Tu n'es rien. You are nothing. *Je te possède maintenant en entier.* I own every part of you, now.

With a low-pitched growl he drove Penelope back against the bed. Covering her with his body as if he could shelter them both.

Anger rioted though his desire.

"Chev—"

"No! Just let me—" Let him what?

Ravage her as he'd been ravaged? Restrain her from touching him while he indulged the restless, demanding ache in his cock?

Be no better than the pirate?

"Touch me," she offered, "if you cannot allow me to touch you."

He released her wrists and crudely went for her breast. He felt her shock skitter through her body. In her shiver, he knew she resisted recoil.

He dropped to his other elbow and rested his forehead against her chin.

"No." She gripped his hips, drawing his body fully onto the bed between her thighs. She threaded her hand through his and placed it back against her breast.

Beats of pain drummed in Chev's elbow. He didn't mind the stabs. He was ashamed. He'd been rough. Which was wrong.

But what the devil was right?

"I don't want to take you in anger." He could barely speak. His words burned in his eyes, on his tongue, in his lips.

"You are not taking anything. I give what I give in love. I love you, Chev. I always have. I always will."

Love.

A feeling like rain. Like a gentle breeze rising from dead calm. Like the soft relief of twilight. Like the circles she drew against his spine.

Penelope.

He listened for her breath. *In. Out.* The rioting anger quieted.

He opened his eyes and gazed down into her hers—half frightened, half longing, all trust. And luminous, even in the early afternoon light.

Sweet Pen.

Her gaze lulled him like a ship's rocking.

"My body knew you at once"—she spoke mildly, tenderly, as if he had not twisted her wrists above her head —"though my mind refused to believe."

He concentrated on her melodic tone. "You—you wanted me?"

"Did you not know?"

He'd known. Or, at least he had hoped...

"I blushed," she said.

Blushed, yes. She had. And often.

Such were the signs of innocence. A language he could no longer speak.

But a language he could, perhaps, still understand.

"I love you, too." He touched his forehead to hers.

He could lie with his wife. He *would* lie with her.

He braced his knee, relieving her of some of his weight. Every muscle in his body screamed, tensed, repelled. She stilled. Frozen. Like a hunted rabbit in brush.

Or a woman seeped in pity.

Then, she circled her fingers down his spine.

He felt like an impostor.

"Cheverley," she whispered, guiding him back.

Chev reached behind him and caught up her hand in his. Her fingers were so long, so thin, so delicate. *Why* did he want to twist her fingers above her head? Pin them painfully while he rode her hard? He hated the very idea of her being helpless.

He lifted her fingers to his lips, greeting each one, learning their shape with his lips.

Gentle fingers. Penelope's fingers.

She threaded her other hand through his hair, light and yet precise, as if she were weaving and then her fingers came to rest on the back of his neck.

His shoulder muscles twitched, waking to tenderness he'd been denied. Want flickered in his belly, feeling almost like hope.

Penelope...Penelope...Penelope...

Silently, he chanted her name as if it were a torch that could keep the fear at bay.

No one had a touch like hers, so why was he frozen? Why did he wish to roar and, at the same time, to weep?

"I saw you," she said, with tears shining in her eyes, "and all my words fell away."

She'd said the same on the night they'd met. The young woman within her reached in and touched the boy within him.

The boy within him responded.

"I saw you, and you became the embodiment of words I never understood."

"What words?" she asked

"Love." He kissed her forehead. His inhale wrecked his body. Two people—children really. Brave-hearted. Foolish. And somehow wise. "I'd never seen anything so exquisite. Not then. Not now. Not ever."

She soothed his neck with firm even strokes.

"This time, I choose you," she said. "If you'll have me."

At stake, his marriage. His future. His heart.

"Yes," he replied. "And I choose you."

Penelope.

A benediction.

He bent his head, kissing the very edge of her cheek-bone, just beneath her eyes. He tasted the salt trail of the tears she'd wept.

Penelope.

He kissed the outer corner of her eye. Her lashes feathered against his skin. Light and feminine. His lips found her brow, followed its curve. Then, he kissed the center of her forehead.

Penelope.

Yearning dipped low in his belly. The kind of yearning that made him believe he would one day be whole.

Penelope.

She glistened with need that had sweat through her pores.

Penelope.

He moved off the bed, allowing the towel to fall. He was naked. Erect. She wet her lips. Her gaze glazed with heat.

Penelope.

"Take off your shift."

She stood, too. She withdrew her arms from her shift and then let it drop.

Nothing remained between them. Nothing but the scars he could ignore.

Her nipples peaked enticingly. He accepted the invitation.

With a greedy tongue he laved her breast, delighting in her involuntary moan. He did not notice that her hands had crept back into his hair, not until her fingers tightened into fists and she whimpered.

A sense of ascendency surged—mutual ascendency.

He walked her back against the bed. She sank down and parted her legs.

Penelope.

His rough, muscled thighs contrasted against her pale ones. He held his cock, positioning it between her legs. He entered her slowly, inch by inch—stopping the sweet torture only when fully inside.

Penelope.

She hooked her legs around his back; he bent forward, claiming her proffered lips in a kiss he'd never forget.

She swathed him with her body, wrapping him up, arms, legs, heat, and heart.

Penelope.

He opened his eyes, synchronizing his breath with hers with every captivating thrust.

Only the two of them existed. Now. Forever.

Her thighs trembled around his waist, her lips parted, her thighs quivered, and she clenched around him with a vital cry.

He closed his eyes, covered her mouth with his and kissed her as he broke open, releasing, spilling into her body as if it were the very first time.

Chapter Seventeen

Once again, Penelope could not find words. For thirteen years, she'd given everything she had to Pensteague and to Thaddeus. Tonight, she'd scraped together any remaining courage and poured her all into Cheverley.

She was exhausted and yet full. Completely drained and yet buoyant and floating on an ocean full of tenderness.

Her husband's return to health would not be easy or short, but the connection they'd just shared made her certain they would find a place of happiness—create that new world he'd always promised they would create.

So long as Chev did not leave her again.

She glanced over at him. He lay on his back by her side, still breathing deep, his body flushed from exertion. He rested his injured arm over his face so that the crook of his elbow fully covered his eyes.

Ah, Chev.

He'd suffered so much in order to survive. Protective, maternal instinct panged in her heart.

Her husband.

Her beautiful, injured-but-not-broken husband. She could hurt anyone who'd done or did him wrong. She, who'd never believed in violence.

"Chev," she said softly.

He lifted his arm.

How different he looked without his beard—the husband she remembered, just older and more weathered.

But had he become more wise?

She swallowed roughly. "You're going to stay, aren't you?"

His silence was a scourge. The longer he did not answer, the further up her throat her heart spiraled.

"You have a plan." She spoke to reassure them both. "Just as soon as we have proof Anthony is smuggling, you intend to tell everyone who you are."

His wide, blue-grey eyes haunted with unending torment. "I don't have a plan."

Chev always had a plan.

Always.

She pulled the sheet up over her body and sat up. "But you will. You and Emmaus and I will—"

"No." He reached out, expression urgent. "*You* are not going to stay involved. Whatever happens between Anthony, me, and the smugglers you are going to keep yourself—and Thaddeus—as far away from any danger as possible."

He reached out with his injured hand, winced and then slammed down his arm.

"In fact," he continued, "you should take Thaddeus and leave at daylight tomorrow." He rubbed his hand over his face. "I'll travel with you to Ashbey's—if we leave early enough and use post horses, we'll be able to get there in a day and a half. Ashbey will make sure you both stay safe."

Her jaw dropped. "Do you actually think I would leave you?" Didn't he know her at all? "I will not allow you to take on Anthony and Thomas and the smugglers alone."

And Thaddeus... *Good Lord.* Even if she resolved to go, she'd not be able to tear Thaddeus away.

She suspected Thaddeus, too, had known his father from the start, even if Thaddeus hadn't fully acknowledged the realization.

She shook her head no. "Thaddeus would *never* leave his home to the mercy of his enemies."

Chev cocked his head, eyes slightly narrowed.

She frowned. And then gasped. "I wasn't comparing him leaving now to you leaving then."

"Weren't you?" he asked quietly.

Not consciously. "I meant that he is protective—just as protective as you. You *can't* expect us to go."

Didn't Chev understand? Pensteague was hers to defend. *Chev* was hers to defend.

A light rap sounded against the door. "My lady?" Mrs. Renton called.

Penelope exchanged an ominous glance with Cheverley. "Yes?"

"Mr. Anthony, Lord Thomas, and their friends have returned. They request your presence in the library." Mrs. Renton paused. "I would not have disturbed you, but you know how Mr. Anthony gets when he's been kept waiting."

"I understand," Penelope replied. She searched Cheverley's blank gaze, unable to read his response. "Thank you, Mrs. Renton. Tell Mr. Anthony I took an early afternoon rest, but I will come down as soon as I am dressed."

"Very well." Mrs. Renton's footsteps withdrew from the closed door.

Again, Chev hit the bed. "Must you go just because Anthony beckons?"

She lifted a brow. "Going down is the most reasonable choice. Anthony's rage is much easier to prevent than restrain. He throws things when angered—he threw a chair at you in the courtyard, remember?"

"Anthony's trained you to prevent his rage."

She stared for a long, hot moment. "Trained me?"

"Yes, trained you."

She whipped aside the sheet, slammed her feet to the floor, swiped up and then pulled on her shift.

"Trust me," he said through his teeth. "I know something about being trained."

A terrible ache weighted her limbs. She glanced up as she tightened her front-lacing bodice.

She sat down on the bed and spoke in a more tender voice. "Perhaps it would be better if we speak about this after I return."

"I cannot stay," Chev gritted. "I promised Emmaus I would see him off—and he plans to depart just before dusk."

"Where is Emmaus going?"

He sent her a warning glance. "He's going to attempt to take a privateer."

"What?"

"Shh," Chev replied. "There has to be a connection between that ship and the delivery we saw last night. If Emmaus is successful, it will help our cause."

"And if not?" she asked.

He pursed his lips. "That's why I must see him before he goes."

She nodded slowly. "Send him my prayers."

"You can deliver them yourself. I am going to go down with you and I'm going to tell Anthony to go to the devil.

Then, you and Thaddeus will come with me to the cottage. We'll leave for Ashbey's tonight."

She froze as her simplest muslin dress settled around her legs. She searched Cheverley's gaze—still raw, still vulnerable.

She'd longed for him to claim his place, dreamed of having him return.

But to confront Anthony now felt...*wrong*.

Chev wasn't ready. And there was no way she was going to allow him to take her to Ashbey.

He stood up from the bed.

"Wait," she pleaded. "You're in no condition to go downstairs."

"*I'm* in no condition?" he asked. "Your lips are swollen, and you look like—"

"I look like what?"

He softened his voice. "Like you've just been thoroughly pleasured."

For a moment, the heat flared between them.

"I *have* just been thoroughly pleasured. But Anthony won't see that. He'll see exhaustion. Worry. And he'll simply believe he's pushed me further under his thumb."

Cheverley flattened his lips. "I'm taking you away."

"Why can't you work *with* me?" she asked. "Must you always forge forth on your own to set things right in some grandiose spectacle?"

His cheeks darkened. His arms fell limp at his sides. "Is that what you believe?" He prowled toward her. "That I have no control? That I'm weak? *Nothing?*"

"That is not what I said!" she exclaimed.

What was happening? It was as if they weren't speaking the same language. She pressed her fingers to her temples.

"Cheverley, Thomas warned me a storm was coming.

205

And last night, we heard the smugglers talking about transporting people. We cannot possibly leave."

"You cannot possibly stay," he replied.

"It's rash—can't you see? If you go down now just because you think I cannot handle Anthony, we may never be able to fully oust the danger."

"*I'm* being rash? *You're* the one insisting you must go down."

"Because I know from experience that if I don't, Anthony will come up, and whatever his mood, it will be far worse."

Devil take Anthony, he *had* trained her, hadn't he?

But just because Chev had been right on that point, didn't mean her decision to go down alone was wrong.

"Chev," she said, "we must be smart. Patient. Anthony may well have murdered Piers—do you think he'd hesitate to kill you?"

"You don't believe I *can* defeat Anthony, do you?"

"Neither of us can—not alone." Her eyes burned. "Please, Chev. Don't go down now. You *aren't* ready."

"You made your feelings about that quite clear."

"I *can't* lose you," her voice cracked.

Chev squeezed his eyes closed and pinched his jaw with tight fingers, as if he were trying to shut something out.

Her?

She went to him, grasped and then lifted his left hand. "I've been delaying Anthony for months...just let me handle him one, last time." She pressed her lips to his knuckles and then held his hand against her cheek. "We can win, but only together. And only when we've properly prepared. You always told me never to accept a challenge you did not define."

He sighed roughly. "What would you have me do?"

"Listen in from the servants' stair. If there is any problem at all, you can come in." She tightened her grip on his hand. "No reckless gestures. Let us be wise."

He nodded. "I will wait," he replied. "But if he so much as raises his voice—"

"He won't." She exhaled. "Help me dress, would you?"

Cheverley assisted with the ties as she wound her hair back into a knot. When she was ready, she turned.

"Thank you." She placed a quick kiss on his lips. "I will see you soon."

"Be careful."

She gazed at him with a long, frustrated glance. "I promise I will. I am *always* careful." She had to be.

She left the chamber.

She'd upset him when all she'd been attempting to do was protect them—and their son. And he'd been doing the same.

She turned to make her way down to the library.

She'd won the skirmish, but the larger battle loomed. There must be some way to show him they worked better together.

At least he'd listened, for now.

The old Cheverley would have swept past her and entered the library with sword raised. And what would bloodshed have solved?

She adjusted her dress before opening the library door.

For now, she'd use the single tactic she'd successfully employed—*delay*.

She entered.

Anthony and his coterie lounged about the room sprawled across chaises and chairs, and, though this was the library, not one held a book. Every single one of them held a glass of deep red liquid.

"Ah, Penelope," Lord Thomas dangled his glass by his side, "you have deigned to join us after all."

Anthony's cold gaze met hers. "Penelope likes to do things on her own terms, in her own time. The right husband could solve that, I wager."

A snicker passed amongst the gentlemen.

"It is not the time to discuss marriage," Penelope replied calmly.

"Isn't it?" Anthony asked. "The duke's condition has worsened, I hear."

"How bad is he?" Thomas asked.

"His Grace is weak," Penelope answered honestly. "He is confused and prone to vomiting."

Anthony mock-toasted with his glass. "What dreams may come, eh, sweet?"

She blinked. "I don't understand."

"His Grace is a ruthless whoreson," Thomas replied, not without a hint of his usual awed respect. "If he's tortured by the loss of his wife and his sons, he has no one but himself to blame."

Penelope censured Thomas with a look. "His Grace needs rest."

"His Grace"—Anthony leaned forward—"needs the future of Ithwick secured. Ithwick and Pensteague flounder on their own. The estates must be reunited. And you, unfortunately, are the key to making that happen. You had best resign yourself, my sweet. I asked the vicar to read the first banns on Sunday."

Thomas raised his brows. "Didn't I tell you the storm would come? If resignation does not appeal, *my* offer still stands.

Anthony's gaze snapped to Thomas. "Don't tell me *you've* been courting Penelope."

Penelope glanced between the men. If Anthony and Thomas were not in league with one another, what the devil was going on?

"Stop," she said with a shake of her head, "*both* of you. I'm not marrying again. *Thaddeus* is heir to both Ithwick and Pensteague. Whether or not the estates are reunited will be up to him."

"Penelope," Anthony spoke with exaggerated patience, "do you understand how a title is passed from one generation to another?"

"Of course," she said, though she did not.

"Birth and marriage records must be submitted, reviewed," Anthony continued. "An easy enough process in most cases"—he swirled the liquid in his glass—"but everything becomes much more fun when things are...murky."

"What do you mean *murky?* The line is clear." Pen stiffened. "My marriage was witnessed. Thaddeus's birth was attended by Her Grace and Mrs. Renton."

"You mean Thaddeus's *early* birth?" Anthony asked. "And remember, the duke never actually gave his consent, not before your marriage."

Penelope clenched both fists at her sides.

"Anthony is correct, I'm afraid." Thomas sighed. "Were he to submit a claim, it could take *years* for the dispute to be resolved."

"Despite your efforts," Penelope said, "I am not without friends."

"Hurtheven and Ashbey?" Anthony asked. "Even if you were to enlist them, there is still *so* much for the courts to review. Thaddeus, for instance, was born *after* Cheverley went to sea."

"We were legally wed," she argued. "Any child born of—"

"And then," Anthony interrupted, "there is Cheverley himself. He never did actually see the child, did he?" He shook his head as if sad. "Seven years and Cheverley never took leave. My guess is that he was ashamed he had to raise your bastard."

She stared at Anthony and the lines of his face became ugly.

He'd played his final card, and the deck had been stacked from the start.

If Cheverley were not alive, her hands would be well and truly tied.

The laws were against her.

The courts were against her.

Even Society would offer little support.

But Cheverley was alive, and with luck, he was still listening.

Cheverley hadn't answered when she'd asked him if he intended to claim his place.

Unfortunately, she would have to force his hand.

He wants this. He needs this.

"Perhaps," she said slowly, "I have delayed too long in making a choice to wed."

Anthony sighed. "That's better, sweet."

"Sweet," she repeated. He had no idea what a lioness she really was, did he?

His loss.

She was a lioness. She had wit, courage, determination, and the wonderful, awesome power of love.

Lord Thomas rose from his chair, went to the sideboard, and poured Penelope a glass of wine. He gave her the drink.

"Here's to choice, Lady Chev."

"Indeed." She took a sip. The rich, spicy liquid calmed as she looked up into his strange expression "Mr. Anthony,"

she said, "both you and Lord Thomas have expressed
interest in my hand."

She strolled closer to the panel concealing the servants'
stair.

"You have been living in my father-in-law's house,
eating his food"—she lifted her glass—"drinking his wine."
She met Anthony's gaze. "And you've been waiting for *me*
to come to *you*. Does that sound like proper courtship to
you? *You've* been taking. A proper suitor gives."

"Gifts?" Thomas grinned. "You want gifts?"

"What kind of gifts?" Anthony asked.

She thought of those men. Of the cargo they secreted
up the side of the mountain. "A lady loves lace." Belgian in
particular. "Perfume." Say, from Cologne. "And, of course"
—she sipped from her glass—"a fine, red burgundy." From
France.

All of which, given the war, would be impossible to
obtain without smuggling.

"Laces, perfumes, wine," Thomas replied. "Seems
reasonable enough."

"Reasonable?" Anthony replied. "We'll plie her with
gifts, and she will *still* seek to delay?"

"It's not as if you can force her to say vows, Anthony,"
Thomas argued. "The vicar wouldn't stand for that. We
have her word she'll finally choose, don't we, Lady Chev?"

"On one condition." She cast her gaze to the hidden
door that led to the servants' stair and prayed that Cheverley would hear and would understand. "You both seem to
enjoy outdoor games." She turned back to Anthony. "After I
have received your gifts, I'll hold a competition."

"What kind of competition?" Thomas asked.

"You cannot expect me to wed a lesser man than my
first husband, can you? You will compete by attempting

to string Lord Cheverley's bow and shoot an arrow through twelve axe handles. And if you can do as he did, I swear on the deed to Pensteague I will wed the winner."

Thomas's laughter started as a snort and ended in a full-belly chuckle.

"That's absurd," Anthony said.

Thomas stopped laughing and wiped his eyes. "Are you afraid you won't be able to win?"

Anthony bristled. "Of course not."

"Then it's settled," Penelope said. "I suggest you begin collecting your gifts at once."

She only hoped Chev would understand the reason behind the gifts she'd requested and see that the gauntlet she'd set up was one only he could win.

* * *

"Can you believe that?" Cheverley asked.

Emmaus continued cleaning the barrel of the largest of his four flintlocks. He'd finished with the musket before Cheverley had returned.

"What was she thinking?"

"I don't know," Emmaus glanced up. "Why don't you go back and ask her?"

Cheverley lifted his brows. "She *begged* me not to confront Anthony and then, and then she invites him to compete for her hand in marriage?! I don't think she was thinking at all."

"And if you don't think she was thinking," Emmaus snorted, "I don't believe you know your wife very well."

Chev folded his arms and scowled into the fire. The very idea of a competition was absurd, even if shooting through twelve axes was something that only he had ever been able to do.

And he wasn't completely certain he could do it again.

Was she?

"You didn't say what kind of gifts she requested," Emmaus said.

"She asked for gifts she doesn't even like. Laces, perfu —" He stopped abruptly. Tingles raised the hair on the back of his neck.

Emmaus cocked a brow. "And, let me guess, wine?"

Chev closed his eyes and exhaled. "Proof of smuggling."

"When's the competition?" Emmaus asked.

"Tomorrow."

"I hope to be back by then."

Cheverley eyed Emmaus with unease. "I should go with you."

"No, you should not. Your place is here."

His place *was* here, wasn't it?

In Chev's heart he knew it was. But when she'd told him he wasn't ready, something slick and twisted had snaked up from the tar of his worst nightmares. And a taste he could not spit out lingered.

"This is almost over," Emmaus said. "I've gathered enough men to take the ship. And, if I'm successful, we'll have further proof the ship is tied to Anthony. Trust me." Emmaus set aside his gun. "And trust your wife."

Chev held Emmaus's gaze—which flickered with the fire of a man about to go into battle.

"Are you certain tonight is your night?"

"The ship has been emptied of cargo. Half the crew are in Penzance. I've two men from Pensteague, and a member of the crew," his gaze slid away, "I convinced to help me. With luck and the right incentives to the rest of the crew, I might not have to fire a shot. What are you going to do about this competition?"

"Go back to Ithwick and have Lord Thaddeus collect the weapons."

Emmaus rose and clamped Chev on the shoulder with a firm hand. "I expect to see you on the morrow."

"I look forward to calling you Captain." Chev swallowed. "God speed—from both my wife and me."

Chapter Eighteen

CHEVERLEY PACED THE length of the secret storeroom beneath Ithwick Manor, waiting for Thaddeus to return with every weapon in the house he could find. He'd thought for certain Anthony would have discovered the room by now, but Thaddeus had produced the single key saying his mother had bid him to keep it safe.

Penelope. Always a step ahead.

The duke had built this chamber separate from the other cellars in order to store the best of his wine. Casks for which, of course, he had not paid customs.

Unlike the cellars beneath Ithwick Castle's ruins, this never connected to the tunnels, and unlike Ithwick Manor's other storerooms, this one could only be entered through a hidden door.

Cheverley had used the room, too. It was where he'd stored his bows. His axes. Nothing he'd constructed at Pensteague before he left had been quite as secure.

So strange to see his bows and other treasures just has

he'd left them. Like some sort of Viking hoard dug up centuries after it had been buried.

And, like a Viking hoard, his possessions would have been left here to rot if he had never returned from sea.

Sobering.

And terrifying.

Almost as terrifying as Penelope and Thaddeus remaining in harm's way.

He'd been wrong to suggest she leave. Wrong to believe he had any other duty more essential than his duty to his wife, his son, and his home. Yes, hunting down the pirate may have brought a measure of relief, but he'd leave her to the Admiralty.

He was not willing to leave Penelope and Thaddeus any more than Penelope and Thaddeus would have been willing to leave him. He'd prove that to her when he won the competition.

He'd tell her, too—he'd been wrong, and she'd been right—just as soon as she returned from the vicar's, where she'd gone to cancel the banns and spread the word about the competition.

He arrested his turn as the cool metal of a pistol barrel pressed into his throat.

"Very good, Thaddeus," he said. "I did not hear you approach. I am impressed."

"Just practice." Thaddeus withdrew the pistol. "However, if you trespass on my mother's trust, you will pay."

He smiled. "I'd be unwise to cross any lady who throws a knife like that, don't you think?"

"She throws brilliantly. Always catches me off-guard."

"Oh?" Chev replied. "Like you just did me?"

"I did, didn't I?" Thaddeus grinned. "And you were the

one who told me never to turn my back to a person with a weapon."

"Yes," he replied. "But next time, remember to cock the pistol before issuing the threat."

"Oh that," he answered cheerfully. "I'd have done so, only I didn't actually wish to hurt you, you see."

Something very much like pride filled his chest.

"We had better get to work."

They moved the guns into the room, carefully stacking them behind the casks.

"I'm not so sure about any of this," Thaddeus said. "What was she thinking?"

Cheverley smiled to himself. "The better question is, *how* was she thinking?" And the answer was brilliantly.

"I don't understand."

"The gifts she requested—none of them can be obtained by legal means, not without an exorbitant price."

"She means to prove Anthony is in league with the smugglers?"

"Yes."

"What of the competition? I've been thinking," Thaddeus lifted one of Chev's more intricate creations. "If I join in the competition and I win, she will not have to wed either of them, would she?"

His gaze softened.

"Valiant," he said. "But unnecessary."

He joined his son and ran his finger over the carving. He'd spent so much time on that bow—making sure it was just right.

"Fancy, no?" Thaddeus frowned. "I don't understand why anyone would put such effort into a weapon."

"Don't you?" Chev replied. "Then let me tell you this— exercise crafts the body, while artistry crafts the mind."

"Is that why you spent so much time on the detail?"

Awareness skimmed Chev's senses, though Thaddeus had asked the question so quietly, Chev almost hadn't heard.

He turned, facing the unspoken plea in the lad's eyes.

He was the only answer to that plea.

"Yes," he said slowly. "It is why I spent so much time on the detail."

Thaddeus launched without warning, crushing Chev with his arms, burying his face in Chev's chest.

He hooked his son close, with both arms, wounded and not.

After a heart-swelling moment, Thaddeus broke away.

They shared the same eyes. They shared the same heart. And they might have shared the same flaws, but Thaddeus had not been raised by the duke.

Thaddeus had been raised by a smarter, kinder, wiser parent.

"I am sorry I deceived you," Chev said.

"Deceived me?" Thaddeus asked.

"By pretending I am someone who I am not."

"Oh." Thaddeus considered. "You are doing so to protect us—my mother and I—are you not?"

"Yes," he said. Although it was only part of the truth.

"Do you intend to reveal yourself to her?"

Chev sent his son a crooked smile.

"Ah," Thaddeus nodded. "Mother knows already. The competition."

He gripped the boy's shoulder. "We are counting on you to be very brave."

"Always," Thaddeus replied.

Thaddeus carried the axes Chev could not hold and,

together, they made their way out of the cellars back into the early evening light.

"Are you coming back inside?" Thaddeus asked.

"In a moment," Chev answered. "You head back—and stay out of the woods."

Thaddeus, walking backward, saluted, and then turned, skipping down the pathway toward the house.

The ruined towers of Ithwick Castle cast a long shadow across the lawn.

Chev envisioned the lives that had come before him—not just his rich and mighty ancestors—but those who toiled in the fields. The blacksmiths that fashioned both plow and sword.

He imagined the need that had pushed them all forward though good times and bad.

Need that joined with observation and led to innovation that created change.

It was the fearful, the haters, the hoarders that held everyone back.

He'd hated. He'd hoarded.

But he could choose another way.

Only, he couldn't choose another way while keeping everything he treasured buried, nor while hiding behind a false name.

He must claim his place and his duchess.

Together, they'd make their mark...and permanently change Ithwick forever.

* * *

Penelope leaned against the carriage door as it rattled up the drive.

Plans for the competition were fully in motion. The

vicar had cancelled the banns. He and his wife were to attend with Sir Jerold. She'd even extended an invitation to Madame LaVoie, who'd lingered on the stairs until Penelope had invited her to join them.

If all went well, most of the county would bear witness to Cheverley's win.

And Anthony—the emperor without clothes—would have nowhere to run.

What had Cheverley quoted earlier?

Nothing could be better in this world than when two minds, husband and wife, are united in harmony and spirit, they bring grief to their enemies and happiness to their friends.

Not knowing if Chev had fully understood her intent, she could hardly wait to return to Ithwick and speak with him.

The carriage came to a stop, but when the door opened, it wasn't the coachman that waited for her in the dusk, but Lord Thomas.

"Forget this competition," Thomas said. "Marry me. We'll take a ship tonight and then, once safely abroad, we'll wed."

"No." Penelope avoided his hand and stepped down out of the carriage on her own.

The coachman drove the carriage toward the stables.

"I mean you no harm," Thomas argued.

"Is that so?" She re-wrapped her shawl around her shoulders. "Anthony was the one who convinced you not to take Thaddeus away and send me to an asylum."

"Did Anthony tell you that?" Thomas sucked in air through his teeth. "I had to tell him *something* when I found out about the smuggling. I wouldn't have *actually* sent you to Bedlam, just far enough beyond his reach to

frustrate his plans. What kind of monster do you think
I am?"

She frowned.

Should she believe Thomas?

Lord Thomas is a bad boy. He tells bad lies.

But Thomas didn't look as if he was lying. He looked
like a man at the very end of a short rope.

"What is Anthony planning? What is going on,
Thomas?"

Thomas eyed her doubtfully. "It's not just Anthony that
has me concerned."

"Then who?"

"You wouldn't believe me if I told you...which I won't,
and don't ask, because I have good reason not to say."

"For heaven's sake, Thomas! What are you talking
about?"

"Penelope, please." He caught her. "You *must*
marry me."

"Do you honestly think I would?" She put her hands on
her hips. "Even if I wanted to, you are having an affair with
that woman—Madame LaVoie."

Lord Thomas blushed. "She told you."

"Yes," she replied. "And she was gracious enough to tell
me you prefer a firm hand."

Thomas's blush deepened. "You mustn't think I had any
true feeling for her. I don't think anyone could."

"Then why did you court her?"

Thomas remained silent.

"I don't have time for this," Penelope brushed passed
him. "I know more than you think I know, and *I* have a
plan."

"Wait. Please, wait." Thomas caught up to her in the
hall. He lowered his voice. "I'll confirm it if it will make you

trust me—I *do* happen to prefer a lady with a firm hand—not that it's anyone's business but my own. Marry me, Lady Chev."

"No," she said. And then more gently, "And not because of your preferences, either. I just—" she glanced up the stairs.

"You aren't considering marry Anthony, are you? Is *that* your plan?"

"*Thomas,* I don't want to marry either of you any more than either of you want to marry me."

"But I *do* want to marry you—if only for convenience. Perhaps we'd rub along well enough. I would leave you to your interests." He swallowed. "And you could leave me to mine. If you marry me—they can't touch Pensteague."

They?

"I'm not completely foolish, Thomas. And who do you mean by they?"

Thomas's shoulders slumped. "You're not foolish at all. You just have no idea what you are up against."

"I would know if you told me!"

Thomas shook his head no. "They made me swear."

"They again? Who comprises this *they?*"

Thomas did not answer.

"Why were you and the widow arguing, then? Can you tell me at least that much?"

Tomas glanced up. "You *really* don't want to know. It's part of why I cannot tell you everything. You've grieved enough. It wouldn't be fair."

Fear painted a wispy-thin line down Penelope's spine.

"Tell me, Thomas."

He lowered his head and folded his hands behind his back. "She told me she'd known Cheverley—and that she'd often taken joy from his *la verge.*"

"Pardon?"

"Manhood." He sighed. "She was telling the truth. She even described that tattoo on his ankle. I'm sorry, Penelope. Madame LaVoie was Chev's lover."

"Madame LaVoie..." The little French widow couldn't have been Chev's jailor, could she?

"She says Chev was a traitor, Pen. And she says she has proof. Do you know what that means? You and Thaddeus— the whole family including myself—we'd all be ruined!"

Well, now Thomas's actions made sense. "How did you meet Madame LaVoie?"

"Anthony introduced us when she came to live with the vicar. And then I found out about the smuggling and I told them both to go to the devil but—"

Penelope grabbed Thomas by his shoulders. "When? When did she come to live with the vicar?"

"December, of course."

Penelope pushed Thomas away.

What if Madame LaVoie had been Chev's jailor? What if she'd been waiting for him to return all along?

Penelope stumbled backward.

She'd just told the vicar that the banns were not to be posted. And she'd told Madame LaVoie she should come to the competition because she'd planned a big surprise.

"Dear God." She took a deep breath. "Thaddeus! Thaddeus!"

Thaddeus's feet thundered on the stair.

"Where is he?" she asked Thaddeus. "The captain?"

"I don't know," Thaddeus replied. "I left him by Ithwick Castle's ruins. He said he'd return straight away, but he hasn't."

Penelope lurched for the door.

"Where are you going?" Thomas caught her.

"I have to find Chev."

"Penelope!" Thomas shook her. "Have you lost your mind? Chev is dead."

"He isn't! Cheverley is alive—and she's here, which means he's in danger—just let me go."

"I *can't* let you go out there," Thomas said. "Not tonight."

"Why not tonight?"

"Because she's out there waiting for the ship to signal—the smugglers are to deliver the first freed French captain tonight."

"Listen to me!" She fisted her hands in Thomas's shirt. "If you aren't on Anthony's side, be on mine. Where will she wait for the signal?"

"The tunnels, of course."

"Show me, show me now."

Chapter Nineteen

CHEVERLEY OPENED HIS eyes to darkness and the damp stench of cave. He was trussed and laying on his side in the dirt. His arms were bound at his back by the elbows. His ankles had been strapped together.

He calmed his rapid heartbeat by deliberately slowing his breath.

What the *hell* had happened?

Last he remembered he'd been making arrangements for the competition with his son. He'd stayed behind to consider Ithwick's long shadow, and then—?

Well, the sting on the back of his head provided one clue.

But who had hit him? And why? Anthony? Thomas?

A man moved to the front of the tunnel carrying a watering can.

But no—the metal vessel the man carried wasn't a watering can, it was a smuggler's lamp, a lamp with a long, thin funnel to keep the light within from being seen from the side—light used to wave in a ship.

Chev lowered his lids, so it would appear he hadn't

awoken. Slowly, he stretched his fingers down toward the binds around his ankles.

"Something's wrong," the man called back from the mouth of the tunnel.

Chev recognized Sir Jerold's voice.

"They should have delivered the prisoner by now," he continued. "The smugglers must have been intercepted. And if they have—"

"It doesn't matter. This one is of far more value to me."

"I don't know what you plan to do with him," Sir Jerold said, "but he can't be worth the three hundred guineas we were promised to free the French captain."

"Bricon!" *Fool.*

The momentary satisfaction of having guessed right evaporated when the woman answered in French.

"Do you not recognize Lord Cheverley?"

Dread's icy fingers seized Cheverley's throat.

"Lord Cheverley! My God. Don't think you can ransom him—Anthony will never pay."

"Non. Il est à moi." *No. He is mine.*

Jerold sighed. "Well, he lost his ship, didn't he? Do what you will. I'll check for the signal."

Jerold's boots crunched on the gravel as he retreated.

The pirate crouched by Cheverley's side. "Bonjour, mon Jouet."

Every muscle in Cheverley's body tensed. Though she was petite, he knew better than to underestimate her.

"Tu m'as manqué." *I have missed you.* She sucked in her angled cheeks. "Et moi? Je t'ai manqué?" *And me? Have you missed me?*

"No," he answered in English. He'd be dammed if he'd make any of this easy.

"Let me see." She reached down toward his manhood.

He jerked away. She laughed as she shrugged.

"I do not need to feel you to see you are not properly impressed," she replied in English. "Do not worry. I will train you again."

"No." It was a vow.

He'd risk whatever he must. He would not be kept from his family again.

"Ah, mon Jouet, you know you do not belong here. You belong with me."

"Go to hell."

"Ah. The fire within you has returned. I am intrigued." Her hard, green eyes glittered in the light of her lamp. "I will make an agreement with you. Come with me willingly, and you can share in all that I have —ships, gold, freedom." She ran her hand down his face. "I am queen of my dominion, and you can be my king."

"No."

"But why?"

"Every day apart from home is a day of suffering."

"Your wife plans to wed another. Just today she confirmed the banns."

A pain seized his chest. *The pirate lies.*

The pirate softened her voice. "Why would you wish to stay where you are not wanted?"

He held her gaze with pleading eyes, ever inching his ankles upward behind his back.

"I've always told you." She brushed his cheek a second time. "You are weak inside."

"I will endure," he replied.

She shoved his shoulder, knocking him onto his back.

"You will survive *only* if I allow!" she shouted. "*Tu es rein!*"

His nightmare's refrain scratched against his heart like fingernails on slate.

"Le capitaine grand et courageux," she shook her head, lip curled in disgust, "impuissant et frémissant." *The great and brave captain, helpless and quivering.*

Yes, he was helpless. Yes, her voice had left him quivering.

However, he would not give up.

Inside, he knew.

Inside, he trusted.

"I will survive," he replied.

She could try and take him. She would not get far.

Sir Jerold swiveled back from his spot at the entrance to the cave.

"We have a problem. Men are coming down the beach —a whole crew."

The pirate cocked her head. "Your soldiers?"

Sir Jerold shook his head. "Not mine."

"Have you signaled the ship? Has the ship responded?"

"Yes and yes."

"Then prepare the dinghy!" She hooked an arm beneath Chev by the shoulder and dragged him toward the opening.

Chev lost hold of the partially loosened knot.

"Help me with him!" she demanded.

"Are you mad?" Jerold asked. "There isn't time. Leave him!"

"No!" She answered in a low, gravelly voice Chev knew well. "I *never* leave a prize behind. He is mine!"

"I said," Sir Jerold raised a sword. "leave hi—"

Sir Jerold crumpled, a look of open-mouth shock still on his face. The acrid scent of saltpeter filled the air.

"Bricon," the pirate said. "Fools—all of you. Why didn't he listen?"

Chev's heart lept. She'd used her one ball. He ran his gaze up and down her breeches—she didn't appear to have a second flintlock...

Chev forced a swallow and attempted to look contrite. "Jerold did not know you like I do."

She smiled, slowly. "That's better, mon Jouet. Soon, we will be back on my ship and you may pleasure me."

She yanked him outside the cave and into the near-dead day, pulling him across the piles of rocks and sand that had, until recently, blocked the entrance to the tunnels. She dropped him by the side of a small boat.

Her ship—with Danish flag still flying—had anchored a few hundred yards from shore.

Had Emmaus failed? Chev's heart sank.

Chev lifted his head above the stones and gazed as far as he could down the shore. There were, indeed, men traversing sand—but they weren't soldiers.

They were a motley collection of former sailors. And at their fore?

A woman whose long blonde hair flowed down her back and past the breeches she'd donned—as beautiful in her controlled fury as she'd ever been.

Thank God the pirate had already fired.

"My wife is deadly with a knife," he warned.

"She is too late." The pirate bent down to lift him into the boat.

Somewhere behind them, a bowstring pinged. An arrow pinned the pirate to the boat by her sleeve. With a cry, she tore the fabric, freeing her arm.

"There are plenty more," Thaddeus said from within the tunnel.

"Thaddeus!" Chev yelled. "Get back."

"He's not alone," Thomas spoke from the darkness at the mouth of the cave. A barrel of a musket raised. "And my aim is just as good as yours, madame."

With a cry of frustration, and a quick, angry glance at Chev, the pirate turned, waded into the water, and then dove beneath the waves.

Thaddeus sprinted toward the shore.

"Let her go," Chev commanded, raw. "She doesn't matter." Nothing mattered but Penelope and his son. "Take cover, Thaddeus."

Cheverley freed his ankles, his eyes fixed on the pirate as she climbed the ropes, shouting commands and slinging insults in French.

Her crew would fire. They were sitting targets. He had to move.

He had to get Penelope and Thaddeus away.

He had to make sure they were safe before—

Suddenly, the deck lit with torches.

Emmaus stood, legs spread, at the center of the ship. A beautiful, equally dark-skinned woman flanked him, her musket—like everyone else in the crew—aimed toward the pirate.

"Traître!" *Traitor.* The pirate yelled at the woman. "Merdaille!" *Scum.* She yelled at the rest of her crew.

"You should have treated them better, madame," Emmaus yelled back.

"C'est fini!" Cheverley cried, voice breaking with fury. "Tu n'es rien!"

The pirate whipped around to look back and her grip on the rope faltered.

And then came a loud boom and the crew was engulfed in a cloud of smoke.

Impossible to tell which one had fired the fatal shot, but with a desperate, guttural cry, the pirate fell. The darkened circle spread outward from her body as her blood pooled in the salt water.

The pirate was no more.

Felled by her own crew.

He couldn't imagine a more fitting end.

The sailors of Pensteague took to the water and Penelope fell to her knees by his side.

"Penelope! Pen! Are you hit?"

"No," she cried working the knots out of his binds. "I can't breathe," she freed him, but—"

"What if she'd shot you?"

"I told you—I won't lose you again."

He caught her by her waist with his elbow and then drew her close. Winding his fingers into her hair he claimed her lips in a searing kiss.

He touched his forehead to hers. "Thank you."

"You aren't alone, Chev." She gripped his face. "For as long as I am alive, you will never be alone."

He held her close, fingers tight against the back of her neck, breathing the night air as one. He closed his eyes, pressed his lips to Penelope's hair and sighed.

* * *

Penelope cast her leg over the side of the pig-skin lined hammock, pushed off from the wall, and then snuggled up against her husband's chest as, together, they swung.

"Is this what it feels like in a ship?"

"A little," Chev replied.

She kissed him beneath his chin. His skin tasted of salt water...or tears. Or maybe both.

She could not describe the terror she'd felt when she realized Madame LaVoie was the pirate who'd kept Chev captive. However, it hadn't been she who had alerted Madame LaVoie to his presence. She'd known he was there and had only been waiting for the right time to signal her ship.

According to her former first mate—now aligned with Emmaus—Madame LaVoie had come close once before. She'd convinced Anthony to set the trap in the same place Anthony had set one for Piers. Anthony had believed the trap was for Thaddeus.

Penelope and Cheverley had settled both Thaddeus and Thomas at Pensteague for the night before taking refuge inside Emmaus's cabin. Thomas, who was not a villain, but a man who'd truly believed LaVoie had proof Cheverley was a traitor and was desperately trying to protect Thaddeus.

"I wish you would have allowed me to take you home to Pensteague, too."

"No," he replied. "Not until tomorrow, when everyone will know the truth. I want to publicly claim you, Thaddeus, and my home in a way that leaves no doubt."

"And then a deputy lieutenant will arrest Anthony?"

"Yes," he replied. "That is all arranged."

She lifted her head. "So you are still going to go through with the competition?"

He lifted a brow. "Are you afraid I will not win?"

"Don't be absurd." She settled back down and traced his collarbone. "I never doubted you. I only counseled patience."

"I understand," he replied. "And you were right. As angry as I was at the way Anthony had ordered you to appear, I might have done him serious harm."

"Why, Chev, are you apologizing?" she asked lightly.

"I am," he replied, all seriousness. "And I am sorry I did not send word as soon as I returned. I was court-martialed, and the Admiralty did insist I aid them, but I—I wasn't well. I wasn't thinking correctly. If it's any consolation, Hurtheven, quite literally, tried to knock me back to sense."

The hammock listed as she sat straight. "Hurtheven hit you?"

Chev ran the back of his hand down her arm. "There now, my lioness. He was right—I thought you and Thaddeus were better off without me. I was haunted by the pirate's repeated insistence I was nothing. And I thought—" He lifted his injured arm. "I thought you wouldn't be able to bear this."

"I love you." She grasped his arm and held his scars against her cheek. "All of you. You are *everything*."

"Not *everything*." He smiled. "You created all of this without me."

She shook her head no. "You were in every thought, in every plan. And every day, I saw more of you in Thaddeus."

His Adam's apple moved as he swallowed. "I love you, too."

She leaned down, kissed him lightly against his lips, and settled back by his side. She made the hammock rock with another kick.

"If you were supposed to help resolve the matter between the admiral, his wife, and his mistress, how did Ashbey end up wedded to the widow?"

"That," he sighed, "is another story. But it certainly helped that she is carrying his child."

"Ash?! Ashbey is going to be a father?"

"And he's so happy, he constantly grins."

"That I have to see to believe." She sighed. "But I'm glad."

So glad. Everyone knew the admiral had long ago scorned his wife in favor of his mistress. And she knew the Duke of Ashbey had vowed never to wed again, even though she'd always known there was something unique and precious under the exterior of the serious duke.

"Well, that's one good thing that's come of this."

"That and Emmaus has a ship."

"I hope he will be happy. Where will he go?"

"I believe the proper question is where won't he go. And, he will be in charge, and for him, that with bring the greatest satisfaction."

"For anyone, no?"

"Yes. For anyone."

"I'm sorry you did not have the chance for vengeance."

He angled his body toward hers. "I'm not."

"You aren't?"

"No," he said sincerely. "It is enough she is gone."

She rested her hand over his heart. "Is it?"

"I rest easier knowing she cannot hurt anyone else," he replied. "As to whether or not the terror will fully fade? I do not know." He kissed her crown. "But I know your love is as fierce as it is tender, and that will be my light."

She closed her aching eyes and inhaled his scent.

"Rest, darling." He made the hammock rock. "Tomorrow you become a future duchess."

Chapter Twenty

THE NOISE OF the crowd swelled in the courtyard. Chev pushed down the cap resting low on his head, and glanced urgently to Emmaus, still engaged in animated conversation with Ithwick's most loyal tenant, who'd heard Emmaus was to leave, following a competition for Penelope's hand.

Chev ran his fingers over the cobalt bead fastened to the special string hidden in his pocket. *Still there.*

As planned, the competition had begun without him. But they were due inside. *Now.*

Readiness surged within his body.

"Patience," Emmaus said. "Do not make a decision of this magnitude in haste."

"Even if there are no other farms to let in the whole of the county," the renter argued, "I will not renew my lease."

"Has Ithwick sunk so low?" Cheverley interrupted.

"Ithwick was never an easy place, but now it's run by unscrupulous men. I cannot in good conscience continue to fill their coffers with my rent."

Emmaus and Cheverley exchanged a glance.

"Listen to Emmaus," Cheverley said.

The renter shifted his position and gazed at Chev in surprise, as if he only just noticed him. His eyes settled on Cheverley's missing hand and then slowly returned to Cheverley's face.

The renter squinted as he studied.

"Lord Cheverley!" The renter paled. "Are you ghost or man?"

"Quiet! I beg you." Chev gripped the man's shoulder. "I am very much a man."

"How can I be sure it is you?" the renter asked.

"You cannot," Chev replied. "When I am duke, Ithwick will have stewardship akin to Pensteague, not greedy abuse of the land. Ithwick and Pensteague will again be one. Her ladyship will guide the transition."

"Lady Cheverley shows excellent judgement," the renter said.

Chev agreed, although he wasn't sure he would have given himself the same second chance as she had given him.

"Well, let us go in then," the renter exclaimed. "What are you waiting for?"

Emmaus snorted.

Cheverley opened the gate and, together, the three of them headed into the courtyard.

All the residents of Ithwick and Pensteague combined lined the courtyard's walls. Cheverley made his way through the crowd, listening to Thaddeus speak.

"Both you and Thomas have failed to even string the bow," Thaddeus said. "If I shoot the arrow through all twelve axes, you will you swear to leave my mother and my land alone?"

"As it is an impossibility, I give you my word," Anthony replied.

Thaddeus stepped through the bow, just as Cheverley had shown him the very first day he returned. He could have easily finished stringing the bow, but he looked up, scanned the crowd and caught Cheverley's eye.

Cheverley shook his head no.

Thaddeus made an exaggerated attempt and then hung his head.

Anthony chuckled. "Looks like you have failed as well."

Keeping his head down, Cheverley stepped out from the hedge. "May I attempt the feat?"

"Why it's the captain-turned beggar!" One of Anthony's coterie exclaimed. "And he's gone to great lengths to clean himself up."

"Insolence!" Anthony cried. He stalked toward Cheverley. "You should not be allowed to set foot on this land, you aren't fit to look on Penelope, let alone compete for her hand."

"Cousin," Pen scolded, "what harm is there in letting him try?"

"Would you wed this beggar?" Anthony asked.

"I don't need to," Penelope replied, because, of course, they were already wed. "He just wants to take a chance at stringing and shooting the bow."

Penelope met Chev's gaze. Her inner smile may not have been visible to anyone else, but it sank in ever-tightening spirals straight into his heart.

"Wouldn't that be beautiful?" Thomas said. "Him winning where we have failed."

"We'd be shamed," Anthony replied.

"Shamed?" Chev queried. "You've wasted another's riches. You've disrespected the duke, his heir, and the women of this house."

Emmaus locked the gate.

"I do not have to listen to this." Anthony turned toward the house.

Thaddeus blocked Anthony's path.

"For all this and more," Chev took off his cap and lifted his face, "you are already shamed."

Anthony froze, jaw slacked.

"Hand me the bow, son."

Thaddeus handed over the bow. Cheverly attached his string to the bottom, and then, stepping through the bow the way he'd shown Thaddeus, he fastened the string to the top.

He nocked his arrow, and he aimed.

A small spot of Ithwick's grey stone was visible through the handle holes.

Around him the sounds of the crowd rushed like the winds over the ocean.

The leather mouthpiece tasted of dwindling hung beef.

His neck swelled as he pulled back.

One shot.

One shot that would raft him back to the great yew bed.

He would bury his face in softness of Penelope's hair and relish her touch.

One shot—not to pierce the pirate's putrid heart but reunite him with his life.

He released the arrow. The slender piece of wood sailed through the holes in all twelve axes, before lodging in the door to Ithwick Manor.

"Cheverley," Anthony whispered.

Chev met Anthony's gaze, bow drawn, a second arrow already knocked and aimed.

"Cheverley—if you are Cheverley—what are you going to do? Kill me in front of all these witnesses? Reclaim your home with violence and bloodshed?"

Slowly, Chev released the pressure in the string. He

grasped bow and arrow in his left hand and spit out the mouthpiece.

"I don't need violence," Cheverley said. "I have the law."

The second lieutenant—now in charge of Sir Jerold's militia—stepped forward. "You had better come with me, Mr. Anthony. By order of the crown."

"On what charge?"

"Smuggling." The lieutenant indicated the pile of gifts that Anthony had presented Penelope. "These match those found in the village, marked by the privateer's brand. And last night, an escaped French prisoner was recaptured on Ithwick land."

Two militia men came forward, each taking one of Anthony's arms.

"How can we be sure this is Lord Cheverley?" Anthony struggled in their grasp. "What if he and Lady Cheverley have conspired to claim the duchy?"

"May I speak?" Penelope's voice quieted the crowd. "Men from the Admiralty, as well as my husband's oldest friends, will vouch for Lord Cheverley. I am certain this man is my husband. But I have no problem waiting for a court's decree to live as husband and wife. However," she paused, "he should not sleep in the game keeper's cottage. If you would, Mrs. Renton, have a few sturdy men bring Lord Cheverley's yew bed to Ithwick."

"My bed!" Chev flushed. "Impossible! No one could move that bed! We crafted that bed together from the ancient yew. The bed is part of our home's very foundation. How could you—"

He stopped speaking.

"Of course it cannot be moved," she said. Then louder. "Does anyone still doubt this is Lord Cheverley?"

The crowd's murmur ceased. Women curtsied. Men took off their hats.

Chev strode to his wife's side.

"Extraordinary woman," he said.

"Extraordinary man," she replied.

The door to Ithwick's conservatory opened and the duke, assisted by Thaddeus, stepped out.

"At last," the duke said roughly. "My son is home." He grasped Cheverley's hand. "You will make a fine duke." He joined Cheverley's hand with Penelope's. "And she will make a fine duchess."

* * *

Cheverley gazed down at his missing fingers in the mirror in his very own bedchamber—fingers still curiously fisted. He stood to the side, moved his arm.

Penelope moved behind him, with looking glass in hand. In the double reflection, his left hand appeared as his right. Intentionally he fisted his fingers. Then, he relaxed.

To his astonishment, the fingers-that-were-not-there, also went limp.

"St. George!" he whispered the exclamation.

"He's the saint who killed the dragon," Penelope said.

"Yes," he turned to her, "St. George killed the dragon."

"And Michael the archangel, too," she added. "Though you never believed me when I told you."

Slowly, he turned. "Michael the archangel *did* kill a dragon. The night I washed up on shore I remembered. I remembered you were right."

"Pardon?" Her brow furrowed.

He wiped away the crease with his thumb. "I swear it won't take so much for me to listen."

He gathered her into an embrace—so warm, so very right.

"What are you thinking?" she asked.

"I cannot decide if I should kiss you or tell you to rest."

"When in doubt," she glanced up through her lashes, "always go with the kissing."

She yelped when he lifted her from the floor. She wound her arms around his neck as he carried her over to the bed. He knelt on the mattress with one knee and gently laid her down.

"You," she said, "are the embodiment of words I've never understood."

"What words?" he asked.

"Home." She arched up and kissed his right cheek and then his left. "And quite definitely love."

He brushed his lips over hers. "Make circles on my spine."

She blinked. "Do I do that?"

"Yes." He nodded. "No matter how long we were apart, I never forgot your touch."

She danced her fingers softly down his spine. "And I never forgot your scent."

"You didn't, did you?" He closed his eyes as her fingers swirled. "That night at fairy rocks you told me I smelled like me."

"No," she said, "I told the captain he smelled like you."

Chev lifted the side of his lip in a lopsided, devilish smile. "Cavorting with the Captain was very naughty of you."

"It was, wasn't it?" she wrinkled her little upturned nose.

He nodded, made a disapproving face and *tsked*.

"You're irresistible." She shrugged against the pillows. "What can I say?"

He locked her in a kiss and rolled them both, so that he was on his back and she was draped across his chest.

He stilled the tremor in his heart by keeping his gaze locked inside of hers.

No hunger for dominion lingered in the depths of her eyes. Only wonder. And love. And tenderness.

Infinite tenderness.

She shifted her weight and her breasts brushed against his chest. She traced the arch of his brow, his cheek bones, his nose.

Desire pooled in his groin.

"Take off your shift," he said.

She rose to her knees drew the white linen over her head.

He undid his falls and lifted out his manhood. Stroking it as she stared until he was fully hard.

"Straddle me."

Shyly, she cast one leg over his body. He grasped her hip and guided her into place. Slowly, she lowered her body over his.

He groaned from the deepest place inside, delighting in her little gasp.

There was nothing harsh or groping in the way they came together—nothing of performance. Just wedded coupling—inelegant, a measure nervous, a measure more embarrassed...but a fully wet, hot joining of man and wife.

Of future duke and future duchess.

He pulled her down against his chest. Her folded thighs gripped his sides.

"I have you," he whispered into her ear. "I won't let you go."

She buried her face into his neck and he inhaled the scent of her hair. He rocked upward until the sensations sent him spinning and he only vaguely heard her satiated cry.

* * *

Penelope grasped her husband's injured arm as they walked together through the coppiced wood that evening.

"What star is that?" he asked.

Of course, he knew the North Star.

"That," she replied, "is the star that guided you home."

He smiled down into her eyes and something inside unraveled. Something long and thin that she'd started to spool up tight the night he'd left.

She cut out this moment and set it apart in her mind.

Happiness was not a state, or an ever-after.

Happiness was a quilt.

Or a constellation...with moments like jewels. Like stars.

A sapphire evening. A Carnelian sunset. Emerald spring.

The brilliant white diamond euphoria—rare, like that rocking carriage ride to Scotland. Like the moment he'd shot that arrow through those axes, forever pinning himself to her heart.

"Tell me," she asked, "do you still have an insatiable thirst for adventure?"

"I've had enough adventure for a lifetime, but I have an insatiable thirst for you."

"You've experienced so much."

"We've a lifetime to exchange stories. And," he paused, "all that matters is you know my heart."

His face was now shadowed by dusk.

There would be time for healing.

Time for passion.

Time to teach one another again.

He was a constellation—bright points, and vast spaces of unknown. An imagined shape, sometimes barely recognizable, but shining in the darkest night.

"I know your heart," she agreed. "And I finally know who you are."

"Who is that?" he asked.

"You are brave and strong and caring. And loyal and wise and good." She held his cheeks and stood on the tips of her toes to kiss him. "And for all that and more, you are my hero."

Epilogue

THE DUKE AND Duchess of Ithwick, the Duke and Duchess of Ashbey, and the Duke of Hurtheven trudged in an uneven line toward a mountain at the very center of Hurtheven's extensive grounds.

Hurtheven, of course, led their party of five.

And, though they were miles from any navigable water and even further from the sea, Hurtheven carried an oar.

Cheverley smiled as Alicia tucked her arm beneath Ashbey's. Ash subtly tilted towards his wife.

Ash and Alicia were happy.

Truly happy.

And—Cheverley threaded his fingers through Penelope's hand—so were he and his duchess.

He stretched out his injured arm as they walked. Occasionally his phantom fingers fisted. But not today.

"Tell me why we have to plant an oar again?" Ash asked Hurtheven.

"Because Cheverley is Poseidon," Alicia answered.

Hurtheven glanced over his shoulder and scowled.

"Hardly a secret society, Ash, if you tell your wife all about it."

Ashbey shrugged. "No secrets."

"No secrets," Chev echoed.

Hurtheven made a sound of disgust. "If that's what marriage means, Lord spare me a woman's love."

"I think he already has," Ash pointed out.

Hurtheven grunted. Cheverly snorted. Alicia sent Penelope a significant glance over her shoulder.

"Boys," she said with a heavenward glance.

"Chev *is* Poseidon," Hurtheven explained. But we are planting an oar at the base of my mountain because that's what Odysseus is told he must do to placate Poseidon."

"Ah, well," Ash said wryly, "*now* everything makes perfect sense."

"Hurtheven is mad," Chev reminded. "He's always been mad."

"And," Ash sent Chev a significant glance, "you waited until we dragged our wives to this mountain to remind me?"

"You know," Penelope interjected, "I'm all for fulfilling the prophecy."

Chev lifted a brow.

Penelope shrugged. "Well it cannot hurt, can it? Just in case there *is* a sea god and he's still mad because you survived and stole his thunder."

"Thunder belongs to Zeus." Hurtheven corrected. "But other than that, you are right. Considering all that's happened, I decided we cannot be too safe."

"What exactly was the prophecy?" Ash asked.

Hurtheven glanced rather wistfully at Penelope. "When the oar Odysseus brings is planted by a people who do not know the sea, then the curse will be ended, and Odysseus and Penelope will grow old and happy together."

"Hurtheven's gesture is sweet," Penelope said. "If you think about it."

"I'm *not* sweet." Hurtheven lifted his brows. "I'm practical."

"Yes," Ashbey chuckled. "Planting an oar is exactly what you'd expect of a practical man."

"Ready Chev?" Hurtheven asked.

"You can do the honors," Chev replied.

Hurtheven lifted the oar and then shoved it down, hard. It wedged between the stones, standing on its own.

"Well, it's done," Ashbey said.

Hurtheven nodded at his handiwork. "And the couple will be long-blessed."

"I, for one, feel much better," Penelope said.

"As do I," Cheverley chuckled.

Together, they made their way back to Hurtheven's castle, returning just before the start of a downpour.

Rain ticked against the windows as Cheverley and Penelope undressed for the evening.

"Come here," Cheverley said by the window.

Tying her dressing gown, she joined him. He motioned down into the courtyard.

Lightening flashed.

"Was that—" She placed her hand against her chest. "Is Hurtheven still out there? In the rain?"

A great crack of thunder sounded and then another flash of lightening lit the sky—bright enough to illuminate Hurtheven's face, upturned to the heavens and smiling.

The rumble of thunder soon followed.

"Should we bring him inside?" Penelope asked, uncertain.

"Oh, he'll come in on his own," Cheverley answered. "When he's good and drenched."

"Aren't you worried about him?" she asked.

"Worried for Hurtheven? Not in general, no." Chev kissed his bride. "But do I hope he finds the happiness we have? Absolutely. Even if he must face a dozen or so labors before he sees the light."

THE END

Excerpt from Her Duke at Midnight

A governess and her secret take an invincible duke by storm...

The Duke of Hurtheven will stop at nothing to protect those he loves. So, when a mysterious new governess captures his godchild's affection, he vows to uncover her secrets. Instead, she sets him aflame.

Miss Hera Bythesea accepted a governess position to secure the character reference she needs to reclaim her secret child. But she did not count on Hurtheven—curious, relentless, and temptation in human form.

In Hera's world, Hurtheven faces a challenge his power and wealth cannot solve. But for the love of unwed mother and child, he'll undertake any Herculean Labor.

Her Duke at Midnight

Her Duke at Midnight is a full length novel of

Excerpt from Her Duke at Midnight

approximately 80 thousand words

Chapter One

"Less than a mile to go, Horace," the Duke of Hurtheven gently urged his hired horse further up the path to his friend Ashbey's seat. The horse neighed in protest but then yielded to the duke's will. Most things did...*eventually*.

The duke understood the horse's reluctance. He, too, was road-weary, with quavering thighs and joints pulsing with pain, and the path he'd chosen—the more direct, but ancient entry—was less easy to navigate than Wisterley Castle's newer, Repton-designed drive. But a promised visit was a promised visit, especially to his godchildren.

He intended to deliver.

As he advanced through weeds left to wild à la the picturesque, the castle's stone tower rose menacingly from a Hawthorne hedge. Truth be told, he preferred an aspect with menace, even if the morning's bright skies rather ruined the effect. A Duke going about his business in daylight tended to be noticed, what with the livery and such.

Which was why Hurtheven preferred night. And rain. And any other atmospheric condition that offered a challenge while repelling the masses.

He analyzed the trees for inverted leaves, then tested the air for the slightest breeze. *No.* Not even a hint of threatening weather. Disappointing, really. Every storm, real or metaphoric, offered yet another chance to test himself against life's vagaries. Test himself, and win.

Of course.

Two lightning strikes had, in fact, forged his life.

The first, at age nine—a literal, blinding current flashed

through his father's carriage, sparing him, though not, benumbingly, his parents. The second, figurative, this time, at sixteen—the sight of a silver-blond woman stunned him to stillness before rushing onward, sending heart-pounding fervor crackling through his veins.

But his long-subdued emotions had roared back to life only to blister beneath his skin, because, in the same moment, the young lady had been equally and mutually captivated by the man standing to his right—his dear friend Cheverley.

Since then, Hurtheven dared the heavens every possible chance, never content to simply anticipate a third life-altering event.

Playing both Hercules and Eurystheus, he'd chosen "labors" that both strengthened him and sharpened the lessons he prized: Keep your friends close. Keep your secrets closer. And stay closed and coiled—always anticipating the next devastating strike.

Schooling his features, he handed off his hired horse to one of Ashbey's grooms with a curt nod of thanks. He emerged into the light, wiping the back of his gloved wrist across his sweat-damp forehead. In the distance, dozens of people milled about the gracefully sloping lawn.

Damnation. Ashbey's annual garden party. How could he have forgotten?

He spotted Ashbey in the distant clearing. Ash's wife Alicia was by his side, and, with them, the third member of Hurtheven's school-day triumvirate, Cheverley, now the Duke of Ithwick. Chev's wife Penelope, though not in view, was doubtless present. Chev hardly went anywhere without Penelope.

Not anymore.

"Now *there's* an interesting expression."

Penelope's voice trickled over his skin, sweet as summer rain.

"I'd forgotten about the party." He turned.

Silhouetted by Ashbey's Castle and looking as majestic as the mythical Queen of Ithaca whose name she bore, Pen advanced up the pathway, both hands outstretched.

"Ah." She smiled tenderly. "You know, I had the strangest feeling you were the lone rider I saw making his way up the old castle trail."

Of course she had. And, of course, she would be the one to greet him—with him smelling of horse and scowling down at Ashbey's guests, no less.

He recoiled, flexing mud-stiffened gloves. "I'm afraid I'm not in any state—"

"Never mind that." She grasped his hands through worn leather. "I may be a duchess, but I'm still a pig farmer's daughter. Besides"—she brushed a feather-light kiss against his cheek—"it's been an age. How good to see you!"

"It's good to see *you*, as well," he replied. His heart spasmed.

Too good, so it seemed.

"You didn't write." She searched his eyes. "Chev has been worried about you, you know."

He *had* written. He just hadn't *sent*—a crucial part of his plan to use his time at the Congress of Vienna to finally and permanently sever the unrequited cord.

Yes, his initial attraction to Pen had been beyond his control—fate-the-trickster's play. But when Chev had been lost at sea and believed dead by everyone, himself included, *he*, not fate, had proposed marriage to Chev's wife.

Pen had forgiven him. As for forgiving himself...

He dropped her hands and took a deliberate step back.

253

"Well..." He cleared his throat. "My presence at the Congress was in constant demand."

"Oh, I see." Her brows rose playfully. "Heaven forbid the world turn without your by-your-leave." She leaned in. "Now, how was Vienna, *really?*"

He closed his eyes, immediately drawn back into the shadows of the old city.

What could he say that would succinctly capture the intrigue, the life-and-map-altering decisions shaped by backstabbing and ever-shifting alliances—not only in official meetings, but in bedrooms and ballrooms?

And what of the people? Each ruthlessly bargaining to retain every possible power? People like the now-disgraced prince Karl? Hurtheven had caught him secreting double-crossing letters in a doll the prince then claimed belonged to his daughter.

How selfish did a man have to be to put treason on the head of a child?

He sighed. "Vienna was war-ravaged and yet glittering. A gathering of kings and emperors likely to remain unrivaled for centuries."

"So the papers said." She tilted her head. "But that doesn't tell me much about *your* experience."

"My experience..." He echoed, resting his gaze on the horizon.

Despite the complications that arose and the rather unsavory role he'd been tasked to play behind the scenes, threatened invasion no longer menaced the blue-grey channel waters shifting lazily in the sun—*that* was something.

Great Britain was safe. His *friends* were safe.

"I'm happy for peace," he added.

"But are *you* happy?" she asked.

Happy. He sniffed.

For himself, certainly not. *Happy* was not an objective, no matter what the unhinged Americans had written in their Declaration.

"I am grateful the war ended." A hellish spring, beginning with Napoleon's escape from exile, had turned into a bloody summer. "Despite the limitations and concessions of the Congress, order has been restored and a Bourbon is once again on the throne." He forced a smile. "Though the peace, I imagine, will render any skills I have acquired about as useless as a frigate run aground."

"Useless? You? Never." She threaded her arm through his.

He braced for a surge of physical longing. Surprisingly, desire did not come.

What did this absence of feeling mean?

Could his initial response to her have been roused, not, as he'd assumed, by the scars of love long denied, but merely by the sight of a dear friend, deeply missed?

Had this particular "labor" been successful after all?

"Worry not." She doubled back toward the castle, pulling him along. "Soon enough, you'll be embroiled in yet another puzzle that you and you alone must solve."

He glanced askance. "Am I being mocked?"

"Of course you are," she replied.

All remaining discomfort evaporated in the warmth of her cheerful expression. He *was* content to be home. Or, at least in a place where he needn't stand on ceremony.

His friends knew his flaws, and yet they took him into their safe hands, chaff and grain together. Despite all that had passed—and perhaps because of it, as well—Ash, Alicia, Chev, and Pen were family.

Family he'd chosen.

And, of course, there were the children.

He lightened his tone. "I didn't ride a rented horse all the way from the ferry to talk about myself"—he flashed a smile—"much as you know I enjoy the topic. Tell me—how *are* my godchildren?"

"My Thaddeus grows more like his father every day." Her eyes sparkled with maternal pride. "He's taller than Chev, now, can you believe?"

"Truly? I had no idea a boy of sixteen could sprout so much in so short a time."

"Like a magic beanstalk." She thrust her free arm upward. "As for Ash and Alicia's wee ones, both seem head over heels for the woman that came to care for them after their nursemaid's abrupt departure just before Christmas last year—Mrs. Montrose."

"Ah, yes." He lifted a brow. "The *incomparable* Mrs. Montrose."

"You've heard of her?"

"The children's last letter mentioned little else." And yet Alicia's note contained nothing of true substance about the woman.

She slowed her steps. "You sound wary. Why?"

He did not relish the thought of *any* unknown person newly and closely attached to his circle—especially one who had arrived in his absence. "Children do not normally accept a stranger so quickly, do they?"

She considered. "In my experience, they do. And they tend to be good judges of character, too. Thaddeus never trusted any of my would-be suitors, the ones who overran Ithwick Castle in Chev's absence. But when Chev returned in disguise, Thaddeus liked him immediately."

He made a sound of disapproval. "Your experience with strangers should make you more concerned, not less."

"Should it?" Penelope tilted her head thoughtfully before wrinkling her nose. "*Everyone* likes Mrs. Montrose, not just the children. She's not only competent, she's also good natured and kind..." She paused, a slight crease between her brows.

"But...?"

"At times, I *have* thought I noticed a certain wistfulness about her expression." She flashed him a quelling look. "However, I could have been mistaken. Ash and Alicia consider themselves quite lucky to have found reliable help on such short notice."

"Do they, now?" He didn't believe in that sort of luck, and his suspicious nature was part of what made him successful in all his endeavors.

Anything *too* convenient should always be suspect.

Intriguing, too, this *wistfulness*. "What led to the departure of their nursemaid?"

Pen shrugged. "Her mother contracted some sort of illness, and the family requested she return home as soon as possible. Mrs. Montrose is"—she paused for emphasis —"*admittedly* more suited to the position of governess than nursemaid, but Alicia considers that an advantage. Fee will need a governess soon—she'll be six next month."

Six! "And how did they find this Mrs. Montrose?"

"I believe she and Alicia were introduced through Alicia's charity work—"

He grunted.

"—*and* Alicia is acquainted with Mrs. Montrose's family, which is good enough for me, and *should* be good enough for you, too."

When he did not immediately agree, she shook her head.

"You are the most cynical man I know. You don't trust anyone besides Chev and Ash."

"It's who I am."

"No," she replied. "It's who you choose to be."

A distinction without a difference, in his opinion. She knew him well—as did his friends—but, no matter what the game, on matter of principle, he never revealed his whole hand. Not even to those he loved the most.

Besides, why shouldn't he be wary?

Felicia and Delmare were his godchildren. If his own godfather had not regarded the role as a grave responsibility, where would he be?

Aural memory rang in his ears.

First, the sound of rain pinging against glass. Then, the squeak of an upended carriage wheel uselessly revolving in a raging wind. Finally, a voice—*his* voice—screaming out in terror and pain.

Again, he settled his gaze on the horizon, this time, just above the top of the Castle tower.

The suffocating sensation would pass. It always did. He refocused on the present with a silent, but deep, inhale.

Pen was, doubtlessly, correct. He had no real reason to mistrust his friends' choice, just an instinctive sense of unease. But not having a definitive reason for concern certainly didn't preclude him from investigating the nurse-maid's past on his own.

He nodded as if Pen had convinced him to let the topic go. "Alicia has a good friend in you."

"Well"—Pen arched a brow—"with you and Chev and Ash as close as you are, we ladies must stick together. In fact, when *you* fall in love and marry—which, by the by, it's high time you should consider doing—our numbers will finally be—"

"Please," he interrupted. Pen was the last person with whom he'd choose to discuss marriage. A decade and a half of denied feelings had been torture enough. "At least let me make myself presentable before you start planning my nuptials."

"Oh, very well, Spoilsport." She released his arm. "I should return to the festivities, anyway."

"Which begs the question...just what *were* you doing wandering around outside the stables?"

She sighed. "If you must know, I was interrupting a tryst."

"You're not serious!"

She nodded. "I didn't think much when Thaddeus disappeared. But then the eldest daughter of the Earl of Witford headed toward the house. I had just sent them back to the party alone, each in a different direction, when I spotted you coming up the drive."

"Thaddeus would never do anything dishonorable."

"Not intentionally, no. Consequences, however, aren't first in the mind of someone sixteen years of age."

"As you and Chev well know," Hurtheven murmured.

"Do not"—Pen cast him a warning glance—"remind me."

"Go, then. I will be down as soon as I'm presentable—but don't tell anyone I've arrived just yet. I'd like to surprise Chev and Ash."

She squeezed his arm before releasing him. "Welcome home, Hurtheven."

"Thank you, Pen," he replied sincerely.

Her enveloping scent faded as her figure swished down the lane.

Suddenly, he, too, was a youth again, watching a sleepy

blacksmith in Gretna Green say the words which placed her forever beyond his reach.

Not that he would change things, even if he could. He'd made his choice all those years ago—friendship over love.

And thank God Pen had never truly given up on finding her lost husband. If she had, she might have accepted Hurtheven's proposal, and then, when Chev had miraculously returned from his ordeal, Hurtheven would have lost Chev twice—a thought too disturbing to contemplate.

He turned back onto the path and trudged onward toward the castle.

Cheverley and Pen. Ash and Alicia. Happiness all around. *So. Much. Happiness.*

But for him?

...when you fall in love and marry...

Another heart spasm.

Although fond of female company, he simply couldn't picture either. The only time he'd fallen in love had cost him only pain, embarrassment, and regret. He'd no wish to risk a second blunder. And no one besides Pen had ever tempted him to risk his heart—*if* he was even capable any longer.

As for marriage... Well, he'd been alone so long the state had become habitual. And leg-shackling himself to some innocent likely to be awed and deferential and obedient, but never able to mean more to him than Penelope, did not seem fair, although an heir was, of course, an eventual necessity.

He shifted his thoughts to a more comfortable vein—specifically, the unearthing of mysteries, the solving of conundrums...

He paused to survey the rear of the castle, sweeping his

gaze across the kitchen gardens, to Alicia's rose bushes, and then, to the more distant cedar labyrinth.

All conundrums were in want of solving, were they not?

Large conundrums. Small. *Domestic*, even...

Like a mysterious new nursemaid who appeared through some loose charity connection and immediately and intimately ingratiated herself into the household of his once infamously reclusive friend.

Now *she* was a conundrum ready to be solved. And investigating her past a worthy effort...certainly less complex—and disturbing—than the contemplation of love and marriage.

"Lady Felicia!" Miss Hera Bythesea, or, as her charges knew her, Mrs. Montrose, sing-songed her youngest charge's name. Then, she paused in the doorway and huffed under her breath, "*Fee!*"

Felicia-sized footprints appeared in the muddied grass just outside the castle kitchen. Hera followed them through the herb garden. *She* stopped at the freshly tilled earth's edge...the footprints, however, continued onto the more elaborate grounds.

Grounds where Felicia's ducal parents and their glittering guests mingled, enjoying the rare experience of coastal sun.

On any other day, Hera would have forced herself to look on the bright side. She might have even *celebrated* the cleverness behind Felicia's subterfuge. But for Felicia to disappear on the day of the Duke and Duchess of Ashbey's grand garden party?

Hera caught her lip between her teeth.

Disaster.

On a shaky inhale, she considered her options. If she continued into the gardens, she might happen on someone she recognized.

Or worse, someone who recognized her.

Fretting, on the other hand, would not keep Fee from harm. She forged onward, sidling toward the rose bushes. At least her frock had a greenish tint. With any luck, her white cap, if seen from a distance, would be mistaken for a cluster of roses.

"Fe-*li*-cia!"

She listened but heard only undulating peals of incoherent society gossip. As a small child, Hera had found the sound of finely dressed gentry chattering amongst themselves comforting, even pleasant.

Now she knew what they really represented—inherent threat.

She looked away from the party, scanning the hedge for any sign of her youngest charge. How, *how* had the duchess convinced her taking over the position of nursemaid in the Duke of Ashbey's household was the answer to her desperate prayers?

Well, there was her answer. *Desperate.* Nothing good ever came from a decision made in desperation, as she, of all people, should have learned by now.

She rested her forehead against her fist.

You just feel like you're going to break apart. You won't. You can't. Swelling panic was nothing more than a wave in the ocean. She breathed in deep, imagining the wave cresting, breaking, and then fizzing back into gentle swirls.

When she'd taken on Lady Felicia and her nine-year-old brother, Lord Delmare, she'd assumed she could manage them much as she had her half-brother's offspring, and, after them, the children of Prince Karl Wilhelm Albert of the Electorate of Heinenberg.

She hiccupped back a sob.

She'd seen herself taking the little lord and lady under her protective wings and lavishing on them all the unused care that had been festering inside of her like a neglected wound since the night she'd had to make the most difficult choice of her life.

A night just a few weeks prior to the duchess's appearance as her slightly tardy guardian angel.

The duchess had assured Hera she'd make every effort to assist—including providing a position and then the necessary glowing reference to prove Hera had "reformed." And she'd also promised Hera, on successful resolution of their combined efforts, a small stipend.

If all went well, by summer's end, Hera would be living in rented rooms in the village near the Wisterley estate, healed, safe, and with her prize.

Sound reasoning, that.

But what if, instead, she became the infamous nursemaid who lost the Duke of Ashbey's beloved daughter? The duchess would withdraw her support and the board of directors would deny her petition.

Breathe in. Breathe out.

Felicia hadn't been snatched up by nefarious persons unknown, or gotten lost in the wood, or ruined the party. She'd merely escaped the schoolroom. All Hera had to do was find the termagant—a-hem—*darling child*, persuade her to come along quietly, and then sneak back into the house with no one the wiser.

While dozens of guests and an almost equal number of servants milled about.

Right.

The alternative, however, was to admit defeat. And no matter how many pernicious reversals life had already delt her in her quarter century, the one thing she'd could count on was her own competence.

Keeping a watchful eye on the crowd mingling over by the pavilion, she crept along a length of the duchess's prized roses. From the edge of the bushes Fee's footprints meandered, not toward the party but the cedar maze.

She sighed.

If the guests remained in their clusters and she rushed quickly across the open space, she'd be able reach the maze with no one the wiser. She lifted her skirt to mid-calf and tucked the fabric into the ties of her apron. Then, the sound of rustling gowns grew more pronounced.

She ducked back down.

"Ah." A woman. "You were absolutely correct, Lady Adelaide. The scent *is* divine. Why, the aroma is *almost* appealing enough to cover the stench of Ashbey's past."

The woman and her companion tittered.

"Darling Elizabeth," Lady Adelaide scolded, "you mustn't say such things. In the end, our host found someone his equal...in scandal, if not in consequence."

As the ladies laughed again, Hera's heart seized.

She'd known, of course, that Ashbey's father had been tried, though not convicted, of murder. She'd also known that, for years, Ashbey had shunned society and lived as a recluse. But that was before his marriage to a war widow of a celebrated naval captain.

Before Lord Delmare and Lady Felicia.

Before Wisterley's garden parties.

He was quite respectable now.

Wasn't he?

"Oh, *my*!" Lady Adelaide exclaimed. "Could that be...? Yes! I am *sure* that is the Duke of Hurtheven!"

Hurtheven.

His name was a second blow. This one knocked her off her heels. She touched the earth—damp and clammy—to restore her balance. Although she'd never met the man, Felicia and Delmare talked about the duke incessantly. He held the same exalted rank as the children's father, but, to them, Hurtheven might as well have been a god.

Perhaps not *God* himself—the children would never be blasphemous—but of indisputable celestial origin...supremely powerful with ubiquitous cognizance.

Like Zeus, for instance. She scowled. The *last* thing *any* Hera needed was a Zeus.

"Where?" The one called Elizabeth asked breathlessly.

"Over there by the hedge. He's..." Lady Adelaide's voice lowered in disgust, "*crouching.*"

Hera leaned to the right, just enough to catch sight of a man's trailing greatcoat. But the man could not possibly be Hurtheven. A *duke* would not be on his knees, crawling along a hedge in the middle of a garden party, would he?

Not unless—*Oh, no.*

"That's *definitely* Hurtheven," the other woman cooed. "He's always been...unconventional."

"Unconventional? *Please.* To have survived as he did when his parents perished in such an unusual fashion *had* to have been a matter of unnatural luck. For years there have been rumors. I believe them. He is the devil incarnate."

"Adelaide!"

"Is calling a fig a fig and a trough a trough a crime? Besides his own exploits, those he chooses to keep as friends should be enough to condemn him."

"You're just angry that he hasn't called on you since—"

An unholy wail interrupted the conversation, washing Hera in a cold sweat.

"Got you, Fee!" The timbre of the duke's voice rang dissonant against a second high-pitched squeal.

Frozen in horror, Hera watched as he swept up a now-laughing little cluster of arms and legs and rose to his feet.

Heavens, he was tall. And large. Shockingly so. His gaze fixed on the ladies, his eyes so black, Hera wondered if they lacked irises. Even holding an impish child couldn't make his presence less intimidating.

You think too much of other people. She heard the words in Karl's clipped accent. *You must remember...we are all just pawns.*

She fortified herself with a deep inhale. Her perfect plan may have hit a rub or two. But she could pivot like a well-trained horse and still come out all right. She had to.

Her life wasn't the only one on the line anymore.

Hope for her deepest desire—the very reason she took this position—flared so painfully she blinked. Immediately, she forced the feeling away—back, for now, into the same lockbox with her memories and her aspirations.

Alright, Karl. We're chess pieces—bone without flesh or spirit moving about in an endless game. What does it matter, so long as we move to our advantage?

...as I moved against you.

Hurtheven stepped between the ladies and the rose bushes.

"Be off," he said.

"Hurtheven, I—" Lady Adelaide began.

"Off, he repeated.

With twin gasps of indignation, the women scuttled back across the lawn.

Impressive. Arrogantly, *horribly* impressive.

Suspicion confirmed. Hera knew everything she ever needed to know about the duke, now...and intended to interact with him as little as possible. She lifted herself to her feet as quietly as she could and then turned away.

"I didn't mean you."

He was close enough for his breath to raise gooseflesh on her neck. Who could steal up behind a person so quickly and not make a sound? A devil incarnate, that was who.

No matter. She squared her shoulders. She'd faced devils before.

She swiveled around with as much dignity as she could muster. "There you are!" She addressed Felicia. "I'm very disappointed in you, young lady."

Felicia chewed her lip, glancing between her nursemaid and the duke. With eyes wide and innocent, she wrapped her arm more tightly around the duke's neck.

"You must be the *incomparable* new nursemaid." Hurtheven's tone suggested he found her anything but.

"Indeed." Though she dropped a quick curtsy, she made certain her tone revealed her own disdain. "I'm afraid, however, *you* have me at a loss."

"Do I?" He revealed a line of white, even teeth in neither a smile, nor a sneer, but a chilling combination of the two.

"Well"—she wet her lips—"I imagine I would remember if we'd been introduced."

"Of course you would."

Ugh. The arrogance. Her initial assessment had, of course, been correct.

Well, if he wasn't going to own up to being a duke, she needn't treat him as one. She fixed a level gaze on him and held out her arms. "If I might have my charge, Mr.—?"

He did not immediately reply. In fact, he didn't speak until the tendons on the back of her knees started to quiver. A useful silence, Karl had called that trick. But she could no longer be tricked. She kept her expression patient, pleasant.

The duke returned his attention to the child. "Hurt?"

Fee scoffed. "No."

The duke exhaled, holding her close for a significant moment.

Hera inhaled sharply. Hot embarrassment prickled in her neck as if she were witnessing something she ought not. He'd been *genuinely* frightened.

"Fee," the duke addressed the child, "you must go back inside...and stay there."

Her little fingers dug into his skin. "Can't I stay with you?"

He angled his head to meet her gaze and his expression softened. "Ah, but if you *do* stay with me, you'd have to be a proper lady and greet every one of your father's guests."

Fee dropped her jaw, widened her eyes, and then violently shook her head.

"I didn't think so." He touched her nose. "Now, you go back upstairs, and I promise I'll be up to see you when the party is finished."

Fee pouted. "You've been gone for*ever*."

He nodded. "An interminable amount of time, I agree. And I *missed* you every day—"

No. *No.* She would not reconsider her judgement of the man just because he looked into Felicia's eyes with tenderness and spoke to her as if she were the most important thing to him in the world.

"—An hour longer is all I ask. Surely the party guests will be leaving by midafternoon. And, if you go quietly, and

Mrs. Montrose tells me you've been good, I promise presents tonight."

Fee considered. "*Good* presents?"

"The best, of course." Fleetingly, he met Hera's gaze over Fee's head. "They're from me, aren't they?"

Hera bit back a groan.

"You *do* give good presents." Felicia nodded. "I'll go."

"And be good?" he prompted.

"And be good." She parroted.

"That's my girl." He kissed Fee's forehead before planting her on her feet.

As Hera reached out to take Fee's hand, her arm brushed his, singeing her flesh. *Fire and brimstone.*

"I trust"—he spoke as if *she* were the errant child—"you will not to lose her again."

"Of course not. She's promised *you* to be *good*." Hera matched his authoritative baritone with her best no-nonsense nursemaid voice. "Good day."

Her still-tucked-up skirts may have belied her bravado, but she turned and walk back to the house, head held high. *All will be well.*

"Mrs. Montrose?"

She stopped.

"That *is* your name?"

His voice dripped with undisguised suspicion.

She glanced back over her shoulder. *How* had he discovered her surname was false? Or—she narrowed her eyes—was he just guessing?

"Why would I lie about my name?" she asked.

"Why, indeed." He lifted a brow, not in the least cowed nor convinced by her insouciance. "I was merely making sure I remembered correctly."

She smiled, briefly and innocently. "Allow me to reassure you...your memory is sound." She tilted her head in a pitying manner. "My father had trouble remembering things in his later years, too."

Without waiting to see his reaction, she returned her gaze to the door and quickened her pace.

Obviously, all was not going to be well.

She could carefully advance across this checkered board while employing every ounce of competence and skill she possessed and *still* find herself ruthlessly knocked aside. This man wasn't a pawn. He wasn't even a rook, a knight, or a king.

This man was *the player*.

And his presence challenged everything.

****End of Excerpt***

Her Duke at Midnight

Author's Note on the Odyssey

I've been fascinated with The Odyssey since I first read it in high school. The epic poem is full of monsters, storms, bloodshed, dramatic confrontation, and divine intervention. However, the simple human themes of coming of age, revenge, and romance make up the story's core.

The disguised hero, a man with super-human qualities —not only is he a brave and clever warrior, he is the best carpenter, sailor, hunter, seaman, marksman—he is not a god, and his discipline fails him at several key points. The son in search of his father is not yet strong enough to protect his home. The besieged heroine is caught between grief and duty, hope and moving on.

I read several versions of the Odyssey for this project, but the one that had the most impact was the recent translation by Emily Wilson, the first translation by a woman. Ms. Wilson's version is direct, raw, and doesn't shy away from the more uncomfortable parts of the story.

My Regency reinterpretation includes characters, situations, dialogue, plot points, and, in one case, a direct quote from the Odyssey. However, I also take liberties. Odysseus, unlike Chev, was not wounded, nor did he kill Calypso, the goddess who had imprisoned him on her island, nor did he have to contend with a smuggling plot. He does not have childhood friends who come to his aid and wasn't forced by his father to go to war. I also moderated the bloodshed that follows the competition, left out the dying dog, and added more kisses (as one does in a romance novel).

Some character parallels include:

-Eumaeus, the loyal swineherd/Emmaus, the gamekeeper.

Though Eumaeus was born a noble and ends up a slave, my Emmaus was born a slave and ends up a captain. As in the Odyssey, Chev meets the swineherd first, is attacked by his dogs, and has a very similar discussion about hunger, strangers and lies. Eumaeus, like Emmaus, sleeps with a knife under his pillow. Although Eumaeus is not former crew—in the Odyssey none of Odysseus's crew survive.

-Telemachus, Odysseus's son/Thaddeus, Chev's son.

Telemachus goes in search of his father in the Odyssey, while Thaddeus does not, but they both struggle with what it is to become a man. As in the Odyssey, Odysseus meets his son in Eumaeus's cottage. Telemachus's life is threatened by Penelope's suitors. Telemachus clears the house of weapons with his father. And Telemachus attempts to string the bow at the competition.

-Antinous, the most aggressive of Penelope's suitors/Mr. Anthony steward and villain.

Antinous threatens Telemachus's life, throws a stool at Odysseus, is chastised by Odysseus (disguised as a beggar) for giving of another's wealth, and encourages Irus the beggar to fight a reluctant Odysseus.

-Eurycleia, Odysseus's nurse/Mrs. Renton, Ithwick's housekeeper.

Eurycleia is very protective of Penelope and Thaddeus. She also bathes Odysseus and recognizes him because of a scar on his ankle (Although Odysseus's scar is from a childhood encounter with a wild boar).

-Calypso the goddess/Calypso the pirate-Madame LaVoie.

Odysseus washes up on Calypso's island and, although she does not torture him, she does keep him there against his will. When we first see Odysseus in the story he is on Calypso's shore, gazing at the horizon, weeping and tearing at his clothes because he wants so desperately to return to his family. Calypso is aware of Odysseus's distress, but does not release him until ordered to do so by Zeus. She offers Odysseus immortality and his answer is no, 'I will endure.' Unlike Madame LaVoie, she does not come after him after he leaves her island.

Penelope, Odysseus's long-suffering wife/Penelope, Chev's wife.

I wanted to give my Penelope more agency—something she had created besides the funeral shroud Penelope weaves for her father-in-law (or, in my story, for Chev), and so I gave her a separate estate (I also had to work out some thorny guardian and inheritance issues specific to the Regency). Like Penelope in the Odyssey, she is wise, caring, kind and clever. Several of Penelope's plot points in Eventide are directly from the Odyssey—her distress at hearing a song about her husband, her calling Anthony a brute and accusing him of trying to murder her son, her insistence that the suitors bring her gifts, and her planning the competition.

Penelope of the Odyssey asks to have the mysterious beggar brought to her. As in my version, Odysseus first refuses, but then meets her at twilight. In that first meeting, she asks him who he really is (a sign she realizes all is not what it seems)—and he asks her not to ask because his grief is too great for him to bear. She urges Anthony to allow the beggar to try his hand at the competition, and, of course, she gives Odysseus one, final test when she pretends to order their unmovable yew bed moved. In the end, they call one another extraordinary, and they take a twilight walk together. Although Penelope, in the Odyssey, is not certain of Odysseus's identity until the very end and does not have any amorous encounters with Odysseus as a beggar.

And so we come to my Odysseus, Captain Lord Cheverley. As already mentioned, Odysseus survives a shipwreck and a raft wreck, was held against his will on an island, returns in disguise as a beggar, interacts with his former staff, his wife, and his son while in disguise, and claims his home by winning an archery competition involving shooting an arrow through twelve axes. Other points taken from the text but not yet mentioned include Odysseus's encounter at the town fountain with the goatherd who insults him, his confrontation with Antinous where Odysseus chides Antinous for giving away another's wealth (Antinous chucks a stool at him in response), and his fight with Irus (egged on by Antinous). In the Odyssey, however, Odysseus is not a second son, has a healthy relationship with both parents (although his mother does die of grief), and is not injured.

Cheverley appeared on the page in *Her Duke at Daybreak* already injured. I imagine that was because I'd been reading so much about Admiral Lord Nelson who had his right arm amputated after suffering a bullet wound. At the time, I hadn't decided to merge Chev's story with Odysseus's story, although Chev's wife was named Penelope and some deep wound (along with the Admiralty's mission) was keeping him from returning home.

Author's Note on the Odyssey

I thought a lot about my father while writing Chev's story. My father was an artist, a gardener and a pianist who lost all the fingers on his right hand in a table saw accident when I was five. While he healed, he often showed us his scars and welcomed questions. By the time I was a teen, he was again painting and drawing, playing the piano and gardening (although he did give up the accordion). I was often surprised when new friends asked about his hand. I no longer noticed, although, on rare occasions, his phantom fingers itched.

My Dad loved history and tragic tales. He even read us Longfellow instead of traditional children's stories. I think he would have liked the idea of retelling the Odyssey, and so the book is dedicated to him and to my mother.

I also thought a lot about my mother, whose right side was, for a time, paralyzed following a stroke this past January (why the release of this book was delayed). Her therapists trained her and my sisters to think of her right side as 'affected'—never 'bad' or any other phrase that would have led to her developing an adversarial relationship with her body. I was awed by my Mother, the therapists, doctors and nurses who assisted her, and her fellow patients who showed such determination while finding their way through the abrupt devastation that often follows a stroke.

As for Chev learning to shoot with his teeth, amputee archers are quite common, and include London Olympian Jeff Fabry. My thanks to the men and women behind the many YouTube videos that describe in detail how bows can be modified. The longbow archers I spoke with gave me conflicting answers as to whether Chev could have managed shooting an English longbow using materials available in the early 19th century, but since the act of shooting through twelve axes is in itself a superhuman feat, I erred on the side of possibility and determination.

As for the special shirt and coat Penelope designed, the idea is based on the Raglan sleeve designed by the British clothing company Aquascutum for FitzRoy Somerset, 1st Baron Raglan, who lost his arm in the Battle of Waterloo. The style wasn't conceived until the Victorian era, but I'm convinced resourceful seamstresses of earlier times could have designed their own seam modifications.

Fitting the shipwreck from the Odyssey into the Napoleonic wars was tricky. As one does not simply *walk* into Mordor, the Royal Navy would not have simply 'lost' a captain and his ship. Navy vessels, unless ordered otherwise, traveled in fleets. The seas were full of war ships, merchant ships, and shipping vessels, and the European coasts subject to raids.

The wreck from the book is a blend of fact and fiction—a version of the loss of the *HMS Repulse,* which had been attached to the Channel Fleet, gave chase to (and caught) a French privateer, but was lost in fog and then hit a rock off the shore of the Glenan Islands (Known then to the English as Penmar). The crew was taken prisoner, (with the exception of a few who had taken off in a cutter). They were eventually released from the French prison at Quimpar (which had been notorious during the War of the First Coalition). And, when the captain returned to England, he was court marshalled for the loss of his ship. The captain was acquitted and allowed to keep his rank, but was never called back into service again, despite the war raging around them.

Smaller nuggets from the Odyssey include the loyal renter no longer wanting to rent, the final prophecy of the planted oar, references to the 'Wine-dark sea,' and 'dawn's rosy fingers,' and, finally, a reference to Athena making the night magic. There are also nods to the Odyssey in the description of Odysseus as 'not just any man' (when Odysseus blinds the Cyclops, he shouts out that he is 'no man'), the fact he tied himself to a mast to avoid death by the Sirens, the river Styx, and the hostility of Poseidon.

Why would I identify Cheverley with the god that is the cause of most of Odysseus's problems (although betrayals by his men and his own hubris don't help)? Well, in the Odyssey, Poseidon hates Odysseus, but Athena comes to Odysseus's aid. I took this as a metaphor—that within which is wild, elemental and prone to rage (Poseidon) can be tamed by wisdom, courage and strategy (Athena).

And healed, of course, by true love.

Acknowledgments

First, I'd like to thank Cora Lee for bringing together the A Legend to Love series. I'm thrilled to have taken part in her vision and was awed by her creativity, organization and patience. Likewise to my fellow series authors.

I'd like to thank Alison Delaine, Inara Scott, and Susan Sey for encouraging me to proceed with the concept, for their advice on the Cover Copy, and for being blindingly talented goddesses.

Thank you to Tamar Bihari, who talked me down from the ledge several times, and to Stacey Adgern who kept texting support, even when I disappeared for a while. Thank you also to Elizabeth Essex and Bill Haggart, who were generous with their knowledge about the Royal Navy. And I wouldn't ever get anything done without weekly check-ins and support from Madeline Iva.

I cannot thank editor Lindsey Faber enough for her comprehensive analysis and notes—I nearly wept with joy when I read them. I couldn't have made the story come together without her. A huge thank you to proofreader Louisa Cornell, a talented historical romance author whose eagle eye for proofing & historical accuracy was a lifesaver. And *merci beaucoup* to fabulous author Adriana Anders for correcting my French.

On the day-to-day life side of things—much love & gratitude to my Mom, who kept smiling as she recovered from a very serious stroke last January, and love and gratitude to my sisters, who have been amazing. Somehow, we've made it through this past year, and I love them all even more for their humor and determination.

And, as always, thank you to my amazing friend Debbie and my husband Richard. I love him madly. And I swear to him that, one of these days, I'm going to learn balance and not panic halfway through projects.

About Wendy

Historical Romance author Wendy LaCapra writes award-winning books reviewers describe as 'heart-pounding, entrancing', 'lusciously romantic and sparkling with wit.' As a teen, Wendy discovered spine-tingling gothics in her local public library, inspiring her to craft her own seductive tales full of secrets and scandal. She lives with her husband in a quirky, historic building in NYC and loves a girls' night in. For new release, sale alerts and other news, sign up at http://bit.ly/GetWendyNews

Author Website

All Books by Wendy LaCapra

Excerpts available for all books on Wendy's Website

The Mythic Duke Series
Her Duke at Daybreak
His Duchess at Eventide
Her Duke at Midnight

The Lords of Chance
Scandal in Spades
Heart's Desire
Diamond in the Rogue

A Free Lords of Chance-related Novella
Mrs. Sartin's Secretary

The Furies Series
Lady Vice
Lady Scandal
Duchess Decadence

A Legend To Love Series

A collection of Classic myths and stories reenvisioned by Regency historical romance authors

When The Marquess Returns, Alanna Lucas
The Lady and Lord Lakewood, Aileen Fish
Lady Soldier, Jillian Chantal
My Wild Irish Rogue, Saralee Etter
Between Duty and the Devil's Desires, Louisa Cornell
A Wulf In Duke's Clothing, Renee Reynolds
The Promise of the Bells, Elizabeth Ellen Carter
Rogue of the Greenwood, Susan Gee Heino
A Gift From A Goddess, Maggi Andersen
The Duke of Darkness, Cora Lee
His Duchess At Eventide, Wendy La Capra

Excerpt from the second book of A Legend to Love series

Chapter One Excerpt from:

The Lady and Lord Lakewood
A Legend to Love
Copyright © 2018 Aileen Fish

Purchase The Lady and Lord Lakewood

June 1818
    Near Glastonbury, England

A violent dream held Vivienne, the widowed Viscountess Avalon, deep within its darkness and wouldn't let her escape. Shadowy figures swarmed around her, threatening and maleficent. Heavy fog kept her from seeing exactly where she was, but some inner sense told her it was the woods near Lake Avalon. The shadows gathered behind her, guiding her—no, forcing her—toward the shore. Her heart pounded in fear of what had taken control of her. She tried to run away, tried to hide in rotting log, but her feet were leaden. Trapped in the fog as she was, she held her breath as if the sound would reveal her location to the enemy, whoever or whatever it was.

When she cleared the trees, the fog thinned, allowing her to see a few feet ahead. Still the shadows closed in, and she stepped into the cold water to stay beyond their reach. Hesitantly she inched forward. First her half-boots grew damp, then her hems soaked up the cold water. Vivienne shivered both from the cold and from fear, but a glance over her shoulder showed the shadows still approached. What evil wanted to control her?

Lake Avalon shimmered in a radiating circle in the direction Vivienne felt compelled to go. Tiny waves rippled outward as if a pebble had broken the surface. In the center a face appeared. A kind, gentle face. Her great-aunt Nimue. She remained just below the surface. Vivienne's heart raced in fear. Was this vision saying her aunt was going to die soon? Vivienne shook her head, pleading, "No, please no."

Aunt Nimue raised her arms and a magnificent sword appeared in her hands. She lifted the weapon above the water while her body and head remained below the surface.

Compelled to reach for the sword, Vivienne hesitated to do so. "What am I to do with this?"

Aunt Nimue was silent, not even sharing her thoughts. She simply lifted the sword again, displaying it with both hands like a gift, and motioned for Vivienne to take it.

As soon as Vivienne did, the last of the fog lifted. The shadowy figures vanished, and her aunt swam away. A gruff voice called her name from within the trees. Merlin, who some claimed was a magician, stood watching her.

"What am I to do with this?" Vivienne repeated, this time directing the question to him.

The old man with stringy white locks blending into his

long, graying beard said, "You will know when the time comes. Since you are having this dream, the time must be soon."

She hated answers like this. You will know... Would she ever trust her second-sight enough to be confident in what lay ahead?

"You will," Merlin said, and Aunt Nimue's voice echoed the words in a whisper from the distance.

Looking down at the magnificent weapon, Vivienne marveled at the workmanship. The bronze grip and hilt looked like a little primitive man. The cross guard curled downward on either side to look like legs, and the arms of the man curled upward around the head to create a pommel. It even had a face of sorts, and a belt etched into the middle of the body. It was heavy, with the broad blade of an old weapon of battle. Someone had put great pride and love into making it. Given the way the metal shone, it was clear others had polished it and cared for it in the centuries since. Who did it belong to?

And as she studied it, it faded away, leaving her hands empty. She lifted her gaze to Merlin only to find him gone, too. She was alone at the edge of Lake Avalon, her skirt and boots wet but nothing else to show for the odd events.

Then she jolted awake in her bedchamber, snuggled deep under her heavy woolen blankets, barefoot and clad in her linen nightgown. Moonlight streamed between the thick damask draperies on her window, and the castle was silent. Her dream was so vivid she felt certain she'd lived it, yet her nightgown was dry.

Vivienne hated these visions and the period of waiting afterward as she watched for clues to guide her toward the meaning. Aunt Nimue might be able to shed light on the clues, but she couldn't visit her until daylight. Knowing she'd never get back to sleep, she got up, pulled on her robe and slippers, and went downstairs to make tea. Not having visited her aunt for several months, she'd enjoy a brief visit. The woman was a font of memories and the history of the village of Avalon, and their family's part in it. Time spent with her was never dull.

* * *

Richard Bedivere, 3rd Earl of Lakewood, rode out at dawn with his friends, Sir Kay and Sir Cador, and their former commanding officer, Major-General Uther Pendragon, 1st Duke of Camelot. The air was brisk for a summer morning, but fresh, and the rising sun promised another beautiful day in Camelot.

They didn't converse, even when they slowed to a walk, but that was normal for their rides. Not a daily occasion, they gathered together at least once a month to share memories of their battles in the Peninsular War and celebrate that they'd come home safe and sound.

That morning, early in their ride, the Duke of Camelot and his horse slowed. He pressed his arm against his belly.

"Are you unwell?" Sir Cador asked.

"Likely something I ate. Perhaps that apple was over-ripe. Or under ripe." The duke gasped and his arm tightened. "I need a drink."

The three men followed the duke to his pond, where he and the horse drank. He knelt on one knee, bracing an elbow there, and rested his forehead on the back on his hand.

"Should we get the wagon?" Lakewood asked. "Clearly you're unwell. Sir Kay?"

"On my way," said Sir Kay, wheeling his horse about and galloping away.

Lakewood and Sir Cador dismounted, Lakewood going to the duke and Sir Cador taking the reins of the three horses.

"His horse is overtired," Sir Cador commented. "He's breathing quite hard."

Paying little attention, Lakewood kept his focus on his friend, uncertain how he could be of assistance.

Camelot was breathing hard, still clutching his midsection. Then he groaned, leaned further over and retched.

Lakewood grimaced and waited for the bout of nausea to pass.

The duke reached a hand into the pond, brought some to his mouth and drank. At the same time, his horse grew restless, neighing soft, short sounds, and pawing the ground.

"Easy boy." Sir Cador patted the horse's neck. "It's almost as if he feels his master's pain."

"Don't become fanciful on us," Lakewood muttered, nodding toward their sick friend.

Camelot grunted, as close to a laugh as he could get. "That horse has no attachment to me. He likely hates me for rousing him so early." He struggled to his feet.

His horse bobbed his head and pawed the ground. Then he began to drool.

"This animal is really sick," Sir Cador said. He tried to lead him to water, but the horse fought the reins.

In the distance they heard the approaching wagon. Lakewood went to the duke, offering his shoulder to lean on. When the wagon drew to a stop, the driver and Lakewood helped the duke aboard, laying him in the back on a dirty blanket that happened to be tucked to one side. Lakewood hopped up beside him.

As they pulled away letting Sir Cador handle the horses, Camelot's mount dropped to the ground, jerking about in a seizure. Lakewood's gut tightened. Had the man and horse eaten something? Was the duke going to get as sick as the animal? "Let's go, quickly!"

Camelot groaned once or twice, then grabbed the lapels of Lakewood's coat and pulled him close. "Arthur."

"He's fine, I'm sure of it. Sir Percival is with him, isn't he? If the boy took ill, they would have sent for the doctor."

The duke's son Arthur was only a babe, a mere three years old and if something happened to His Grace the boy was doomed to live without either parent, his mother having died giving birth to him. Someone would be appointed guardian until Arthur came of age, and his father's men would protect him with their lives, but Lakewood's heart ached for the empty future the boy would face. If the worst happened, it would be up to the duke's friends to make sure Arthur knew the great man his father had been.

Lakewood's thoughts tumbled and rolled with questions that didn't need to be answered just then. His gut told him this wasn't a simple illness, nor a rotten apple. This was a serious attack oon the duke.

Sir Kay met them at the door to the great hall and helped carry Camelot up to his bedchamber. "The doctor was called for. How is he?"

Lakewood shook his head to indicate not well, and not to discuss it then. The castle was oddly quiet, even their footfalls fell silently as they climbed the stone spiral stairway, as though any noise might disturb the duke. No footmen scurried about their duties. No chambermaids ducked into hiding as the three reached the end of the hallway. It was uncomfortably still.

When they entered the duke's bedchamber, the older

man stirred, and as they laid him in bed, he again had a seizure.

"How long will the doctor take to arrive?" Lakewood asked.

No one answered.

The room reflected the way Lakewood felt, dark and somber, the heavy curtains blocking the daylight. In the pale glow from the candle beside the bed which the valet had lit, the duke lacked color, his eyes were sunken and shadowed. His brow was furrowed with pain. His breathing was rough, labored.

Being unable to help made Lakewood restless. If Camelot had been shot or stabbed, he'd know exactly what to do. Apply pressure, decide whether or not to remove the bullet, clean the wound and bandage securely. The duke had no wound to clean, nothing to bandage. Lakewood was of no use whatsoever.

It felt like hours before Dr. Miller arrived led by Sir Cador, but it had likely been less than one. After examining the duke and asking questions of the three men who'd been with him, the doctor said, "Let's hope it's a severe stomach ailment. It should pass quickly if it is, and he'll grow stronger. For now, you should let him rest."

The doctor crossed the room to the single chair and sat, leaving no room for discussion of who would remain with Camelot. As Lakewood, Sir Kay and Sir Cador left the room, Cador said, "The horse died."

Lakewood felt his blood pool at his feet, he was sure of it. He turned quickly and returned to Camelot's bedchamber and informed the doctor. "What could have sickened them both? And if it killed such a large animal..."

Dr. Miller nodded. "It would be worse in the duke. I know of no illness that would pass from horse to man this way, or the other way 'round. Could they have been bitten by a snake? But a man would have seen the horse react and know to move out of the way."

"His horse was fine until Camelot became ill and we stopped at the pond. The duke vomited, and his horse seized."

"Hmm." Crossing his leg, the doctor folded his hands around his knee and frowned. "That suggests ingestion of poison. Water, or food. Has anyone else become ill? Any of the animals in the stable?"

"No one has reported it. I'm sure Sir Kay would have heard something when he ordered the wagon be driven to the pond."

"That's right," Kay said from inside the doorway. "No one said anything."

He and Sir Cador entered the room and stood beside Lakewood. The three men watched Dr. Miller.

The doctor looked from one man to the next. "What would the duke have shared with his horse? He wouldn't drink the same water or eat the horse's oats."

Remembering what he'd seen when the duke vomited, Lakewood said, "Apples. Camelot had eaten an apple before we went out."

Dr. Miller stroked his chin, then shook his head. "A rotten apple might make a man ill for a time, but it wouldn't bother a horse." He lifted a hand to ward of the question he expected. "Yes, even a few bad apples wouldn't kill a horse."

The duke's valet suddenly cried out. "Doctor!"

Camelot was having another seizure. When the valet reached to hold him down, the doctor ordered him back. "Let it pass, that is all."

When the trembling ended, the duke was fast asleep. Or unconscious. His chest rose and fell, and the doctor reached for Camelot's wrist. After a moment or two, he nodded. Turning away, he said, "There's not much I can do but watch to see if this runs its course, or if new symptoms arise. I can send word if anything changes."

Lakewood continued to watch his friend on the bed. Only the deep crease between his eyebrows showed his pain. Sir Kay and Sir Cador also watched, their worry clear on their features. "Come," Lakewood said and left the bedchamber.

Once again in the hallway, he said, "You two question everyone in the household, in the stable. Ask for anything unusual, any strangers. Someone has to have seen something. I'm going upstairs to see the boy, then I'll join you."

Lakewood climbed another flight of stairs to the nursery where young Arthur played. The lad waved a wooden sword at his nurse, who was on her knees performing an adequate rendition of a dragon. The innocence of the scene was poignant.

"Die, dragon," Arthur cried valiantly, gently pressing the wooden blade to his nurse's neck. She gasped and moaned, then rolled on her side and lay with her eyes closed. The boy laughed.

Suddenly noticing Lakewood's presence, the servant jumped to her feet and smoothed her skirt, brushing a stray lock of mousy brown hair off her cheek. "May I help you, my lord?"

"No, I came to see how Arthur's faring. He grows so quickly."

"Yes, sir. He's already learning to write his letters. Soon the duke will need to hire a tutor." Her face softened and her fear for the duke's wellness showed. News always spread quickly through the servants.

"Arthur will be fine. He has many uncles to watch over

him until Camelot is better. We all feel as though he is our own son. I've heard the other men say it."

Arthur looked solemnly at Lakewood, meeting his gaze. "My father will be dead. Lord Percival says so," he said, nodding to the large man standing in the corner. Even garbled as a three-year-old's words could be, his message was clear.

Lakewood spun to face the other man, frowning, disbelieving while questioning.

Percival shook his head. "I only said his father wasn't feeling well and might not be up to see him today."

"I will be Duke of Camelot," Arthur continued.

Sir Percival jumped in. "Your father will be duke for many years to come, and when he's old and dies, then you will be duke."

Rivers of chills coursed over Lakewood's skin. It was as though the boy knew the future. No, that was foolish talk. One of the servants must have said something and the boy overheard. Arthur was three, for goodness sake. He couldn't understand.

Still, Lakewood shivered as he rose. "I believe your dragon is escaping, young lord. You'd better go after it."

Arthur yelled and posed with his sword high before running around the room shouting gibberish. Lakewood nodded at Sir Percival, took one last look at the boy, and left.

*** End of excerpt The Lady and Lord Lakewood ***